Praise for the novels of *New York Times*
bestselling author

FERN MICHAELS

"Fern Michaels shines."
— *Publishers Weekly*

"Michaels' writing is as intriguing and fast-paced as ever."
— *Booklist* on *Vendetta*

"The concluding triathlon, in which Michaels's likeable heroine
shows her stuff, is a strong finish to a frothy read."
— *Publishers Weekly* on *Pretty Woman*

"Michaels is a master at family tales.... She craftily combines
humor and emotions into a truly enjoyable novel."
— *RT Book Reviews* on *Family Blessings*

"Another fast-paced and engaging novel from
the prolific and entertaining Michaels."
— *Booklist* on *The Real Deal*

Other unforgettable reads by

FERN MICHAELS

Sea Gypsy
Golden Lasso
Beyond Tomorrow
Nightstar

FERN MICHAELS

Dream of Me

HQN™

ISBN-13: 978-0-373-77424-1

DREAM OF ME

Copyright © 2009 by Harlequin Books S.A.

The publisher acknowledges the copyright holder of the individual works as follows:

PAINT ME RAINBOWS
Copyright © 1981 by Fern Michaels

WHISPER MY NAME
Copyright © 1981 by Fern Michaels

www.HQNBooks.com

Printed in U.S.A.

CONTENTS

PAINT ME RAINBOWS

stories that she wanted. Quietly, subtly, Deke had agreed to become Jake's wife.

Twenty-Three was time to get married. It was time to start a family and put down roots. This, she thought, looking around the toy apartment, was hardly what a person should call roots. But just while she saved for the future, it could work out nicely. Eventually she wanted to work she didn't know if they temporarily let loose would she like it or not. It her boss was a good he

CHAPTER ONE

JILL BARTON WAS oblivious to the loud knocks and the hysterical shouts of her bridesmaids. She had to use all her concentration to keep her own hysteria under control. Jilted! She had been left waiting at the altar! What a fool she had been, standing there like some ninny, waiting. It was the pity in the minister's eyes that finally told her what she had been dreading. Deke wasn't going to show up. It was hard to be believed— Deke had been so insistent, so certain, telling her she needed a man in her life—that *he* was that man. She could almost hear his voice, so close to her ear: "You need me, Jill. The business world is no place for a girl like you. We can make it together. I know we can. I've wanted to ask you long before this, but there were always financial considerations. Now, with that little inheritance of yours, those problems are solved. Trust me, Jill, bells aren't supposed to go off in your head when I kiss you. That kind of love comes later, after marriage." His persuasive voice had whispered those words, banishing her doubts, gratifying her inner longings for marriage and family. "All your friends are married," Deke had continued, his lips nuzzling her ear. It was true, when they went to visit friends she was uncomfortable, feeling left out, as though she were missing something or someone. It was the intimacy, the sharing, that she wanted. Quietly, with a kiss, she had agreed to become Deke's wife.

Twenty-three was *time* to get married. It was *time* to start a family and put down roots. This, she thought, looking around the tiny apartment, was hardly what a person could call roots. Her job, while assured for the moment, could never be labeled as security. Each day she went to work she didn't know if her temperamental boss would fire her or not. If her copy was good, he would smile; but if it wasn't up to par, he would say there were thousands, yes, thousands of people who would jump at the chance to work for the Vancouver Advertising Agency. It was true. And they could all have the job if they wanted it. She didn't like the job, didn't want the pressure. Marriage would have been a graceful escape from it all. *Would have been.*

"Jill, open the door! Please! We can't leave you like this. Come on now, open the door!" It was Nancy Evans, her maid of honor.

Jill walked on leaden legs over to the door. She opened it a crack and spoke softly. "Go home, Nancy. I just want to be alone. I'm all right. I plan to have a really good screaming and yelling tantrum where I cry and throw things. I might even roll around on the floor. After that I'll be all right. Don't worry about me. Tell Sue and Mary to take all the food home with them and thank them for being so understanding."

"I will, Jill. You're sure, now, that you'll be all right?"

"No, I'm not sure if I'll be all right. I'm going to try." Her voice cracked and then became firm. "I might just take off for somewhere. I'll send you a card or call you. Please, I want all of you to leave now." There was desperation in her voice. What would she do now? She had already left her job and had been disgraced in front of her friends.

"Okay, Jill. If there's anything I or the girls can do, just call us. Promise me and then I'll leave."

"I promise, Nancy." Tears were burning her eyes again. Leave, her mind shrieked. Leave so I don't have to hear the pity in your voice.

Jill gasped when she heard the filtered words through the door. "I knew it was too good to be true. You owe me five dollars, Sue. I bet you that Deke wouldn't go through with the wedding, and I was right. What a rotten thing for him to do. The least he could have done was call Jill and tell her the wedding was off and not put her through this humiliation."

"You're right, Nancy. I don't know why I even bothered to make the wager. Everyone in the office was so sure this wedding would never come off. Jill was the only one who didn't seem to have even one small doubt. I feel so sorry for her. I just wish there was something we could do, but I know that Jill needs to be alone now to sort out her emotions."

"Forget the five dollars. I'm just sorry that I ever made that silly bet in the first place. It was a terrible thing for us to do. Jill is our friend. What we should have done was tell her what a bounder Deke really is. That would have been a real favor for our friend."

"I didn't have the nerve, Nancy," Sue all but squealed. "Besides, there was always the hope that Deke was serious about the wedding and truly did love Jill. Whatever, it's over and done with now. The best thing we can do is leave Jill as she suggested. In her own way she'll cope with all of this. If she needs us for anything, she knows where we are."

Jill closed her eyes. They all knew. Even the people

in the office. How they must have watched the wedding preparations proceed and even counted down the days. Would he or wouldn't he go through with the wedding? How degrading, how humiliating.

A long sigh escaped her as she waited for the sound of the apartment door to close. They meant well, but the look in the minister's eyes was all the pity she could handle for one day. Her eyes fell to the stack of luggage next to the door. She was packed. All she had to do was walk out the door behind the girls. Everything had been taken care of. The elderly lady down the hall had promised to come in every day to feed her tropical fish and water the plants. The post office was going to hold her mail. Even the newspaper and milk deliveries had been canceled.

The loud sound of the front door closing made Jill's shoulders slump. They were gone and she was truly alone. Alone to take out her hurt and humiliation in the small apartment. What was it she had told Nancy? That she was going to throw a tantrum and kick and scream. Why? What was the point? It was over, finished. Why make herself more miserable, more angry? She had to start new, get on with her life! If she didn't do it now, this minute, she would stay locked up in this apartment that was full of Deke and memories of him. Before she could change her mind, she opened the bedroom door and then picked up the two suitcases.

The tweed luggage, her gift to herself, rested in the back of her yellow compact car. Her pocketbook was in the bucket seat on the passenger side. She took another deep breath, turned the key and maneuvered the small car from the curb. She would drive until she was exhausted and then stop.

Deftly, without a wasted motion, she slipped a

cassette into the tape deck. Strains of romantic music rose and soared within the confines of the small car. Hastily, Jill withdrew the cassette and replaced it with her new disco tape. That was better.

She drove steadily north, her mind blank as she kept her eyes on the road and the beautiful autumn colors.

It was three hours later when her neck began to ache that she realized for the first time that she was still wearing her wedding gown and veil. A rich bubble of laughter escaped her. Some new life she was starting. Dumb. It was a dumb thing to do. No wonder people had smiled at her whenever she slowed down for traffic. She would have to risk the amused glances of gas station attendants when she stopped for gas.

She drove for another hour before she saw what she considered to be a suitable gas station. "Fill it up, and please let me have the key to the ladies' room," Jill said in a firm voice that brooked no questions. She slid from behind the wheel and gathered up her long train. Regally, she tripped her way to the washroom, only to remember halfway there that she needed her suitcase. A grimace on her face, she made her way back to the car and grabbed for the smaller of the two cases. "Please check the oil too." Not for the world would she let her eyes meet those of the attendant. What must he be thinking? Someday when I'm old and gray I'm going to write the memoirs of Jill Barton, she muttered as she fit the key into the bathroom door. The room was clean but cramped. Impatiently, she struggled and tugged at the heavy satin. Free of its stranglehold, she felt a hundred percent better. She balanced the suitcase on the sink and manipulated the numbers of the combination lock to her birthdate. Just the sight of her jeans and the pullover shirt made her feel better. This was her style. A pair of sneakers for added comfort was all she needed. Now, what was she to do with the gown and gossamer veil? There was no way she could fit them into her suitcase, and she just couldn't leave them in a gas station washroom. She would throw them in the backseat for the time being. Perhaps the day would come when she could put all of this behind her and have a use for them again. Her back straightened and her eyes spewed sparks. It would be a very long time indeed. She had made a fool of herself. Once was enough. There wouldn't be a second time.

The heavy gown and veil were on her arm, the suitcase in her other hand, as she made her way back to the car. She offered no explanation to the curious attendant as she paid for her gas and a quart of oil.

Back on the highway she realized she was getting hungry. She didn't want to stop, because that would mean talking to people and she wanted only to be alone with her thoughts. She wanted to be insulated from everything and anything. The car was working its own brand of quiet magic as it ate up the miles on the highway.

She drove for another two hours and then pulled over to the side of the road. She would just take a little catnap. She couldn't keep her eyes open another minute.

It was still dark when she woke. The digital watch glowed with red numerals. It was 3:30—the middle of the night. After rubbing the sleep from her eyes with one hand while she turned on the ignition and lights, she continued to drive steadily north with no destination in mind.

DAWN BROKE SOFTLY, casting streams of reddened sunlight across the dew-drenched countryside. Jill

Barton yawned sleepily, tightening her hold on the steering wheel of her mud-splattered car. Squinting her eyes, she forced herself to concentrate on the stretch of road in front of her. She had been driving aimlessly for hours and realized suddenly that she hadn't passed another car for miles. Instead of feeling threatened by the thought of having the road to herself, she was buoyed by a thrilling surge of freedom. Even a flat tire at this point wouldn't dampen her spirits. Jill smiled as she thought about the prospect of such a mishap. She was totally prepared for any mechanical disaster her car might decide to present her with. Night classes at the community college had made her an expert on the basics of servicing motor vehicles. She could change a tire faster than a twenty-year man at a mechanic's shop. Her knowledge of all the intricacies of just what made her car purr along so happily was so impressive that even Deke had had to admit that she was a born grease monkey.

Now that she had been jilted—must have something to do with her name—and had burned her bridges behind her, it was time to look her situation full in the face. And it was time to take a look at Deke and what had happened to her yesterday.

Deke had never been perfect, far from it. He was bound to be a success, there was no point in denying it; his drive had earned him a secure position in the advertising business. Deke had started low in the ranks only five years previously and used his wit and charm to his own advantage. Jill had been enticed by him from the start. His personality was almost overwhelming. Assured and confident, he seemed to lack any faults or idiosyncrasies. His face was actually quite unremarkable, but his blue eyes gleamed with a boyish mischievousness, making him the prime target for all the single girls in the office. Some of the girls were so blatant in their approaches to him that Jill had learned with a jolt that she wasn't the only one who harbored coffee-break fantasies about him.

Of course, Jill held no secret hopes of being singled out by him. It wasn't that she didn't consider herself worthy of his attentions; she knew that she had the type of looks that turned men's heads. Her hair cascaded down her back in silken blond strands. The practice of confining the length in plaits before bed each night gave the tresses a beautiful series of waves, causing some of her friends to refer to her teasingly as Rapunzel. Her eyes were a muted green, sparking into flashing embers when someone tried her temper. In an age of elaborate makeup and chic hairstyles, Jill felt content to pat a smidgen of face powder across her countenance and dab just her lips with color. In many respects Jill was a woman who combined a little of the good old-fashioned ways with an ample helping of liberated ideas. She enjoyed her independence, yet knew that she craved a real family life. At times she chided herself for her thoughts of puttering around a kitchen stocked with an array of copper pots, potted herbs and bubbling concoctions from exotic cookbooks. She could almost picture herself in a red gingham apron, greeting that special someone at the door with a long, romantic kiss. But just as quickly as it would seize her, the vision would shimmer and fade.

There was another side of Jill that seemed in complete contradiction to the rest of her. Some people called it impulsiveness, but Jill knew that she had been blessed with an adventurous spirit. Whenever things caught her fancy, she pursued them. On a dare once she had joined a friend in a sky-diving course, ending up promising herself that learning to fly would be next on her agenda. She followed whims with a passion, never passing up a chance to learn something new.

Jilted! Left waiting at the altar! That was new, wasn't it? How humiliating. If she had to blame something for Deke's desertion of her at the critical hour, it was probably her impulsiveness. He wanted a doormat, someone who would yes him to death and never have a thought of her own. Even her ten thousand dollars wasn't enough to make him want her on a forever basis.

In all honesty, Jill knew in her heart of hearts that she had been less than wholeheartedly enthusiastic about the wedding. Things had moved so fast that she hadn't taken time to examine her inner true feelings.

She should have run like a deer the day the office started to buzz about a new advertising account that all the head executives were hoping to land. The competition had been fierce, the reward a hefty commission and a step up the corporate ladder. When word had reached the floor that Deke had pulled off the biggest coup of his career, the oohs and aahs had seemed almost perfunctory. Jill had remembered thinking that it would only be a matter of time before this advertising whiz had reins on the entire company. For some reason she felt a surge of anger take hold of her when he had paused beside her desk that night as she was covering her typewriter and sorting out her work for the next morning. She had looked up at him, trying to feign boredom as she waited for him to speak. No doubt he wanted some last-minute typing done for his new account, and Jill was silently coaching herself to be assertive and refuse him outright. Instead, he had laughed, almost nervously, a lock of his hair falling out of place and across his eyes.

"Ummm, yes...Miss Barton," he had said haltingly, "I suppose you've heard about my landing the Becker account."

"Yes, Mr. Atkins," Jill had answered dutifully. "Congratulations."

"What I'm trying to say, Miss Barton...Jill, isn't it? I'd like to ask you to help me celebrate this evening."

"Mr. Atkins," Jill whispered. "You don't even know me except in passing...."

"Before you turn me down flat, let me explain." His eyes dancing with a contagious enthusiasm, Deke had begun to shift his weight from one foot to the other, reminding Jill of a teenager eager to learn a new dance step. "I'm so elated about landing that account that I can't waste it just on me. So I told myself, 'Go out and find the prettiest girl you can and take her out on the town.' So, of course, I thought of you immediately. What do you say? Make it your good deed for the day. I promise you, it'll be a night you won't forget. We'll hit all the high spots. An elegant dinner, dancing, the whole schmeer!"

Feeling a smile tug at the corner of her lips, Jill had relented. "All right, Mr. Atkins, your talents as a salesman do seem to be above par."

"You'll accept, then?" Deke had grinned.

"Chalk it up to your winning ways," she had answered teasingly.

When word had filtered down that Deke had lost the account, Jill had found herself in complete sympathy with him. She had pampered him, coddled him, told him over and over that it was a minor setback and he would learn from his mistake. Long walks, with her doing all the talking to rebuild his confidence and catering to his every wish and whim so he wouldn't dwell on what he called his "personal rejection" by his superiors, seemed to be all she had had time for for weeks on end.

As far as the office was concerned, Jill and Deke had become a definite item.

She had found herself becoming more and more involved in his life, yet somehow she had been nagged with the feeling that the Deke she was seeing was only part of the man. Quick glimpses of him when he had had all his barriers down had made Jill wonder if there were facets to his personality that he struggled desperately to keep in check. His impatience with Jill's involvement in night classes at the university and club meetings that took her away from the apartment had been one cause of many a ruined evening and countless bruised feelings. Deke had referred to her interests as flights of whimsy, seeming not to realize or care how much his judgments wounded her. A part of her had felt love for Deke, and another had felt resentment and annoyance that he didn't even bother to try to understand her and her needs. While he had acted oblivious to her inner turmoil, his concern had centered on company obligations. Jill had been convinced that he loved her; after all, he had said it so easily. He had found time for her and had told her that she made everything in his life seem worthwhile and enjoyable. That was what convinced her in the end.

And then had come the big day and the big check. How readily she had fallen in with his plans. She hadn't balked when he had suggested Hawaii for a honeymoon. What was three thousand dollars when she was starting off on a whole brand-new life? And she did love him, didn't she? She always had a queasy feeling in her stomach when Deke was due for a date, and her heart pounded when he called her on the phone. And the final argument in favor of love was that her eyes had misted each and every time he had whispered, "I love you."

This recollection, this journey to what might have been, was something she had to put behind her. From now on, each day would be regarded as the first day of the rest of her life.

The tape deck kept her company for the next several hours as she guided the smoothly running car farther north. If she stopped for lunch and spent half an hour eating, she would still make the border of Rhode Island by midafternoon. She hummed her approval along with the music.

The rich golds and browns of the autumn leaves were having a hypnotic effect on Jill. She felt peaceful, almost content, as the minutes sped by. It was a miracle that she wasn't weeping and wailing, and near to total collapse, at what had happened to her yesterday.

Jill drove on, hour after hour, stopping at midafternoon on a wide shoulder of the road. Her intention was to close her eyes for only a few seconds to ward off the bright afternoon autumn glare.

CHAPTER TWO

THE CRUNCH OF GRAVEL beneath the car wheels stirred Jill from her restless slumber. Raising her head to peer out at the source of the commotion, she grinned sheepishly at an elderly woman tapping on the windshield.

Rolling down her window just far enough to enable her to hear the woman speak, Jill said groggily, "What is it?"

The old woman squinted her eyes, a gnarled finger coming up to her nose in an unconscious gesture as she pushed her bifocals up and leaned down for a closer inspection of Jill. "My lord, honey!" she squawked. "I thought you were dead...looked it from the way you were slumped over that steering wheel. Can't tell these days, you know. Seems like girls your age are always barking up the wrong tree and getting themselves in trouble. You're taking your life in your hands sleeping in your car like that, dearie."

Jill felt a scalding blush start at her neck and flow upward. Imagine being scolded by a complete stranger!

"You mark my words, young lady," the woman continued as she marched back to her own car, "you'd best be more careful next time. In my day you had to worry about being carted off by gypsies. Goodness knows what fates you're tempting nowadays!"

It took Jill a good ten minutes to recover from the

woman's well-meaning tirade, and as she straightened her hair as best she could without digging in her tote bag for her hairbrush she promised herself that her immediate goal was to find a place to stay for the coming night.

Pulling back onto the road, Jill glanced at her surroundings. The road snaked out in tight curves, hinting that her hasty retreat from southern New Jersey the day before hadn't brought her too far. A mist shrouded the countryside, making the smell of dampened earth permeate the inside of the car. Jill always drove with the window down, even in the most inclement weather. Traffic began to pick up, and she glanced toward her gas gauge. She was down to a quarter of a tank, which didn't mean much since her car had never registered correctly. For all she knew she could be close to running on empty. Coasting around a bend in the road, Jill smiled as she saw signs of a town up ahead, recognition lighting the pupils of her eyes as the next sign she passed stated simply, Mill Valley. A small, picturesque village community, Mill Valley had become a popular retreat for artistic people of all sorts, or so the roadside plaque proclaimed.

It didn't take long for Jill's unease to melt into enchantment as she guided her car along the narrow streets of Mill Valley. Passing several establishments she knew she had to inspect more carefully, she spied a tight parking place along the main boulevard and eased her car into it with enviable expertise. Her first adventure came in the guise of a combination curio shop and clothing store. Making a point to ferret out the predictable rack of postcards by the cash register, Jill picked out several at random, garnering local information from them. Knowing that the wardrobe she had packed was mostly resort wear, Jill purchased two hand-embroidered sweater tops and a rather unique denim skirt that had been fashioned out of a pair of old jeans and extended with a floral print material. Tourist prices had taken their toll, and Jill held back a gasp as the girl behind the checkout counter let a hefty sum roll off her tongue to punctuate the clanging jangle of the old-fashioned cash register. Watching the girl methodically fold her purchases and slip them into a paper bag, Jill couldn't help but feel that for the price she was paying the goods should be packed in velvet and delivered to her door with a complimentary bottle of champagne.

As she clutched the bag to her side, Jill's rumbling stomach reminded her that lunch the previous day had been her last acquaintance with food. Directly across the street was a health-food store that from all appearances seemed to be doing quite a brisk business. Dodging traffic, Jill eyed the outside of the shop. The windows were filled with all kinds of greenery and rough-hewn log siding gave it a quaint look of being from another time. A swinging sign hung over the opened doorway, and Jill could imagine the sound its metal hinges would make in a stiff wind. Nature's Bounty was the name the proprietor had chosen for the establishment, and as Jill stepped inside she found herself agreeing with the christening. Barrels overflowed with offerings of all kinds. Herbs grew happily in hundreds of little pots, waiting to be clipped for use, and a large refrigerated bin lined the back of one wall, laden with yogurts, natural juices and milk products. Jill decided to introduce her taste buds to some new fare, so on an impulse she selected an avocado sandwich on whole wheat bread and a small carton of a strawberry health drink made with yogurt. She had always preferred yogurt over ice cream, feeling righteous when she satisfied her cravings with fresh fruit stirred into the plain variety instead of weakening to a hot fudge sundae with nuts. Accepting the offer of a straw as she paid for her late lunch, Jill opened the drink and took a preliminary sip. It tasted good, tart and sweet at the same time.

Tucking her sandwich into her tote bag to be sampled when she had settled back into her car, Jill hung her bag on one shoulder and wedged her package under the same arm so she could sip her drink more easily. Closing her eyes as she savored the next swallow, Jill stood poised in the doorway to the shop. A gruff jostling was her first indication that she was blocking the entrance. Before she could react, she had been roughly pushed aside, some of the drink splashing against her shirt.

The culprit who had so rudely broken her trance walked with long strides up to the counter, his presence demanding immediate attention. Jill stared at the man's back, willing him to turn around to acknowledge what he had done so she could have the satisfaction of demanding an apology. As though sensing the intensity of her thoughts, the man turned, fixing Jill with a cold, penetrating gaze that made her words catch in her throat. He was undoubtedly the most attractive man she had ever seen. His hair was dark, the color of a moonless night. His eyes smoldered black, sparking a luminous shade as he let them travel the length of her, coming to rest even with her eyes in a penetrating challenge.

"You could have at least said excuse me!" Jill stated with more conviction than she felt.

The man seemed to consider her for a moment

longer, a mocking grin curling along his lips. "On the contrary, miss," he cooed in a flagrant tease, "you were the one blocking the doorway." Without another word he turned back to the counter, having issued what he considered to be an appropriate dismissal.

Jill knew the urge to throw something—anything— just as long as she could make it hit its mark. Deciding reluctantly against violence, her quick mind devised another plan. Walking slowly to where the man stood, Jill paused for a brief second before she slowly and deliberately poured the remaining contents of the carton over his shoes, creating little puddles of cream where he stood. Not waiting for his reaction, she turned and left the shop, jogging out to her car.

"Men!" she mumbled as she struggled with the key, finally turning over the ignition with more power than necessary. "The arrogance...just because they're born male they think all women are put on earth to suit their whims."

Trying to squelch the anxiety that the incident had spurred in her, Jill occupied her mind with thoughts of a place to stay. There were countless accommodations in town, but none seemed to suit her basic prerequisites. First of all, it had to be cheap. She had to be frugal now since she had made the decision not to go back to the office. But more important than anything else, it had to be far enough away from the mainstream. Whenever she needed to think things out, she found that long, lonely walks helped. Jill knew that there must be a beach within close distance of Mill Valley, so she turned her car in that direction.

Certain that her search was going to prove totally futile, Jill had almost resolved herself to turning back to Mill Valley and settling for one of their tourist-class motels when a stark black-and-white sign along the side of the road caught her eye. The lettering on it was sharp and clear: Woodmeire Cottages. There was no telling how old the sign was, but Jill decided to follow the road until it ended. She had traveled more than a mile up the graveled road when she saw a cluster of buildings ahead, one boasting a clothesline that danced merrily with an array of shirts and pants.

Even before the car had sputtered to a stop, the door to what appeared to be the office opened and a squat little woman waddled out of the doorway and onto the porch.

"Get yourself lost?" she inquired happily as Jill stepped from the car.

Jill shook her head, knowing immediately that she liked the woman. "Actually, I was hoping to rent one of your cottages for a few weeks."

The old woman stared at Jill and at her long golden hair. She grimaced slightly. "It doesn't exactly work that way, Miss…what did you say your name was?"

"Jill Barton. I don't understand. You must have—" Jill looked around "—about twenty cottages here. Are they all full?"

"Lan'sakes, no, child. You must be from out of state, otherwise you would know what this place is." Her eyes twinkled as she watched a play of emotion on Jill's face.

"You mean…this quiet, beautiful place is…?" Disbelief glowed on Jill's face. "I didn't know. What I mean is, there isn't any kind of sign to indicate…" she finished lamely.

The old woman laughed, this time doubling over. "This place has been referred to as many things, but I don't think it's ever been called what you're thinking.

You was kind of thinking this was a nudist colony. Is that it?"

"You mean it isn't?" Jill answered the question with a question.

"Lordy, no. This is an *artists' colony*. I should have told you straight off. Living here for sixty-odd years makes me forget that everybody in the world don't know about it. By the way, my name is Agnes Beaumont. Everyone hereabouts calls me Aggie. I'm the housekeeper for the main house. See, that's the main house over there," she said, pointing to a white clapboard house nestled between evergreens. "I'm just sitting here in this little office to answer the phone till Mr. Matthews gets back. He went into town for some supplies and should be back any minute. He's the one you gotta talk to about staying here. You one of those artist types? What's your specialty?"

"My specialty?" Jill asked in amazement. She still hadn't gotten over the shock that the place wasn't an out-and-out bordello.

"What do you do? Do you write or do you paint? We've got a sculptor here all the way from Los Angeles."

Jill's mind raced. "Write. Right, that's what I do. I write." She decided she could be comfortable with the small white lie. In a way she did write at the office. There was no need to tell anyone that she was no longer employed. As long as she had the money to pay the rent, what difference did it make? It wasn't going to be one of those long-term visits. She was just going to stay long enough to get her head on straight and her act together before she moved on.

"I thought so. I can spot a writer a mile away," Aggie said knowledgeably. "You writers all seem to have a vague kind of look, like you're always thinking about something and just waiting for a pencil to scribble it down."

"You're so right," Jill agreed hastily. "I'm always thinking and I never seem to have a pencil." Frantically, she tried to bring her thoughts into focus. "Do you think I'll have any trouble getting one of the cottages?"

"Shucks no, child. Long as you're one of those artsy people, no offense, you won't have no problem. Look, would you mind doing me a favor of sorts?" Not waiting for Jill to reply, Aggie rushed on. "I got nine blueberry pies ready to go in the oven. Logan, he loves my berry pie, and I want them properly cooled before dinner. That stove over at the main cottage has a mind of its own, and I couldn't take the chance of the pies spilling over and then smoking up the kitchen. We don't have any fire department around here to rush out to put out a fire. You just sit there. There's coffee in the pot—see," Aggie said, pointing to an ancient enamel pot sitting on a hot plate. "You just put your feet up on the desk the way Logan does and wait for him. I'll be seeing you at the dinner table."

"At the dinner table?" Jill asked, puzzled.

"Yep. We all eat in the main dining hall. I do the cooking, and I'm a pretty darn good cook. I don't know what's going to happen at the end of the week. I got to go to Seattle to help my niece have her baby. Logan is just going to have to get another cook or something. You just sit there now and wait for Logan; he should be here any minute."

She was gone, the screen door banging against the doorframe. Jill frowned. How did you help someone have a baby? If there was a way, she was sure the gregarious Aggie would know of it.

Jill poured herself a cup of coffee. She stared at the

thick syrupy mess, trying to decide if it was indeed coffee or some kind of new black syrup. Tentatively, she sipped at it and choked. It tasted like turpentine and tar. If Aggie made blueberry pie the way she made coffee, it was no wonder the cottages were mostly empty.

Thumbing through tattered, dog-eared magazines, Jill chose a vintage copy of *Psychology Today*. She did as Aggie instructed and placed her feet on the desk and started to read the magazine.

"Where's Aggie?" a cold, hard voice demanded.

Jill blinked, taking in the tall form standing in the doorway. Her spirits plummeted when she recognized the man from the health-food store. Of all the rotten, miserable luck!

"Aggie is baking pies," Jill answered defensively. Quickly, she removed her feet from the battered desk. "I would like to rent one of the cottages." Thank God, he didn't seem to recognize her as the person who had dumped the strawberry yogurt drink all over his shoes.

A fly buzzed impatiently, its blue-black wings circling Logan Matthews's legs. Impatiently, he brushed at it, his face full of annoyance. "Damn pests," he muttered angrily. His eyes narrowed slightly as he advanced farther into the room. When he was inches from her, recognition dawned on him. Again, he lashed out at the offending fly. "It's your fault that this fly is driving me crazy. Look for a flyswatter—there must be one around here somewhere." It was an order, a command.

"You…you deserved to have that drink dumped all over you. Manners and a little courtesy would have helped. You just…you knocked me out of the way. You did. I almost fell," Jill snapped.

"Women! You're all alike. You want to be liberated.

You want all of these rights, and then you complain when you get them. If you had stayed in the kitchen where you belonged, this wouldn't be happening."

"In the kitchen!" Jill shrieked.

"Yes, the kitchen. That's where women belong. Besides, you were blocking the doorway, drinking that mess without regard to who was coming or going. I didn't knock you over, I brushed past you. End. Fini. I don't want to hear another word. Get the flyswatter!"

"Get it yourself," Jill snapped as she gathered up her tote bag. "Just tell me where I register."

"You don't understand. You only register if I say you register."

"What does that mean?"

"That means you can't stay here unless you're an artist. What do you do?"

"I write," Jill said loftily. "How much is it for a week?"

Logan Matthews determinedly swatted at the angrily buzzing fly. "Let me see your credentials," Matthews said arrogantly. It was clear he didn't believe her.

"I don't have any...any credentials. I'm just starting out, and so far I don't have anything published. I'm reliable; I won't break your furniture and I don't have wild parties."

"If you don't have credentials, you can't stay here. How do I know you aren't some sort of runaway house-wife out for a lark? We get them all the time. Sooner or later a husband shows up, and then there's hell to pay. If you don't have something to verify who you are, you can't stay here."

"That's just great. It's a good thing James Michener or Norman Mailer didn't stop here. You would certainly have pie on your face. Just look how famous they are. What I'm saying is, how can I ever hope to get to be like them if you won't give me a chance? They had to start out somewhere. I need the peace and quiet of a place like this." Her tone was desperate as she pleaded with the arrogant man standing next to her.

"What is it you're writing? Show me something, a draft, an outline, that will verify the fact that you're serious about all of this."

Jill noticed that his eyes were lowered to her left hand, looking for some sign of a ring.

"I haven't even started, so how can I show you something? All the ideas are in my head. I can pay."

Logan Matthews snorted. "This place is free. We don't take money. All the guests take turns with the chores. We don't have any freeloaders here. Right now, since summer has ended, we've only three artists in residence, so there's plenty of room. But the rules are the same. Everyone has to pull his weight. Why don't you tell me what it is you're writing? Then I'll make a decision."

Jill's mind raced. "My memoirs," she said softly.

Logan Matthews threw back his head and howled with laughter. "Your memoirs? What makes you think anyone would be interested in *your* memoirs?"

Jill's dander was up. "It doesn't make any difference if anyone is interested or not. That's what I'm doing. I have led a very…a…diff…what I mean is, it's been a challenging kind of life. I think that I'm more than qualified to write about myself." Jill couldn't believe she was saying these things, lying actually. But somehow it was urgent that he believe she was a writer because it had suddenly become important that she be allowed to stay here in the colony.

There was humor in Matthews's face. "I get it—one

of those trashy exposé things. Somehow, you don't look the type."

"You have no right to type me in any way. All I want is a cottage so I can start on my...on my book. Either you're going to give it to me or you aren't. What is it?"

"And you're feisty too. What kind of typewriter do you have? Electric or portable? Some of the cottages have electricity and some don't."

"I don't...have a typewriter, that is. I told you, I'm just starting out and I plan to work in longhand till I get the hang of the whole thing. What's wrong with that?" she asked defensively.

Matthews grinned. "I can hardly wait to read this work of art when it's finished. I'm going against my better judgment, I want you to know that. But you can stay. If I find out that you're in some sort of trouble or one of those runaway wives, you'll leave so fast this place will go up in smoke. Do we understand each other?"

Jill let her breath out in little doses. "Perfectly."

"You can have Briar Cottage. It has electricity. Let me see," he said, thumbing through a ledger. "I'll have to assign you to some chores. You will do all your tasks at the assigned time. When you pursue your...literary career will, of course, be up to you. Is that agreeable?"

Jill nodded.

"Starting in the morning, you will have latrine duty. When Aggie leaves for Seattle, you will have kitchen duty. And two of the guests are men who like to eat."

"Now, just a minute," Jill sputtered angrily.

"Take it or leave it. By the way, what's your name?"

"What's latrine duty? Jill Barton."

"Bathrooms, Jill Barton."

"Are you saying that the cottages don't have private bathrooms?"

"Right. Everything here is a communal project. We have a dining room, a workroom where each guest is assigned his or her own space and, of course, the bathrooms. Showers, one tub. Then, of course, there's this office, and we have a motor pool of sorts. The men handle the yard work. Do you have any questions?"

"And if I did, what good would it do me?" Jill muttered under her breath.

"We breakfast at seven, lunch at noon, and dinner is served at six on the dot. Punctuality is a virtue. Can you remember that during your stay?" There was a mocking light in the dark eyes as Logan Matthews waited to see what her reaction would be. "Do you want to stay or not?"

"Okay. Okay," Jill said through clenched teeth.

"By the way, about the bathrooms. Cleaning supplies are in a closet at the main house."

"I thought they would be. What time do I report tomorrow?"

"Sunup should do it. Of course, if you want to get a head start and clean the bathroom before you turn in for the night, that's up to you. All I'm telling you is I want a clean bathroom when I get up in the morning. I shower at five-thirty in the morning."

Jill's eyes widened. "No one gets up that early."

"I do. Now, sign the register and I'll show you to your cottage. By the way, it's fairly secluded, allows for privacy. It's clean and comfortable."

Jill's hands were shaking so badly that she could barely sign her name on the dotted line. What in the world had she gotten herself into? By the time Aggie left for Seattle she would be right on her trail. Kitchen duty! It was a wonder he didn't call it KP. Latrines and KP. He must have been in the military at some point.

Just who was he anyway? She made a mental note to quiz Aggie the first chance she got.

"Come along, then, I'll show you to your cabin. Where did you park your car?" Logan said, snapping his ledger shut after he had carefully scrutinized her writing.

"My car is…" A vision of her bridal gown in the backseat forced her back a step. Wedding gowns would no doubt fit into the same category as runaway wives. "Why…ah, why don't we walk to the cottage? That way I can look around and come back later for my car. I think I would like to walk. In fact, I know I would like to walk. Let's walk," she babbled nervously.

Logan noticed her uneasiness. "You don't have some kind of problem you aren't telling me about, do you?"

Jill looked at his knitted brows and blanched. "Me? Problem? Certainly not. My life is an open book. In fact, it's such an open book that's why I am so willing to write about it." She was babbling again.

Logan opened the screen door and a large Irish setter bounded into the room, heading straight for Jill. He skidded to a stop and then daintily placed both paws on her shoulder. He licked her face affectionately, his tail wagging furiously. "This is Doozey. He's always been fond of girls, but I have to admit I've never seen him quite so smitten. Usually, he has more manners. Down, Doozey."

Jill wiped her face with the sleeve of her shirt. She liked dogs, and Doozey seemed the perfect companion to take on the long walks she planned.

"Go pester Aggie," Logan said warmly to the dog.

Hrumph, Jill snorted inwardly. Guess you have to be a dog to get any kind of friendliness from this guy. How handsome he was when his chiseled features softened. She liked the warm tone in his voice when he spoke to Doozey. For a brief moment she compared him to Deke and wasn't surprised when Deke came up short. But then, next to a man this handsome, most men would come up short.

Jill's nerves were atwitter as she walked alongside Logan, each intent on his own thoughts. He unlocked the door to Briar Cottage and stood back. Jill loved its rustic, cheap comfort. She would be more than comfortable here. "You were right, it's very clean. I'll be sure to keep it that way."

"The bathrooms are at the end of the compound. To the left of the office is the dining room. In one sense it's inconvenient for Aggie because she has to cart all the food to the dining area. She does all the cooking in my kitchen. If I have the time, I help her or some of the other men pitch in."

"Wouldn't it be more efficient if you had a complete kitchen over there to work in?" Jill asked hesitantly as she visualized herself lugging heavy pots of food across the compound.

"The plans are underway. Aggie's getting older and I can't have her working so hard. The work should be completed by the end of next summer. Until then, you're young, hale and hearty, so you should have no problems. Just think," he said coolly, "this experience might take up a whole chapter in your memoirs."

He was baiting her. There was little doubt in her mind that Logan Matthews didn't believe a word she had said about writing a book. She bristled slightly and then relaxed. For now, she was safe. Hard work never killed anyone. She could and would survive. As soon as he left, she would set out on that promised walk. And before she returned she would stop and see Aggie.

Aggie should be a wealth of information on Logan Matthews and this colony. First rule of a writer: Always know what you're writing about. Certainly, that rule could be applied to this situation.

"If I stretch it out, I might be able to make two chapters," Jill answered tartly. "By the way, are you the manager of this colony, or exactly what do you do here?"

"Is this for your book too?"

"One never knows," Jill quipped.

"Why don't we just say I'm a patron of the arts and let it go at that?"

"If that's what you want to say, it's okay with me. I myself don't exactly need a patron, not at this point anyway," Jill said hastily.

"Do I take that to mean you are financially and economically independent?" Logan queried.

"More or less," Jill hedged. This was no time for him to delve into her background. So far, she had lucked out with a minimum of background on herself. But she had to get that gown out of her car as quickly as she could before he saw it and made an issue out of it.

"I'll see you in the dining room. Six sharp. Aggie has a lot to do, so perhaps you could help her clean up after dinner."

"Is that a suggestion or an order?"

"Whatever you want. Just do it," Logan said coldly as he closed the door behind him. She heard the dog bark happily and watched as Logan picked up a stick to toss in the air. The setter bounded off happily while Logan strode across the compound with long, purposeful strides. Jill knew in her gut that everything Logan did he would do purposefully.

Thirty minutes later the yellow car was parked

outside Briar Cottage. The mound of white satin and the lacy veil were in a heap on the floor of the tiny hall closet. She hadn't realized how tense she was until the closet door clicked shut.

She still had two hours till dinner. She could take a walk over to the main house and visit Aggie. She would even magnanimously offer to help her if the older woman looked as though she could use another pair of hands.

CHAPTER THREE

DOOZEY TROTTED ALONGSIDE Jill in companionable silence. Every so often he would woof at a stray squirrel or chipmunk but make no move to chase it away. She was following him, Jill realized as they came near the compound. A rich, tangy aroma tantalized her senses. It was a rich New England kind of smell and one with which she was vaguely familiar. What was Aggie cooking? Evidently, Doozey was as curious as she was. He broke into a run and headed for the back of the Cape Cod house—toward the kitchen area, Jill surmised. She followed the dog and wasn't surprised to see Doozey in his begging position near the screen door.

"Hi, Aggie, it's me, Jill. Mr. Matthews said I could stay. I'm in Briar Cottage. May I come in?"

"Of course. My kitchen is open to anyone and everyone. Here, have a peanut butter cookie. Made them fresh this morning. Give one to that fool dog before his tongue falls out. He's just like Logan, can't keep either one of them away from my cookies. If I didn't keep an eye on this cookie jar, them two would eat them all before the day was out. Logan likes to take them with him in his knapsack when he goes off to do his thing."

"What smells so good, Aggie?"

"New England clam chowder, Aggie Beaumont

style. What that means, child, is I put strips of bacon and a dash of celery seed in it. That makes it authentically mine. Everyone around here just calls it Aggie's chowder. Even that hound sitting next to you likes it. Where did you come across him?"

"Actually, he found me while I was walking and he sort of led me here. I would have sought you out myself; he just made it easier for me."

"So, you're in Briar Cottage. Been a long time since anyone's been in that place. Clean as a whistle, let me tell you." Aggie frowned. "I can't believe that he let you stay there. There are some cottages that aren't so far away."

"Is there something wrong with Briar Cottage?" Jill asked fearfully.

"Heavens no, child. It's just that Logan's fiancée lived there last summer. When she up and left, he closed it, and no one has been near it since."

"Mr. Matthews isn't married, then?"

"Nope, single and free as the breeze. Isn't that what you young people say? He's all caught up in his work. He's a very busy man. Runs a mighty big law firm in Boston when the spirit moves him. Come summer, he comes here and runs this place. He's rich as Rockefeller; that's why he lets everyone stay here for free as long as they pull their weight. He's a painter himself. Mighty fine artist. Does seascapes and trees. He paints a tree like an angel."

"Really? He didn't look like a painter to me."

"He's one of the best—right up there with Andrew Wyeth. Things here can tend to themselves. Come along to my room and I'll show you a picture he did just for me. His daddy and my husband used to run this place, and then when Logan came of age he sort of took over, him being a painter and all."

Jill followed Aggie down a hall and then down a small flight of five steps to a tiny apartment.

Aggie's apartment was furnished quite sparsely. There were none of the grandmotherly touches of old framed pictures, afghans and lace tablecloths. Instead, there was an array of casual decor, a floor devoid of carpeting of any kind and scattered pieces of art that had been fashioned from driftwood and sea rocks. The only picture in the room was an angry rendition of the sea, giving the wall an almost foreboding look. Catching Jill staring at it, Aggie clucked like a chicken over a brood of chicks she was particularly fond of. "Logan painted that for me," she said with the pride of ownership, "and I guess it's just about my favorite thing in the whole world."

"It takes my breath away," Jill said honestly as she admired the turbulent sea scene.

"Haven't you ever seen any of his work in the galleries in New York?" Aggie asked. "He's had showings all over the country."

Patting Jill's hand in a motherly fashion, Aggie reached out to adjust the picture from its crooked stance on the wall. "You will soon enough, my dear. He's got a showing coming up in Boston in less than a month's time, and if it's the success it promises to be, he'll sign a contract for a display in a Paris gallery."

Jill had tried to act enthusiastic, but she found herself itching to get back to her cabin. The day's events were beginning to take their toll, and she craved the chance to stretch out on a real bed.

"You look about done in. That's what this country fresh air does for you. Why don't you go back to your cabin now and catch a few winks of sleep? I'll come and get you when it's time for dinner, or else I'll send

Doozey to wake you. We'll have lots of time to talk before I leave for Seattle."

Jill was tired. A short catnap would work wonders. "I think I'll do just that. I'm going to help you with the cleanup after dinner. Mr. Matthews...ah...suggested it when he left Briar Cottage."

"Did he, now?" Aggie's eyes twinkled. "More like he ordered you to do it. Logan is a great one for issuing orders and getting people to obey them. Funny how no one ever defies him. Makes a body wonder somehow how he does it. Scat now. I have to get back to my cooking."

Jill laughed. She liked the talkative older woman. Liked her a lot. A pity she was going away. Who would be her ally, her confidante, when she was gone? Doozey, who else? Besides, the setter couldn't take sides.

Coming back to Briar Cottage alone was like seeing it for the first time. She hadn't even opened the checkered curtains.

Her fantasies left her totally unprepared for reality, and the moment the parlor light was switched on, Jill felt as though she had committed highway robbery. The front room was the largest, accommodating a brass bed with a homey, star-stitched quilt and a pair of lace-encased pillows. A few feet from the end of the bed was a round breakfast table, covered with a checkered tablecloth. Two wire-backed chairs were pushed up against it, a ready invitation for an impromptu snack. Jill was reminded of her uneaten avocado sandwich. The bathroom was complete with a pull-chain commode and a bathtub that boasted clawed feet and ornate silver fixtures; regrettably, neither worked.

Jill could only nod her approval silently, thanking the fates for guiding her car down that long, seldom-used road.

Jill whirled about the room, allowing herself a contented sigh. Eyeing the bed, she knew that she was too wound up to consider sleep even though she was tired. Slipping on a sweater, she latched the door behind her and set off in the direction she supposed would most quickly lead her to the sea. The short walk around the compound had just been her way of acquainting herself with her immediate surroundings. This walk, her second of the day, was to buoy her spirits, to revitalize herself in some way.

The terrain was mostly mottled with patches of the type of beach grass found along most beaches in the area. It wasn't long before she hit the dunes, clambering up even the steepest of them in a promise to herself that she wouldn't head back until she had caught her first glimpse of the sea. The beach stretched out in a flat, infinite landscape, hypnotizing Jill as the granules of sand caught the orange glow of a fast-approaching sunset. Spotting a formation of rocks a few hundred yards ahead of her, Jill made that her goal. Selecting one of the largest, more contoured boulders, she sat down and positioned herself so she could absorb the view at her leisure.

The sun bounced along the horizon, hanging for a moment before sliding into the sea. A low sound heralded its descent, and Jill sat up abruptly, convinced that the sounds she was hearing were not entirely those of nature. Her suspicion gave way to conviction as the muted sounds of a song reached her ears. She couldn't decipher the words, but the melody haunted her. The whispering cries of scattered sands drew her attention to a spot a few yards away. There, perched on the sands, was an easel with a man beside it dismantling his canvas and storing his brushes in a satchel he had slung over one shoulder. Logan Matthews preferred late-afternoon light in his efforts to find inspiration for his painting.

Jill contemplated speaking, for surely he would hear her across such a short distance. But something made her remain silent. In the next instant she was glad she had followed her instincts, for as the man turned his back on the sea his face was as angry as the seascape in Aggie's room. Jill fought to hold back her gasp of something akin to fear. Never in her life had she seen such stormy emotions and yet there was a shadow of pain beneath it all. But he had been so warm, so contented-looking, when he was with the frolicking Irish setter.

Quietly, Jill withdrew. She made her way back to Briar Cottage with her thoughts in a turmoil. Logan Matthews was a man to be reckoned with. A man of contradictions, as changeable as the sea itself—tranquil one moment and turbulent the next with emotions whipped to a frothy fever.

AGGIE WAS AS GOOD as her word. Promptly at three minutes to six Doozey whined outside the cottage door. Jill gathered up her sweater and dutifully followed the dog across the compound. Sounds of laughter and easy camaraderie greeted her as she entered the door. One-on-one introductions were made, with Jill saying her name over and over. No one asked what she did. It was evident that if Logan Matthews accepted her she was all right in their eyes.

Jack De Marco was a wide-eyed, freckle-faced sculptor from Los Angeles who shook hands gently. His grin was infectious as he released Jill's hand and turned her over to Aaron Michaelson, who claimed to be the best photographer on the East Coast. It wasn't just his opinion, he went on to say; *Life* magazine backed him up one hundred percent. Pat Laird the journalist shook Jill's hand firmly and then warmly embraced her. "Nice to see a fellow female. I've been feeling slightly outnumbered around here with all these guys. Welcome aboard, or whatever it is you say in the creative world."

They accepted her completely and Jill felt right at home amidst the busy chatter as they waited for the food to be brought to their table.

Jill settled herself in a round captain's chair and waited to be served. Thick bowls of tantalizing clam chowder were set down on the table along with a heaping plate of crusty bread. Round scoops of golden butter, sitting in a pyramid, graced the middle of the red checkered cloth. Jill binged with the rest of her table companions. She felt stuffed when the last drop of the creamy chowder slipped down her throat. She was further amazed when a heaping platter of fried chicken and a gigantic bowl of salad appeared. Jill groaned as did the others. They fell to it, murmuring their approval of Aggie's expertise in the kitchen.

No sooner were the dinner plates set aside than the biggest slices of pie Jill had ever seen were placed in the center of the table. "Homemade ice cream," Aggie announced. "I made it myself last night. Eat up."

More groans as the diners attacked the luscious pie and creamy ice cream. There were choruses of, "I'll have to run for two hours tonight," "I'll have to do two hundred sit-ups instead of one hundred," and other general comments about waistlines.

Out of the corner of her eye Jill noticed Logan Matthews staring at her. There seemed to be an amused glint in his eyes. He was testing her. She knew it and so did Logan. And from the grinning faces of the others they knew it too. He knew she couldn't cook like this. She wasn't a seasoned salt like Aggie. Jill's back straightened. He wanted her to fall flat on her face so he could say, I told you so. He was the kind of man who would step over her when she did fall and go about his business. After all, she had seen that angry face by the water. She shivered as she looked around the dining hall.

Jill decided she would give her stay at the colony her best shot, and if that didn't work, she would leave. At that point it would matter little if Logan wanted the money or not. Her best shot. "Male chauvinist," she muttered to herself as her companions scraped back their chairs in preparation for the long evening of athletics ahead. Jill seriously doubted if any of them would make good on their promises to work out later. Speaking strictly for herself, the kitchen duty she was assigned would be all she could handle.

It was an exhausting two hours. The crockery seemed to weigh a ton. Jill lost track of the number of trips she made from the dining room to the makeshift kitchen with its cold-water sink.

She was drying the last piece of silver with a soaking dish towel when Logan motioned for her to meet him outside. Aggie gave her a sly wink and set about stacking the dishes on the shelves. "Go ahead, honey, you're the prettiest thing Logan has seen in a long time. Enjoy the evening. Jill?"

It was a question and Jill waited.

"Jill, Logan is a hard man to figure out. He might seem callous and hard to some people when he's really not that way at all. He's been hurt to the core and doesn't want to be put in that position again. I heard the two of you sniping away at each other this afternoon. Voices carry across the compound, remember that. He's a man."

Outside, the air was chill, almost cold; tastes of the coming winter were sharp in the night. Jill shivered slightly, pulling her sweater closely around her shoulders. "Brrr…gets cold early here."

"Here?" Logan questioned. "Where's there?"

"Oh, the southern tip of New Jersey. I suppose it's cold enough there right now, but this is different."

"Perhaps it's being so close to the ocean. The air is damper, you feel the cold more."

"No, that's not it," she told him quietly. "I've lived near the ocean all my life. We do have a seashore in Jersey, you know. It's just different here—like a Currier and Ives painting about to be drawn. It's like expecting the sweet taste of maple syrup before you open the bottle."

"I like that, what you just said. Perhaps you'll make a writer after all."

Their steps were taking them in the direction of Briar Cottage, and somehow Jill felt like a girl being walked home from school, only Logan wasn't carrying her books. She wasn't exactly looking forward to the next morning and latrine duty, as he called it. During the cleanup after dinner, she had seriously considered leaving Mill Valley. Surely, there must be someplace she could stay where she wouldn't be expected to work so hard. At this point, and with all the thinking she had to do, she would be more than willing to pay her way someplace where she could get her thoughts and feelings together.

Not that she was lazy, far from it, but seeing the feast Aggie had set before them that evening had scared the dickens out of her. There was no way she could ever hope to equal that good home cooking, and she was dreading the thought of portending failure.

She could leave and, more than likely, she *should* leave. But walking under the trees with the brine of the ocean in the air and the peace…Jill knew without a doubt that she would stay, must stay. She felt inexplicably drawn to Mill Valley and strangely curious about the enigma that was Logan Matthews.

"Penny…"

"What? Oh, my thoughts. I was thinking how peaceful it is here."

Logan nodded, agreeing.

"There's a beauty here, a kind of healing."

"Healing? Funny you should call it that."

The tone of his voice deepened; there was a sadness, a mournful quality, in his words, and Jill believed he was thinking of his own broken romance.

They continued their walk until the dim light of her cottage was visible through the trees. Doozey barked and scampered on ahead, expecting his master and Jill to follow him to the cottage.

"I'll leave you here," Logan told her. "Doozey will see you the rest of the way."

Again, that mournful note in his voice. Was he trying to tell her that he was sorry he had put her in the cottage that had been closed ever since the girl he loved ran out on him? Did his mention of Doozey remind him that he and his setter had walked this trail to the cottage many times—happier times?

"Good night, Logan," Jill heard herself say, looking up into his handsome face, seeing pain in his eyes.

Suddenly, without warning, he scooped her into his arms. His mouth took hers, searing her lips with his own. His arms were strong, drawing her close, holding her fast, preventing her escape. And Jill clung to him, needing him, wanting to make him believe that she was a woman, a woman and worthy of love. She demanded that he erase all thoughts of Deke's rejection from her mind, her heart.

Logan's embrace tightened. His lips moved over hers, evoking a never-before-imagined emotion from deep within her. A sound formed in her throat and was silenced by his kiss. His arms were bands of steel, holding her fast, pressing her against him, making her aware of his masculinity, his dominance.

Doozey was howling; Logan was muttering something, something she couldn't understand. As quickly as he had seized her, he set her free, making her feel as though her legs would buckle under and she would fall to the crazily whirling ground.

His hands reached out to steady her, his hands warm against her chilled flesh. For an instant she thought he was going to take her in his arms again. Instead, he stared at her, a frown creasing his brow, his dark hair falling over his forehead. It was his mouth that fascinated her and held her attention. It was grim, tight with sorrow, taut with rage.

Abruptly, he turned on his heel and left her alone beneath the trees with only the light from her cottage to show the way.

JILL AWOKE EARLY the next morning, her mind holding groggy images of the day before. She could remember coming back across the dunes, having waited long after Logan left with his easel.

Propelled by thoughts of a hearty plate of bacon and eggs, Jill rolled off the bed, wrapping the quilt around her as a makeshift robe. The room was unbearably cold, the morning breezes from the sea curling under the door and seeping through every affordable entrance the cabin offered. Jill remembered with a groan that breakfast was only a fantasy until she could get to the dining hall.

Gritting her teeth to try to control their chattering, Jill tossed the quilt back onto the end of the bed. Undressing as fast as she could, she decided to wear one of the blouses she had purchased in town, along with the unusual skirt that somehow appealed to her more every time she looked at it. Completing the effect with her new cork-colored boots, she then covered her chill-bumped arms with the warm comfort of her sweater.

In an action prodded more by duty than choice, Jill sorted through the confusion in her tote bag to try to locate the postcards that she had bought. Choosing a rather dated photograph of Mill Valley's main street, slashed across the middle with a furled banner that read Welcome to Mill Valley, Jill poised her hand over the blank message area on the back, not sure just what to say or how to say it. Something that the elderly woman by the roadside had said to her jumped into her mind, and she wrote to Nancy Evans:

> Kidnapped by gypsies! Caravan camped out at Woodmeire Cottages on the outskirts of town.
>
> Jill

Jill glanced at her watch. She would watch the sun come up. A chilling, bracing walk would do her a world of good. She could even jog and try to work off some of Aggie's dinner from the night before. And she could try to put the memory of Logan's kiss behind her, try to put from her mind the memory of how his arms felt around her. Try. It was like giving her stay here her best shot. All she could do was try.

Her legs felt like Jell-O as she slid them into her skirt. Just thinking of the handsome man was turning her weak-kneed and silly. No doubt there was even a stupid look on her face in the bargain. Aggie had been so right. Never in her life had she been kissed so soundly, so thoroughly. What all the romantic magazines said was true. The earth did tilt, the fireworks did shower the heavens. Deke had told her bells would ring *after* marriage, but Logan Matthews had made them ring with his first kiss. Deke had lied. She should hold her rioting emotions in check, Jill cautioned herself. She should be wary of Logan and of all men. It was so soon since she had been disappointed, humiliated. But all that seemed to be a different time, a different place. Also, it was true that nothing could perk up a battered ego like the attention of a new man, especially an exciting man like Logan Matthews. And the fact that Logan could excite her and salve her pride proved to Jill that whatever she had felt for Deke, it had not been love.

Satisfied that she had fulfilled her obligation with the postcards, Jill laid them on the table by the front door to be mailed sometime in the future.

Closing the door behind her, she found herself wondering if Logan Matthews was awake or slaving artistically over a blank canvas. Scolding herself for allowing her thoughts to be occupied by the man, Jill marched across the tiny porch and down the steps to the road. The sound of an engine barreling down the dirt road that led to her cottage caught her ear. The car definitely needed a tune-up. She looked up just in time to see a baby-blue Porsche roar past, skid to a stop and then race backward and come to a grinding, screeching halt within inches of where she was standing.

Jill stood transfixed as a tall, redheaded woman slid out of the car. The woman oozed sophistication. Her clothes were obviously of designer quality, and Jill could almost swear that her long legs boasted the luxury of real silk stockings. A single golden chain around her throat matched the belt about her tiny waist that accentuated the jade material of her dress. Her hair bounced in a style that Jill regarded with envy; a pair of sunglasses were pushed up on her head.

The woman was out of the car and fishing in her bag for what was obviously a key. Jill said nothing but watched as she then leaned over to take a petit-point bag from the bucket seat on the passenger side of the sports car. With no wasted motion she walked up the steps and fitted her key into the lock. She showed no surprise when the door opened to her touch. Puzzled, Jill followed her into Briar Cottage.

"I know this is going to sound odd, but what are you doing in my cottage?" Jill demanded.

The woman's perfectly manicured eyebrows rose into a graceful arch. "Your cottage?" She made the words sound obscene.

"Yes, my cottage. I'm staying here. I arrived yesterday and Mr. Matthews himself brought me over here. Where I come from, we don't walk into other people's lodgings without knocking. Who are you and what do you want?"

The woman laughed. It was a musical tinkle of a sound that chilled Jill to the very bone.

"I am Stacey Phillips." She made it sound important, as if she were some sort of celebrity.

"I'm Jill Barton, but that still doesn't tell me what you're doing in my cottage." Jill hoped her voice was as firm-sounding as she intended.

Stacey Phillips laughed again.

"Darling, I have a key. See!"

Jill saw the single key hanging from an expensive Gucci chain and wanted to die on the spot.

"This," she said, motioning her hand around the small cottage, "is mine. The key says it's mine. As to what I want, it's simple. I want Logan Matthews. Now, Miss whatever-your-name-is, get your things out of here. Immediately. I'll be staying here from now on."

Jill was thunderstruck. This couldn't be happening to her, it just couldn't. What was she to do? Where should she go? Aggie. Aggie would know what to do.

Squaring her shoulders, Jill gathered her belongings together and stuffed them into her carryall and tote bag. She looked around to see if she had forgotten anything. Satisfied, she stared at Stacey Phillips for a moment. She must be the woman that Aggie had told her about. Jill's stomach lurched and then settled down. Stacey was as beautiful as Logan was handsome. They must make a handsome couple, Jill thought sourly.

Dejectedly, Jill tossed her belongings into the back of her car and then trudged across to the Cape Cod house and Aggie.

Aggie turned from her stance in front of the stove.

"I saw the car," she said sourly. "Expect Logan heard it too. What are you doing here so early?"

"I've just been tossed out of Briar Cottage. She had a key on a Gucci chain and said Briar Cottage was hers. She also told me she wanted Logan Matthews. I can only believe she meant it. That's why I'm standing here. Can I help you?"

"You sure can. Start spooning out the jam into those little dishes. You can bunk in with me. I've got twin beds in my room. Come the weekend, you'll have the whole place to yourself. That solves two problems. Now all we have to do is figure out what *she's* doing here."

Aggie's voice was full of disgust as she turned the long strips of bacon on the grill.

"She said she came for Logan," Jill said with a catch in her throat.

"She probably came because of business. I'm not saying she doesn't want Logan. I'm sure she does. Miss Phillips works in an art gallery in New York. Her father is the one who arranges for all of Logan's showings. Wouldn't surprise me a bit if she turned out to be the one who is going to arrange and handle Logan's Paris show."

"Will Logan be going to Paris, do you think?" Jill asked in a small voice.

Aggie grimaced. "Probably," she said curtly. "She's here, in the front parlor. Listen," Aggie commanded.

"I can't eavesdrop," Jill protested.

"Well, I can. I have no scruples when it comes to Logan. I love him like he was my own son. Here, you watch the bacon."

Aggie tiptoed over to the door leading to Logan's dining room and stood with her ear pressed against the white panel. Jill felt sick.

The loud voices reached her ears. She listened, forgetting her rules against eavesdropping.

CHAPTER FOUR

"STACEY! WHAT ARE YOU doing here? Whatever it is, forget about it. I told you a year ago that I would only do business with your father. We have nothing to say to each other."

"You're a fool, Logan. Haven't you heard? My father is in the south of France recuperating from a coronary. I'm in charge of the gallery. I had my secretary write you three separate letters, all of which you ignored. I made this trip up here purposely to talk to you. It's time we mended fences. Logan, I'm sorry about the way I left you, but—"

"Spare me, Stacey. I'm busy. It's almost breakfast time. If you recall, we do things on a schedule around here. Now that you're here, I can see that I'll have to make arrangements for you."

"Don't worry your head about a thing. I made my arrangements. I moved into Briar Cottage a few moments ago. And yes, darling, I recall many, many moments, all of them ecstatically happy, with you at Briar Cottage."

Jill's eyes popped open as her gaze met Aggie's forlorn look.

"You what? I assigned that cottage yesterday—"

"That's what she said when she left. Possession, darling…"

Jill could just imagine the stunning Stacey waving her Gucci key chain with the key to Briar Cottage under Logan's nose.

"You can just move yourself right back out. You can stay in the Wynde Cottage. You can't come here and upset the routine I've established. I won't have it. You left once. Coming back entitles you to nothing but what I choose to give you. Move to Wynde Cottage!"

"Not on your life. I like Briar Cottage. It holds too many memories for me to give it up to some slip of a girl in tacky denim. We have a contract, Logan. A contract that you signed. It's true that you signed it with my father, but I now have his power of attorney. You and I will be working together. In order for us to have a harmonious relationship I will stay at Briar Cottage where I am comfortable."

"She's got him over a barrel," Aggie hissed.

Jill nodded mutely.

"I don't need you to advise me on my legal rights. I'm an attorney, remember?" Logan snapped.

"Darling, as if I could ever forget." Her voice was suddenly cold and hard, just like Logan's. "You have a contract with my gallery, and I plan to see that you live up to it. To the letter! How do you expect me to plan anything if I'm not allowed to be involved with the pieces you're doing? It's convenient for me, Logan."

"And forget about the girl as long as you get what you want, right, Stacey?" Logan thundered. Not waiting for any response, he continued. "Pieces! Is that what you think art is? So many 'pieces' to be delivered by a set date? You can't time creativity, Stacey. You know nothing and care nothing about art aside from its monetary values."

"Honestly," Stacey retorted, "why I put up with your temperament..."

"Because it makes you money," Logan barked. "It enables you to whiz around in your fancy Porsche and it got you into that exclusive country club you always wanted to drag me to. Stacey, you wouldn't know how to live any other way."

"Temper, temper, Logan," Stacey cooed.

"Aggie!"

It was another bark, a demand for immediate attention. The door to the kitchen slammed open, almost knocking Aggie from her eavesdropping position. Logan's eyes took in the scene and his jaw tightened.

"Evidently, you heard."

If he was surprised to see Jill, he said nothing. Jill turned away, unable to meet his angry gaze. The hot bacon grease hissed and sputtered. Jill sniffed as she lifted the strips of bacon and laid them on several layers of thick paper towels to drain.

"Aggie?"

"Yes, Logan," Aggie said in a motherly tone.

"I want you to take—"

"I already told Jill she could bunk in with me and when I leave on the weekend, she can have the room to herself. I figured that was what you would want."

A look of relief washed over Logan's face. "What would I do without you, Aggie?" was all he said as he left the kitchen.

"Aggie, I've been thinking," Jill said as she put the finishing touches to one of the heavy trays. "Maybe I should stay in the Wynde Cottage till you leave. It's not that I don't want to stay with you, it's just that I want to be alone to do some thinking. I hope you don't mind. I thought I might wander by the cottage after breakfast and take a look. If I change my mind, is your offer still open?"

"Of course." There was genuine affection in Aggie's voice as she too finished up another of the heavily laden trays. She looked around to see if she had forgotten anything.

"Now watch, Jill, this is how it works."

She gave a bell hanging near the ancient stove a long pull. The sound was deafening. Within minutes Jack and Aaron whizzed through the door and literally raced to the dining hall, the heavy trays extended in front of them.

"I get the coffee urn ready the night before, and the first person in the dining hall plugs it in. We have a generator over there, did you know that?"

Jill shook her head.

The photographer and the sculptor were back for the second load. Aggie handed Jill a basket holding the breakfast rolls, and she herself carried two jugs of orange juice. "That about does it. You'll see, everything will be piping hot when we sit down. Want to know the secret?" Again, Jill nodded. "I keep the plates warming in the oven."

She would never remember all of this, Jill thought morosely as she trudged behind Aggie.

The breakfast atmosphere was a repeat of dinner the night before. The only exception was that Logan Matthews was not in attendance. Nor was Stacey Phillips.

The washing and cleaning up were completed by nine o'clock.

"Is there anything else you have for me to do, Aggie? No? Show me where the bath…the latrines are. That's my job, you know. I have to clean them. I almost forgot, what with Miss Phillips arriving and all. Even Mr. Matthews didn't chew me out. I expected he would. I suppose he forgot too."

Aggie nodded sagely. "Everything you'll need is in the cupboard inside. It's really no big mess. Most of the guests are respectful of each other and try to leave the bathrooms clean. Once in a while we get a messy one like Miss Phillips. She smears the place from one end to the other, and when she comes out she looks as though she stepped off a magazine page. What people don't see is the mess she leaves behind. All the cottages have bathrooms, but Logan was running into such expense with the separate drains, he had all the plumbing turned off a couple of years ago. Now we have this one community room, and it does seem to work better. Logan said this was a communal kind of living and everyone was to share. I think he was right. At the time I wasn't all that hepped up on the idea, but now I like it just fine. You will too after you get used to it. The left side is for the ladies, right side for men."

"Okay, Aggie. Thanks for everything. It's okay, then, if I move into Wynde Cottage till you leave? Do you think I should tell Mr. Matthews?"

"It will be all right. I'll tell him myself. I have to go into town for some supplies. That is, if that confounded pickup is working."

Jill's ears perked up. "What's wrong with the pickup?"

"Engines are a mystery to me. All I know is it grinds and then stalls. Makes me crazy is what it does. I spoke to Logan about it and he said he would take a look at it the first chance he got. That was near three weeks ago, and he still hasn't gotten around to it. I just cross my fingers each time I get into it."

"Want me to take a look at it?" Jill asked hopefully.

"Honey, you can look at it all you want. If you like dirty old engines, I guess it can't hurt anything."

There was hope in the older woman's voice when

she asked suddenly, "Jill, do you know anything about engines, or do you just like to look at them?"

Jill grinned. "A little bit of both. Let's take a look."

Aggie seated herself behind the wheel and waited to do Jill's bidding.

"Again, Aggie. Start it up again. Okay, I see what it is. Now start it."

Aggie turned the key and grinned from ear to ear. "What did you do to it?" she asked in amazement.

Jill withdrew her head, her face wearing a matching grin.

"Oh, I just…"

"Yes, I'd be interested in hearing what you did. This truck hasn't worked right in months," Logan Matthews said quietly.

"Well, this old engine is purring like a kitten, and it only took her two hours. Isn't it amazing, Logan?"

Jill looked sheepish. Her hands were full of grease and her shirt had a streak of grease, which resembled a streak of lightning running from the neckline to her waist.

"I know I didn't clean the bath…latrines yet. But Aggie said she wanted to go into town, so I thought… what I mean is, I wanted to…" Seeing Logan's steely eyes, she wiped her hands on her jeans and backed off several steps. "I'm going to do it now. Right now," she said emphatically. "Go easy on the choke, Aggie, when you start off," she called over her shoulder.

Jill set about making herself presentable. Then she cleaned the bathrooms. Her mother would have been hard pressed to find fault with the completed job. Now she was on her own. Now she could do whatever it was she wanted to do. She would move into Wynde Cottage and then go for another long walk.

Might as well drive her car to the cottage and save

herself a trip later. Besides, her bags were in the back-seat. No point in making more work for herself.

Even though she felt tired, Jill decided to give the cabin a complete cleaning. The only vixen that had escaped Aggie's scouring hand was dust. A peppery film of it layered almost everything, and Jill hummed silently to herself as she set about a campaign to banish it from existence.

The hours passed swiftly, Jill stopping only long enough to snack on a chocolate bar and some peanuts in her handbag.

Deciding to wash off the grime that she had accumulated on her person during her frenzied housecleaning, Jill headed for the sanitation station. She grinned as she discovered that Aggie had thought of every pleasure; a tall canister of bath oil sat hidden behind a fold of the shower curtain. Dumping an ample amount into the one tub, Jill turned on the tap, watching the crystals dissolve into a frothy pink foam. Stripping quickly, she stepped into the inviting warmth and leaned back. The water continued to gush forth, massaging her feet in a rhythmic whirlpool. She closed her eyes, moaning in satisfaction as she felt the water inch up across her body, waiting until it almost reached her chin before she lifted one foot and turned off the spout with her toes.

Daydreaming, Jill began to sing as she soaped her arms and shoulders. When she cleaned, she had failed to see something that now caught her eye. Wedged beneath the sink sat a trunk, the type Jill thought belonged more in an attic. Ignoring her Pandora pleadings, Jill tried to persuade herself that Aggie had probably stocked the case with bathroom supplies. Lecturing herself for feeling snoopy, Jill rinsed off and grabbed the fleecy towel that hung on a rack beside the sink. Without bothering to dress first, she pulled the trunk out to the middle of the bathroom floor. It was too heavy to hold just towels and washcloths, and Jill found herself stifling a giggle of excitement as she lifted the lid. Books! The entire box was filled with books. Greedily devouring the titles, Jill knew she had found a treasure store that would comfort her through many a long, lonely night. Selecting one of the largest bound treasures, Jill read the title out loud: *"A Study of Gothic Architecture."* Flipping through the gold-edged pages, Jill marveled over the beautiful illustrations that had been etched in pen and ink. Knowing that she would want time to examine each page one by one, she laid the book aside and secreted the rest of the bounty back in its hiding place.

Lunch seemed the furthest thing from her mind as Jill settled down at the table in the sitting room of Wynde Cottage. A quick search for the Irish setter had found him snoozing beneath her bed, his ears twitching as though his dreams had carried him across the dunes in pursuit of a gull.

It was late afternoon before Jill closed the book and paid heed to the dog's whining. Nature bidding, she realized when he trotted to the door and barked assertively. Feeling the need to stretch her legs herself, Jill joined the animal as it bounded out toward the beach.

The wind was brisk and the surf was up as Jill and Doozey romped up to their knees in the surprisingly warm water. Gulls swooped and screamed, keeping them company during their search for pretty shells.

Today there was no sign of Logan on the beach, and with a pang Jill considered that he was probably with the fiery-haired Stacey Phillips. From what she had heard of the argument between them that morning it had seemed that Stacey was trying to apologize but that Logan kept interrupting her. Perhaps by this time they had kissed and made up. Stacey Phillips looked to be the kind of woman who always got what she was after, and her female instinct told Jill that Miss Phillips was after Logan.

Knowing by the low growl in her stomach that it was close to dinnertime, she whistled for Doozey and followed him back to the main house where Aggie was cooking. Jill felt revived by her walk, and although her assigned chores didn't require her working the dinner hour, she decided she would give a hand in helping the older woman get the meal on the table and cleared away.

"Honestly, Doozey, I'll never know how Aggie does it! Even with my help it took almost two hours to get everything cleared away last night." She groaned inwardly. How many hours would it take her to do Aggie's job all alone?

ALL THROUGH DINNER, Jill kept a wary eye on Logan's empty chair. Miss Phillips also was missing from the dinner table. He had probably taken her to some posh restaurant, she thought. Aggie's home cooking isn't good enough for our resident art dealer.

Still, even with all the commotion and camaraderie at the table, Jill felt Logan's absence. "This is silly," she scolded herself, pushing away her half-eaten dinner. "You've only known the man for a day, and yet you lose your appetite because you miss him!"

Too tired from her long day to consider reading herself to sleep, Jill readied herself for bed. Having had little else to choose from in her luggage that was appropriate for sleeping other than filmy, whisper-soft negligees, she hastily allowed the peach-colored silk to slide over her body. Grimacing as she looked at herself in the mirror, she felt a dull pang of sorrow. This nightie was a part of her trousseau and she had chosen it with the thought of pleasing Deke. Stiffening her upper lip and pushing aside her regrets, she admitted that the nightgown still pleased *her,* and that was really all that mattered.

Fastening the little satin ribbon at the plunging neckline, she saw how revealing the nightie was as it hugged the soft curves of her figure and fell with subtle allure to her ankles.

Crawling beneath the covers, she realized with a laugh that she hadn't thought of Deke all day, until just this minute. Surely, that proved something. Weren't you supposed to constantly think about the someone you loved?

Ignoring her own question, she turned on her side, inviting sleep. She was lost somewhere between dozing and deep slumber when a noise from outside made her eyes flash open. She could swear someone was walking by her cottage. Holding her breath to make her hearing more acute, Jill waited for the sound to come again.

"Doozey!" came a call, making Jill bolt upright in bed.

"Doozey! Where are you, dog?"

This last demand was followed by the whistling of a master for his dog. Lying back against her pillow, Jill found herself smiling and admitted that it was because Logan Matthews was back in the compound and thinking of his dog, not Miss Phillips.

Drifting back into a light sleep, she was again

awakened, this time by an insistent scratching on the front door.

Forcing herself to climb out from beneath the warm covers, Jill went to investigate. The source of the disturbance took immediate insult at being ignored and, with a resounding thud, pitched itself against the bottom half of the door. Peering out from behind the curtains hanging from the small window beside the door, Jill spied a wagging red tail.

The greeting Doozey gave her when she opened the door always bowled her over, and she could see that the poor beast was hungry for affection. At first, the dog seemed to be content to languish against her legs, his eyes radiant pools of gratitude as she stroked his coat and cooed to him. Jill laughed as his nose poked around the air, sniffing out the origin of her snack of hours ago.

"You big baby," she teased, "hoping for an invitation to share my snack? You're too late; it's all gone."

The dog barked, issuing an affirmative to Jill's question.

"Come on, I suppose I can find a Chunky bar for you."

Leaning back in the cottage's one chair, she watched in fascination as the setter began to dine on his chocolate. She had expected him to gulp down the offering in one voracious bite. Instead, he savored it a morsel at a time, showing Jill he was a dog gifted with class.

"Doozey! Where are you?" a hushed voice demanded just outside the cottage. Logan Matthews.

"You'd better get going, Doozey. Your master seems to be in a vile mood," she told her guest as she opened the door and tried to shove him out.

"So this is where you've gotten to," Logan said sternly, surprising both girl and dog to find him right outside the door. "You get home now!"

Doozey whimpered and tried to hide himself behind Jill's legs.

"Don't talk to him that way!" she scolded the artist. "It's little wonder the poor creature is afraid to go with you. Look at him!" she pointed to Doozey, who was now crouching fearfully, his wet black nose pressed between her bare feet.

"Don't let him fool you, Jill. He's an Academy Award-winning actor, believe me."

"The poor baby was starved and came begging for food," she argued. "Don't you ever feed your pets, Mr. Matthews?"

Somehow she couldn't tell this man that she didn't believe it was food Doozey was looking for but affection. Jill couldn't bring herself to betray the dog that way. Logan Matthews wasn't a man who would yield to begging for his favor.

"The 'poor dog,' as you call him, had a very fine dinner," he said coldly, penetrating her with a steely glance.

"There's more to life than just food, you know. Doozey was lonely for affection." She gulped. She had said it. Darn, darn....

"We all need affection, Miss Barton." His voice had become husky, stealing her attention away from Doozey to himself. "Do you dole it out in large doses as you do candy?"

She could see that his eyes had noticed the Chunky bar wrapper in her hand. Suddenly, she was aware of the filmy nightgown she was wearing. If Logan had seen the candy wrapper in her hand, what else could he see? A rush of heat warmed her body, seeming to make it glow against the darkness outside. A sudden chill made her shiver—or was it just his cold blue eyes flicking over her body?

"You'll catch your death," he told her, seeing her shiver. "Get inside and I'll haul Doozey out of there."

His hands closed over her shoulders as he led her into the cottage and closed the door behind him. Somehow those strong fingers never released their grip. Somehow they gathered her close to him and held her in an embrace.

Another shudder took its hold, and this time Jill was certain it wasn't from the cold. It was from the nearness of him, the strength of him. With a creeping dismay, Jill realized how remote this cottage was from the rest of the compound and how alone she was with Logan. The size of his body made her feel even more defenseless.

"You'd better take your dog and go," Jill told him, her voice becoming a whisper.

She pulled out of his grasp, backing away, ready to run if she had to. His strong hands bit into her upper arms and bands of steel made her his prisoner. She struggled helplessly against his strength. His face was carved into bitter lines. His mouth was hard and un-yielding as he brought it closer to hers and finally covered her mouth in a demanding kiss.

Against her will, her lips parted beneath his, giving themselves up to his demand, yielding to his searching hunger. She was swept up in a haze of confusion, her mind directing her one way and her body betraying her to another.

Her body was molded against his closer, closer, as his lips became more demanding. His hands made ex-cursions along her spine, heightening her response. Nothing stood between his hand and her flesh other than a film of silk. A riot of emotions raced through her. She had never been kissed this way, had never re-sponded this way. Fires were ignited deep within her being, revealing hidden recesses of sensuality that had never made themselves known to her before.

Where a moment ago she had tried to escape his embrace, she was now trapped in the throes of her own desire. She felt herself melt against him, molding herself to him, seeking to fill a hunger, a yearning, that this man created in her.

Beyond reason or thought, she knew he was picking her up and carrying her to the bed, never lifting his mouth from hers. She was dimly aware of his weight beside her on the covers. Her heart pounded in rhythms without pattern, beating against her breast, just beneath the touch of his fingers grazing over the sheer silk and her warm flesh. Rapturous sensations became her world, as though she had never known any other. Fulfillment beckoned to her across miles and miles of fleeting caresses and burning kisses. His hands left burning trails on her body, and she offered herself to him. All rational thought ceased. Only thoughts of Logan persisted in penetrating the fog that surrounded her.

His teasing lips were searching, seeking, finding. His gentle hands demanded, stroked, worshiped. His warm body was pressing, covering, shielding. Smoldering senses, all of them her own yet alien to her, begged for the touch and kiss of this man, Logan.

An insistent whining, deep and throaty, shattered the silence. For an instant Jill believed she was the origin of those primeval sounds until a weight threw itself against the bed, breaking the ecstasy. Doozey!

Logan rose from the bed beside her and stood looking down at her.

"You have no idea what you do to a man, do you?" he asked huskily.

Without him beside her, warming her, setting fire to her senses, the air was suddenly cold, instantly chilling her. She wrapped her arms about herself to ward off the chill. Logan seemed to take it as a gesture of modesty.

"Don't ever hide yourself from me, Jill. You don't realize just how beautiful you are."

His look was almost a physical touch as it branded her body from the sleek length of her thigh where her nightgown was rucked up to the plunging V of her neckline where her breasts were full and heaving.

When he leaned toward her again, she instinctively wrapped her arms around his neck, her fingers raking through the thick, dark hair at the nape of his neck.

Instead of resuming his embrace, he picked her up and moved her to the pillows, where he put her down again, tucking the covers around her.

"Doozey!" he called to the dog. "You stay here with Jill and watch over her for me."

He snapped his fingers and pointed to the little rag rug beside the bed. Obediently Doozey went to his designated place and rested his head on his paws.

Without another glance in Jill's direction, Logan left the cottage, snapping off the lights before he closed the door behind him.

For a long while Jill lay quietly, thinking of the man who had carried her to this bed and who had ignited passions in her that she had never known existed. Her body still felt warm from his touch and her lips felt burning and ravished. She blushed as she recalled her own wanton responses to his lovemaking.

Pulling the covers up tightly around her neck, his words buzzed through her brain.

"Don't ever hide yourself from me, Jill," he had

said, his voice throbbing with urgency. "You don't know how beautiful you are."

JILL WOKE EARLY and lay still, her thoughts jumbled. Perhaps she had only been dreaming. Perhaps Logan hadn't come to the cottage looking for Doozey at all, and perhaps he hadn't taken her into his arms and taught her new depths to her own sensuality.

Lightly, her fingers touched her mouth, tenderly falling upon the place where Logan's mouth had so greedily kissed her. Trailing a path down her neck to the place between her breasts, she felt a flurry of excitement bubble. "Don't hide from me…." His words were spoken softly, huskily, meaningfully. She could never hide from Logan, she told herself. Just being with him, in his arms, made her completely his.

Doozey slinked from his position beside the bed and stood staring at her, bringing new color to her cheeks. Doozey! Living proof that it hadn't been a dream. It had been real—those moments alone with Logan—here on this very bed.

Doozey's impatience prevented Jill from lying back against the pillows and recalling each and every wonderful moment in Logan's arms. The dog's tail wagged furiously, accompanied by a low whine.

"I know, I know, you want out. Could you wait a few more minutes? No, huh? No time to think, is that it?"

Shivering against the morning chill, Jill climbed from her nice warm bed and opened the door for Doozey, who rushed past her barking gratitude for his freedom.

Sighing wearily, Jill closed and locked the door. She really shouldn't go back to bed. She had the bathrooms to clean and her cleaning-up chores with Aggie.

Yawning widely, Jill dressed quickly, adding the heavy sweater at the last minute. She would take her bath later, after her chores.

Skirting the dense shrubbery at the entrance to the sanitation building, Jill stopped in her tracks. What was that unholy racket coming from Logan's house? She listened another minute, fully expecting Doozey to rush up and explain the disturbance.

Jill looked around. There was no one in sight and the compound seemed to still be sleeping. What was that noise? Deciding her daily chore of bathroom cleaning could wait a while longer, Jill set out for the back of the house and the ensuing racket. It was enough to wake the dead.

Aggie was trying frantically to stanch the flow of water on the back porch. It took only one quick glance on Jill's part to figure out the reason. The water pump on one of the pipes leading to the ancient washer was broken.

"I heard a loud snap, and then the water started to rush out of the machine. I can't get near enough to the plug to turn the power off," Aggie shouted in agitation. "This infernal racket is enough to drive a body to drink. What do you think it is, Jill?"

"Where's the main fuse box?" Jill shouted back.

"Outside around the corner of the house. Now, why didn't I think of that?"

Jill trotted off and with the first rays of dawn was able to make out where the fuse box rested high on the side of the house. She turned off the power and raced back to the now quiet screened-in porch.

"Breakfast is going to be late," Aggie said fretfully as she started to wring out the mop.

"So is latrine duty!" Jill grimaced as she set about to help Aggie. "I think we'd be better off if we just swept the water out the door and down the steps instead of trying to sop it up. I'll start on breakfast while you do that. What's on the menu today?"

"We were going to have blueberry pancakes and waffles with scrambled eggs," Aggie said dejectedly. "If there's one thing Logan hates, it's to have meals served late."

"There are some things in life Mr. Logan Matthews had better get used to, and the first one is that we're having cold cereal for breakfast. If he's lucky, I might throw in some orange juice. And do you know something else? I think your boss is a slave driver expecting you to kill yourself the way you've been doing. You aren't getting younger, Aggie. You could have a stroke working the way you do," she added virtuously.

"You just might be right, Jill. I'm looking forward to this trip to Seattle in more ways than I can tell you."

"It's okay for your boss to be a patron of the arts and to indulge himself with all his rules and regulations but not at someone else's expense. I'm mad, fighting mad," Jill complained as she set about pouring milk into jugs. She looked at the clock and winced. Quickly, she gave the bell next to the side of the door a vicious yank.

Jill's tired eyes defied the residents to say a word about the trays they picked up. Deciding to go all out, she called to their retreating backs, "One word from anyone and I'll take the milk back and you'll eat it dry."

Aggie burst out laughing. "Is this what you writers call rebellion or mutiny?"

"Either/or, take your pick. Let me take a look at the machine now. Do you have a toolbox handy?"

"Right here. Next to the machine. This blasted thing is so temperamental I can't stand it anymore. If we don't get it fixed, I'll have to go into town to wash the towels."

"I have a better idea. I think we should let Mr. Matthews go into town to do the wash. Hold that flashlight a little lower, Aggie. There, you see, you need a new water pump, and the belt came off. I think we can patch it up if you have some electrical tape. Oh, oh, the piston is shot. Lower, Aggie. Maybe if I hook up… that's it, Aggie, now hand me that little screwdriver. What's wrong with you, Aggie? Lower, I can barely see. Okay, I got it now. Hand me the pliers. I can see it now, the macho Logan Matthews doing laundry. I bet he doesn't even know how to fold towels, and he's probably one of those guys who dries off with three. Never stops to think about who has to wash them. I'm telling you, Aggie, if I hear one peep out of him about that cold cereal, I'll…I'll…there, I got it. Whew! I didn't think I could do it there for a minute. Do you have any machine oil? Aggie, is there some reason why you aren't answering me?"

"I can give you two very good reasons right off the bat, but I doubt if you would want to hear either of them," Logan Matthews retorted. "I thought I had assigned you your duties. What are you doing inside that machine? Women's work is in the kitchen where they belong."

"You're right," Jill said, withdrawing her head from the inside of the washing machine. Deftly, she snapped down the outer rim and then closed the lid.

"About what?" Logan demanded.

"That I don't care to hear them—your two reasons. Now, if you'll excuse me, I have latrine duty, or did you forget?"

Jill hadn't formulated exactly what she expected from Logan after last night, but this definitely wasn't it! How could he behave as though she were another of his slaves, like Aggie, ready and willing to do his bidding?

Logan's eyes danced with laughter. "You certainly are a busy one, aren't you? When do you have time to write?"

"In the middle of the night," Jill answered shortly without thinking. Seeing the laughter rekindle in his gaze, she flushed hotly. His hand reached out to lift a golden curl from her cheek.

"And do you also gather research for your memoirs in the middle of the night?"

Jill's knees felt weak, barely able to hold her weight.

"I think," she stammered, "you…you better do something about this machine. It must have come over on the Mayflower. It works now, but for how long I can't say."

She fought for composure, hoping to change the subject…anything!

"Jill?"

She liked the way he said her name. It sounded so soft and feminine when it came from him. When other people said her name, it always sounded so tomboyish.

"Please, whatever it is, can't it wait till I finish the bathrooms?" she pleaded.

There was no way she wanted to hear him chastise her this morning. Why couldn't he be nice to her as he was with the others? Why did he always have to mock her?

"I want to thank you for reminding me about Aggie. I have been neglectful of her. I know how to wash clothes, and believe it or not, I folded towels when I was in the marines. If you want to be really startled, I can square bedsheets and a quarter will flip. You will also notice that there has not been one peep out of me concerning that…cardboard you served for breakfast. What really is amazing is that no one else complained either.

What I'm trying to say, Miss Barton, is, you made your point."

Jill was stunned. She shifted from one foot to the other as she stared at him. Not trusting herself to speak, she merely nodded.

"By the way, how's the book coming?"

"Book?" Jill repeated stupidly.

His eyes were dancing again. "You know, your memoirs. *That* book."

Jill nodded. "*That* book. Fine, fine. I worked all night," she lied. She crossed her fingers as she swept through the door. Outside in the fresh morning air, she let her breath out with a long sigh.

An hour later Jill let her eyes rake the bathroom area. Spotless. It was a job well done. The chrome sparkled, the sinks glistened and the floor was squeaky clean. Deftly, she added several deodorizers and gave a final squirt of Lysol to the general area.

Aggie marched in, towel in hand. "Good job, Jill. I've never seen these bathrooms so clean. Your mother can be proud of you and the way you know how to do things."

"Thanks, Aggie. I'm going to find Doozey and go for a nice, long walk. I might even go all the way into the village and get some breakfast." She lowered her voice to a bare whisper. "I hate cereal."

Aggie laughed as she turned on the water in the tub. "Will you fetch me the new *Cosmopolitan* if it's in? I like to keep up to date on the sexy side of life."

Jill doubled over with laughter. "I'll be sure to look for it. Enjoy your bath."

BY THE TIME Jill found herself in town her stomach was rumbling. She was really hungry and would have cheerfully parted with one of her back teeth for one of Aggie's breakfasts. The sign on the one and only diner in town proclaimed it was closed on Tuesdays from October 1 through May 1. Disappointed, she picked up Aggie's copy of the slick magazine at the corner drugstore along with a cup of coffee and a Danish and headed back to the compound.

Now that it was a little warmer, she went to Wynde Cottage to remove her sweater. She was annoyed with herself for not having made her bed earlier. It was the force of habit, she supposed, for she always made her bed upon rising. Something had always grated on her about walking into the bedroom and seeing the bed unmade. It seemed sacrilegious to forgo the ritual.

Smoothing out the quilt, Jill laid it across the back of the only cozy chair in the cabin. Determined to make a lazy day of it, she put reading number one on her list. And then an entire afternoon of relaxing. Tucked inside the quilt, she would be able to stave off boredom as well as the cold.

It was while she was hanging up her clothes that Jill first heard Doozey at her door. His announcement was entirely recognizable and she found herself weakening immediately.

She hurried over to the door to open it before he scratched it down, but her greeting for the dog died on her lips. Two feet away stood Logan Matthews dressed in a pathetic-looking turtleneck and a pair of spotted jeans.

"I was wondering if you could cook a late breakfast for Doozey and me. Aggie is loaded down with the wash and I don't want to ask her. I'm not very good in the kitchen—"

He halted abruptly, "Say, if you're busy writing, I don't want to interrupt you."

"No...no! What I mean is, I was just making notes. I was going to walk down to the beach today," Jill hedged, but something in Logan's eyes made her respond. "Still I can't have my good buddy going hungry, can I, Doozey?" She patted the dog affectionately and was rewarded with a big smooch.

"We're grateful, aren't we, old boy?" Logan stated. "I thought for a while we were going to have to go the day on that cold cereal. Good as it was," he hastened to explain at Jill's piercing look. "I rarely eat lunch, so I've usually eaten a hearty breakfast ever since I was a kid...."

Was this *the* Logan Matthews? At a loss for words? Jill grinned; she couldn't help herself.

"Winsomeness, Mr. Matthews, does not become you. Somehow, I can't imagine you ever being a little boy. You were one, weren't you?" she asked anxiously.

"Scout's honor. My parents said I was the best boy on the block." He grinned. "Actually, we lived on a ranch in Wyoming. I was a good kid. Never got into trouble in the wide-open spaces. I broke my collarbone when I was ten, jumping off the shed roof. When I was twelve, I broke my leg bronco riding. At thirteen I fractured my elbow riding my new bike. Jenny Carpenter broke my heart when I was fourteen by going to the harvest square dance with Luke McCoy. I never fully recovered. Did I leave anything out?"

Only the part about Stacey Phillips, Jill wanted to say.

"No, I guess not; that about covers it. If you're ready, I guess I am too."

On the walk across the compound Jill was acutely aware of his nearness. She wanted to reach out and touch him, to remind him that she was real, flesh and blood, and that she had responded to him once and would again.

It seemed to take hours to finally complete the breakfast and set down a plate in front of Logan, who had sat and watched her through his lowered lids while she had worked. By this time her nerves were frazzled from his watching her that way. Each time his eyes touched her they left a burning brand, making her aware of her every movement, making her more clumsy than usual.

"Breakfast is served," she announced finally, her voice dripping sarcasm.

As he dove into his meal Logan seemed immune to the anger he had aroused in Jill.

"You know," he said matter-of-factly, waving his toast in the air as he spoke, "I find I much prefer the granola and honey bread that Nature's Bounty stocks. It toasts better."

Jill felt her heart begin pounding, her muscles tensing, and she knew it was useless to keep still any longer.

"Listen, Mr. Matthews, white bread was all we had and white bread is what you got. If you like granola and honey bread so much, see that you get yourself into town to supply it. Aggie has enough to do around here, so you can just quit demanding—"

"You find me demanding?" Logan pretended hurt.

"Yes," Jill maintained, "I certainly do."

Logan seemed puzzled by her admission and rubbed the palms of his hands together in an unconscious gesture.

"Some people have said I was abrupt, eccentric, egotistical...but never demanding."

"I said it and I meant it," Jill told him emphatically.

"And you stand by your convictions, right?" His eyes held Jill's in a challenge, and she could see a glimmer in them that said she had been baited.

"And what is it you're running away from, Jill?"

Sneak attack! He was trying to find out more about

her. "Running away? Who said anything about running away?" In spite of herself, her voice faltered.

"You did."

"When?"

"Your eyes, Jill," Logan said softly. "They're said to be the mirror of the soul. I'd guess your soul is running away from love."

Jill laughed, a nervous sound to her own ears.

"You couldn't be more mistaken!"

Abruptly, she rose from the table and began to clear the dishes, refusing to listen to another word. She couldn't look at him, wouldn't. His artist's eyes had seen too much already and had guessed her secret.

CHAPTER FIVE

"GOODNESS, JILL, I CAN'T remember when I've had so much fun!"

A soft breeze brought a spray of sand up to tickle Jill's bare legs as she hurried over to where Aggie sat sprawled on a beach towel in tribute to the last days of Indian summer.

"I can't take all the credit," Jill said with a laugh as she sat down on the corner of the towel that Aggie had reserved for her. "This picnic was your idea."

A chuckle rumbled from deep down inside Aggie's chest as she strained forward to rub suntan oil over her legs.

"Believe it or not, Jill, I get lonely. I know I don't seem to be the clinging grandma type...waiting around for cards and letters that never come. There are times when being around people drives me clear up the walls. You don't come across too many honest folks these days. Most of them just care about how large a house they can latch on to...how many cars they can have in their garages for the neighbors to drool over. Maybe it was the way I was raised, but I just never cared for those things. Guess I was lucky when I found my Harry, because he saw things the same way. Plain and simple, that's how I like life. Sitting on the beach...working in Logan's garden...that's what makes me happy."

"You've lived here for a long time, haven't you, Aggie?"

"Seems like I was born here," the woman whispered, her eyes misting with a veil of memories. "My Harry helped Logan's pa build these cottages. They said Mill Valley was going to be put on the map by catering to artists and the like. He was right, too. Never came a season when they were alive that all the cabins weren't full. I think it was Harry that made them want to stay. He always understood their moodiness, made them feel like he was a kindred spirit. It's hard for me to believe that he's been dead almost ten years. I almost packed up and left when he died, but it would have been like running out on Harry and Logan…giving up on their dreams."

Afraid that she would break the spell of the past, Jill remained silent. If she hadn't come to Mill Valley and met Aggie, she would have missed something special. She realized that the brief touching of their lives would remain with her forever.

"I knew right from the first moment I saw that man that I wanted to marry him," Aggie announced finally. "And you know, Jill, when I think how close I came to passing him by, I know that him and me were just meant to be. You wouldn't know it to look at me now, but honey, I used to be just as pretty as you are. I was engaged to another man when I met Harry. The date had been set and my folks had come all the way out here from Oklahoma to see me get married. Two days before I was due in church, I suddenly knew that I didn't really love my intended. So you know what I did? I ran. I got myself a Greyhound ticket and ran. Ended up in Eureka with no job, nothing. When I called my ma, she just cried and cried, telling me I'd gone crazy. Bless her soul, she never did understand me or forgive me. Anyway, that's how I met Harry. I got a job in a diner waiting tables. Harry was the owner. All us girls used to make fun of him and his dreaming…telling us how he was going to have his own place with rooms for rent and a restaurant. None of us knew that he'd been salting away money for years!"

Jill felt shaken, overwhelmed by the uncanny likeness of Aggie's life to her own. "Did you ever regret your choice?"

"What?" Aggie asked blankly, still caught up in her recollecting. "Oh, you mean choosing Harry over the other fella? No, honey…I can honestly say that I never did. Weren't no man that could ever compare with Harry. I never met a man who could hypnotize me like he did…except maybe Logan. Now, there's a man that could've held a candle to my Harry. If I was thirty years younger, I'd give that Stacey Phillips a run for her money."

Jill turned, trying to hide the fact that all the color had drained from her face.

"Miss Phillips…you think she'll stick around?"

"I don't know," Aggie said slowly, as though trying to reach a conclusion just inches from her grasp, "but she seems to be settling in here. Makes me kind of sad, to tell the truth. She doesn't love Logan. Anyone can see that. She's just hungry for what she can get out of him. She left him once. Now she's saying they just picked up where they left off."

"Seems to be they deserve each other," Jill offered angrily. She flinched as a series of giggles erupted from the woman beside her.

"Oh, my, Jill! Don't tell me Logan has cast you under his spell!"

"I don't know what you're talking about!" Jill retorted through her teeth.

"Come on, honey," Aggie prodded. "It ain't nothing to be ashamed of. Being vulnerable and in love is what life is all about. Feel sorry for the people who don't take risks in life, Jill, because they aren't really living… they're merely existing."

"I don't know why you insist on saying I'm in love with Logan Matthews," Jill retorted.

"All right, Jill," Aggie relented. "I'm just telling you that you couldn't pick anyone finer. He's a good man. I've lived around him for a long time, long enough to know that despite his spells of brooding, he's a gentle and considerate human being. Look at the art he creates. A soul gifted with that much talent is bound to retreat from life now and then. Especially when all the people that are drawn to him see only what they can get…not what they can give."

Jill clambered to her feet, pulling her T-shirt off to reveal a salmon-pink bathing suit.

"I don't want to argue with you, Aggie. But it appears to me that the Logan Matthews you know and the one I've had recent dealings with are two different men."

Without another word, she turned and jogged toward the water.

AFTER MANAGING TO SALVAGE the rest of their afternoon, Aggie and Jill walked over the dunes and headed homeward. Parting at Jill's cabin, Aggie gave Jill a smothering hug.

"Take care of yourself, Jill. Follow your heart always…it'll never lead you astray."

A leisurely bath to wash away the sand still holding

fast to her body was Jill's top priority. Almost an hour had passed before she forced herself from the soothing balm of the water, her toes and fingers wrinkled and pink. Dressing methodically in her jeans and one of the embroidered tops, Jill loosened her hair from the strict confines of the braids she had worked earlier that morning. Her hair flowed down her back in a shimmering flaxen wave, and Jill closed her eyes as she brushed through its length until her arm ached with the effort. Selecting a book of poems by Emily Dickinson from the chest beneath the sink, Jill renewed her promise to herself of a long evening of reading.

Back in her cottage and well into the small biography that preceded the selection of poems penned by Miss Dickinson, Jill heard a telltale scratch at the door. Ignoring it, she armed herself against the inevitable whining to come. It was hopeless, for she had missed Doozey all day. Cursing herself for her weakness, Jill opened the door and saw Doozey sitting primly in the shaft of light from her lamp. A single red rose was clenched between his teeth. So taken was she with his courting that she almost neglected to see Logan Matthews standing in the shadows behind the dog. Jill felt a glow of pleasure seep through her being as she noticed his appearance. He was clean-shaven, his dark hair combed neatly. A burnished copper sweater had replaced his dingy turtleneck, and his paint-splattered jeans had been traded in for a brand-new pair. But it was what he held in both arms that made Jill laugh aloud— two bulging grocery bags, one with a truce flag fashioned from a gnarled stick and a ragged white handkerchief.

"How about it?" Logan said with a grin. "Is the apology for my nosiness accepted? I spoke out of turn when I said you were running away. Am I forgiven?"

The evening was one that Jill was convinced she would remember forever. In complete turnabout from his request for breakfast several days before, Logan settled Jill into one of his kitchen chairs. Bowing playfully, he began to unpack the paper bags that had been filled to the top.

"My dear Miss Barton," he said as he searched the kitchen for a vase in which to deposit his surrender flag, and set it on the middle of the table, "I'm about to prepare a dinner for you that will make your dainty little taste buds stand up and holler. We'll start off with a Caesar salad and then plow into the main course."

As if to accentuate his promise, Logan held up two of the thickest steaks Jill had ever laid eyes on.

"I've got French bread and garlic butter. And chocolate chip ice cream for dessert."

Jill leaned back in her chair, her eyes dancing as she taunted him, "Actually, I prefer cherry vanilla."

Not for all the tea in China would she tell him she wasn't hungry.

It was Logan's turn to laugh and he did so heartily.

"You're a paradox, Miss Barton. One minute you're shooting mental daggers at me, the next you're oozing honey."

"I think it's a peculiarity we both share, Mr. Matthews."

Logan nodded, his smile suddenly fading as he appeared overcome by a paralyzing thought. "Wine!" he shouted dramatically. "I forgot the wine!"

"Don't fret so," Jill teased. "There's a bottle in the fridge. I bought it in town the other day."

"Ah," Logan answered as he opened the refrigerator to inspect her selection, "don't tell me you indulge in a nip once in a while. It's quite out of character. I thought you'd scream in vegetarian horror when I brandished those steaks!"

"They smell delicious."

"They'd better!" said Logan as he stabbed the browning meat with a fork.

Dinner was as luscious as Logan had predicted; Jill's appetite returned with each bite of the succulent meat.

"Tell me, Jill," Logan inquired as he cleared the table, pouring Jill another glassful of wine, "How do you rate my cooking?"

"Well," Jill smiled in response, "the salad was heavenly, but you have to confess that anyone could have produced the same results with the steaks…it's no major feat. So, taking that into consideration, I'll give you an eight on a scale of ten."

Doing his best to look wounded, Logan sat two bowls on the table. "We almost forgot the crowning glory… dessert!"

Suppressing a smile, Jill forced her face to remain stern.

Logan watched as Jill took a bite of the chocolate chip ice cream he had scooped out for her, patiently awaiting her critique.

"If it was cherry vanilla, you'd have yourself a ten. But since it isn't, the best I can do for you is a nine."

"How about if I do up the dishes and sweep up the floors?"

"Oh, Mr. Matthews," Jill taunted, "you mean you'd actually humble yourself to do woman's work?"

"I don't see why not," Logan answered, making a grand play out of retrieving one of Aggie's frilly aprons from a peg on the wall and tying it about his waist. "There's only one thing I want you to know."

"And what is that?" Jill asked on cue.

Stiffening his back, his face devoid of mirth, Logan divulged, "I don't do windows!"

Jill found herself assigned to the role of spectator as Logan held true to his promise. She sipped her wine, content to remain quiet while he clattered about quite efficiently. About to empty her glass with one last swallow, Jill looked up as Logan reached out and grasped her by the wrist, giving it a gentle press.

"Hold on a minute. I'd like to share a toast with you."

Watching as Logan filled his empty glass, Jill shook her head in refusal as he sought to replenish hers. Holding his glass out to the middle of the table, he waited for Jill to join him in the ceremony.

"I'd like to make a toast to a new start between us. Let's say that tonight is the first time we've met."

Mesmerized by the indefinable look on Logan's face, Jill clinked her glass against his. This was the Logan Matthews that Aggie evidently knew. He seemed in total contrast to the image Jill had garnered of him. She knew she was being seduced, and she found herself suddenly hungry for his attentions.

"Don't tell me I interrupted your reading again."

Jill followed the direction of Logan's gaze to the book she had carried with her just before his arrival, the small bound book of poems.

Not waiting for Jill's response, Logan strode to the chair and began thumbing through the pages.

"My," he said finally, "this stuff is pretty dreary."

"It depends on how you look at it," Jill answered defensively.

"I suppose you're right. I was never one for poetry, although some say I should be able to relate to a writer's drive. We're both the same when you come right down to it. When we create, we're totally alone with our inspiration. There's no way to share what comes from within…only a piece of paper and a slab of canvas can be party to the act."

Depositing himself with a thud into Aggie's kitchen rocker, Logan fixed a somber glance in Jill's direction.

"Now, tell me. Just who is Jill Barton?"

"I could very easily ask you the same question," Jill answered coolly.

"Ah." Logan laughed, shaking his finger at her in a scolding manner. "But I asked you first!"

"There's really nothing to tell," Jill said as she got up and started to pace the room.

"You want to remain a woman of mystery."

"It's not that. I just don't think dinner entitles you to be presented with my life as though it's one of my books you can thumb through and discard with a disparaging comment."

"I wouldn't do that, Jill."

Startled by the intimacy Logan's voice suggested, Jill gave herself leave to examine his motives more clearly. She stared at him, his eyes fixed on her in an unwavering dare.

Before Jill could speak, a resounding knock at the door jolted them both from the moment they had shared. Jill gasped in shock as the door opened without further hesitation. Filling the doorway stood Stacey Phillips.

"I saw a light in here, Logan. Whatever are you doing in the kitchen?"

Realizing Stacey hadn't even registered the fact that she was sitting in the chair, Jill took a step forward in preparation to leaving.

"You've hidden out long enough, Logan. We have to

talk, and I'd like to do it now." Stacey's voice was kitten soft, her tone urging, pleading. She stepped forward, shyly reaching out for Logan, her hand touching his chest just above his heart. Logan's fingers closed over Stacey's, holding her hand there, and he moved a step closer to her.

Jill felt her heart wrench at the hungry expression in Logan's eyes as he looked down at the voluptuous woman with the sexy name. Neither of them seemed to notice when she slipped her arms into the sleeves of her heavy sweater. They ignored her as she called Doozey softly and then left the comfort and light of Logan's homey kitchen.

Seething with frustration that she recognized as illogical jealousy, Jill jogged down the road with Doozey at her heels. Running was supposed to take all the starch out of a person. It was working—she was exhausted.

Slowly, she walked back to her cabin. She made careful note to let her eyes stare at Briar Cottage. It was dark. Logan's house from the front was also dark, but the light was on in the upstairs bedroom area.

CHAPTER SIX

"Ah, if it isn't our little writer!"

Jill turned in time to see Stacey Phillips, with a large lavender bath sheet over her arm. She nodded curtly and waited.

"I was just going to clean the bathroom," Jill volunteered quietly. Withdrawing the bucket and mop from the closet, she ignored the beautiful, if petulant, Stacey.

"In that case I'll wait. I hate to use a dirty bathroom."

"I'd hardly call this a dirty bathroom," Jill said tartly.

"Well, I would. Look, there're long black hairs in the bathtub," Stacey said, pointing a three-inch bloodred nail in the general direction of the sparkling tub.

Jill grimaced. "Are you going to stand there or what?" she demanded. "By the way, exactly what is your chore around here?"

"Chore?" Stacey said haughtily. "Sweetie, I am a guest. I don't do chores."

"But you've been eating here and using all the facilities. You should do your share like everyone else," Jill said irritably.

Who did she think she was anyway? She grimaced again. She was Logan Matthews's lady friend, and possibly much more. Her own question and answer stung her to the quick. Jill grew more annoyed by the minute as she scoured out the tub and then ran clean water down the drain to wash away the residue left by the abrasive powder.

"You'll have to back out so I can mop the floor, Miss Phillips."

Stacey backed out, holding her luscious apricot dressing gown above her ankles.

"I do hate that pine smell. Do you have any Chanel you can spray around to cover the odor?"

Jill clenched her teeth. "I'm afraid not," she said politely. "If you wait another ten minutes the floor will be dry."

"Darling?"

Jill turned. "Yes?"

"How long are you planning on being here?"

"At least another week or until Aggie gets back," Jill said shortly.

"Then you'll still be here for Logan's going-away party, won't you?"

"Party?" Logan was going away. "Where is Mr. Matthews going?"

"Why, to Paris with me. Silly girl, didn't you know? Didn't someone tell you all about it? Usually you commune people spread rumors like wildfire."

Jill mumbled something unintelligible and left the room, her eyes blinded with salty tears. He really was going away. Now what was she going to do?

Suddenly, she was no longer hungry. Even Aggie's delicious homemade waffles couldn't tempt her this morning. She would go for a walk, timing her return for the end of the breakfast hour so she could help Aggie clean up.

How unfair life was, she thought morosely as she trudged down the sandy strip of beach. First, she was jilted at the altar. Then she was rejected before she even got to first base. Life was unfair. Why did girls like her always finish last? Why did the superelegant creatures like Stacey Phillips always walk off with the prize? For a while she had actually deluded herself into thinking that Logan might—and it was a big might—be just a little interested in her. He had kissed her as though he meant it. Surely, he had enjoyed those few intimate moments as much as she had.

Jill flopped down on the sand and stared out across the water. She forgot everything and let the waves hypnotize her. She lost all track of time and was only shaken from her thoughts by Doozey's loud barking. She turned and waved to the Irish setter. Doozey advanced, barked and then retreated. He repeated his frantic actions three more times till Jill got his canine message.

"Oh, you want me to come with you. Okay, Doozey, I'm coming."

She glanced at her watch. She still had time till breakfast was officially over. No sense in giving Logan Matthews cause for concern. She was doing her share, for that matter, more than she bargained for.

Doozey appeared to be upset. First he would bark, then growl and start to run. Every few feet he turned to see if she was still behind him.

"Don't tell me they forgot to feed you again," Jill mumbled as she skirted a sweeping yew at the beginning of the compound.

Startled by her close encounter with the spreading evergreen, Jill didn't see Logan Matthews until she collided with him.

"Oh, I'm sorry. It's my fault. I wasn't watching where I was going. I'm sorry."

"Come with me" was all Logan said.

Jill stared after the tall form. Now what? She hadn't done anything. She stood her ground.

"Where? Why?" she asked loudly.

Logan turned, his face cold and hard. "Because I said so."

Jill shrugged. He was calling the shots, or so it would seem. He was back to being his arrogant, obnoxious self. Puzzled at his attitude, she trotted along behind his long stride, Doozey in her wake, whining pitifully. Evidently, he didn't like his master's attitude either.

They stopped at the sanitation building. Logan held the door open for her and marched into the side that said Hers. Jill followed, more puzzled than ever. The sight that met her gaze stunned her. No wonder he was angry. Talcum powder was everywhere. Toothpaste oozed down the side of the sink and all around the faucets. A greasy, scummy oil with particles of hair from someone's razor lined the tub. The floor was saturated with water and dirty footprints. Jill gulped.

Logan crossed his hands over his chest. Jill had never seen such cold, dead eyes in her life. He said nothing, but waited.

"I cleaned it, truly I did. Then I went for a walk."

Logan's eyes clearly challenged her.

"You don't believe me, do you? Well, I don't care. I cleaned it, and when I left it was sparkling clean. Take a look at the other side, the side you men use. It's clean. When I left here your...your Miss Phillips was waiting to take her bath. She was here all the while I cleaned. She waited because she said she refused to bathe in a dirty bathroom. Even before I cleaned it, it didn't look like this. Don't ever, Mr. Matthews, call me a liar again."

Jill turned and ran as fast as she could back to Wynde

Cottage. It wasn't until she was inside that she remembered she had to go to the dining hall to help Aggie. She couldn't even run away and pretend she had a class act. Now she had to go back and risk facing the artist and his steely eyes.

WAVING TO AGGIE, Jill began clearing the table, careful to avoid Logan's eyes. He and Stacey had their heads together talking in low voices. Stacey's hands touched Logan again and again, picking imaginary lint from his sweater and smoothing his collar. Together, they made a cozy twosome.

Struggling with the cumbersome utility cart, Jill hunched over and started to push it across the dining hall. Her eyes were downcast to be certain the wheels didn't settle into the grooves in the plank floor. Before she knew what was happening, Logan had shouldered her aside and was pushing the cart into the back room where Aggie waited.

"I can do it. I've been doing it all week. If this is the way you apologize, you can just forget it, Logan," Jill hissed.

"It is an apology. I was hoping you would notice." His eyes twinkled and he reached out his hand. "Friends?"

How could she stay angry with him? Her heart soared, and then she remembered the lone light in the upstairs of Logan's house and the darkness at Briar Cottage. What had she expected? He did say *friends*. She nodded curtly and turned her back on him.

"A mite hard on him, weren't you?" Aggie said quietly.

"You didn't hear the way he talked to me, Aggie. He might just as well have called me a liar," Jill said defensively.

Aggie stopped what she was doing and stared at Jill.

"Logan is different from most men, Jill. He's caught up in his painting world. His eye only sees what it sees. What I'm trying to say is when he made his morning check his eyes saw a dirty bathroom. In all fairness to Logan, you cleaned up a half hour early today. Be fair."

"Okay, you've made your point, Aggie," Jill said, slightly mollified.

"What do you have planned for today? Anything special?"

"I thought I might write a little," she fibbed.

Aggie's eyes danced and her chins wobbled with mirth. "How is your book coming?"

"It's coming, but that's about it," Jill hedged.

"Do you think you'll be finished around four this afternoon?"

"Probably," Jill continued to hedge. "Why?"

"I thought if you weren't doing anything you could go with me to the show tonight. Cocktails and everything."

"What show? Cocktails where?"

"Gracious sakes, I forgot you didn't know. Miss Phillips arranged a showing in town this evening for Logan. He kicked up his heels, but Miss Phillips was adamant. Seems there's to be a lot of art critics coming at her special invitation. Mine is engraved. If you stop by the kitchen later, I'll show it to you. Think about it. Why don't you run along now and work on your book for a while? It will get your mind off this morning."

"Are you sure this isn't too much for you?" Jill asked, looking around.

"Good heavens, no. All I have to do now is wipe off the tables and I'm finished."

"If you say so," Jill said dubiously.

Now she was stuck with her lie. She would have to

hide out at Wynde Cottage for a couple of hours and pretend she was working. There would be no walk for her this morning.

Straightening up the tiny cottage and making the bed took all of fifteen minutes. What was she to do with the rest of her time?

If she was careful she might make it to her car and take a ride around the countryside. This way she would be out of sight of the artists' colony and able to explore a bit at the same time. Aggie would never notice if she stayed in back of Logan's house, and Logan himself would probably be down at the beach painting. If Stacey noticed her leave, she could always say she wanted to make penciled notes or something equally stupid.

Jill roamed the countryside for several hours but did not appreciate the beauty of Rhode Island. How sad, she mused, that she couldn't relate in any way to the beauty surrounding her. She might as well go back. The car ate up the miles on the backcountry road more quickly than she would have liked. Driving through the gates of Mill Valley, Jill had to inch her car over to the side of the road, almost going into a ditch. A battered Mustang, with its hood standing sentinel, was almost blocking the road. Jill pulled her car over and climbed out. She recognized the writer and grinned.

"What's wrong?"

"Beats me." Pat grinned back. "It just died on me. I can write about it, but I can't tell you what makes it tick. You don't by any chance know anything about engines, do you?" she asked hopefully.

"A little. Let me take a look," Jill said, grabbing her emergency tool kit from the luggage compartment.

For the next hour and a half Jill lost herself to the

inner workings of the internal-combustion engine. She emerged with a grin stretching from ear to ear. The journalist laughed.

"You look awful. You have grease in your hair and all over your face."

"That's okay. I really enjoyed tinkering with your car. I must say it was a definite challenge. Let's see if it works. Start the engine. I want to see how it goes."

She was spared further comment when the baby-blue Porsche skidded to a stop. The horn blared, stopped, and then blared again. Jill walked away from the car and stood in the center of the road, her face a mask of dislike.

"You'll have to wait a minute until we see if it works."

The journalist turned the key and the sweet hum of a contented engine filled the quiet afternoon. Jill laughed delightedly.

"You really need a good overhaul," she said, slamming down the hood of the decrepit car.

"You must be one of the seven wonders of the world. Did you see and hear that engine?" the writer called out to the occupant of the Porsche. The door swung open and Logan Matthews stood towering over the small sports car.

His steely eyes were doing strange things, or was it the light coming through the maple trees? Jill was aware of how she must look and suddenly she didn't care.

"You said everything here was free." She laughed. "I'm just doing my thing."

She laughed again and the writer joined in as her engine turned over. Jill watched as the old car purred through the gates and out to the main road.

"Well, you can just do your thing somewhere else.

You've held us up long enough. Your car is blocking half the road, or can't you see? That car, or pile of junk, should have been compacted ten years ago," Stacey Phillips shouted angrily.

Jill smirked; she couldn't help it. She always felt good when she made something work.

"If you can't maneuver that submarine out of here, I can do it for you." She giggled. "I didn't learn to drive via Sears Roebuck. Be my guest," Jill shouted as she bowed low with a wide sweeping of her arms.

Logan Matthews threw back his head and roared with laughter.

"Well done, Miss Barton. Well done. I, for one, applaud you. Perhaps you would be kind enough to take a look at my engine tomorrow. That is, if your book isn't going to occupy all of your time."

Jill giggled again. "Mr. Matthews, I would be delighted to look at your engine, your etchings, or whatever you want me to look at."

She waved and the Porsche burned rubber as it sped through the gates. Jill alternated between fits of laughter and giggles all the way back to Wynde Cottage. She gathered her towel, soap and bath oil together, along with a stack of clean clothes. She was back at the cottage an hour later with a book in her hand when Aggie walked through the door.

"I thought you were going to stop by?" she accused.

"I was, but I got sidetracked. That little journalist had some car trouble and I helped her fix it. Then I took a shower and lost track of time. By the way, what time is it anyway?"

"Almost time to leave for Logan's show. Are you ready?"

"Aggie, I can't go. I wasn't invited."

A vision of Stacey Phillips greeting her at the door and then pushing her back outside swam before her eyes.

"Of course you're going, Jill. If you don't go, I won't. And nothing is going to make me miss out on Logan's showing."

Aggie stood in the middle of Jill's sitting room, her face purple from frustration as she shook an engraved invitation at Jill.

"It says that I and a guest of my choice are invited to attend the gallery showing of Logan Matthews's seascapes. So don't say another word about it, Jill. You're the guest of my choice!"

TWIRLING IN FRONT of the bathroom mirror, Jill knew without a doubt that she had achieved perfection. Adjusting the tortoise-shell combs she had used to pull her hair back from her face, she watched as her reflection smiled back at her. It had taken her only a minute to select the mulberry jumpsuit from the depths of the suitcase. Jill's eye had been caught by the creation the first moment she had seen it. The material was a type she had never seen before, giving the appearance of velour, yet lighter in weight. The shoulders capped the top of her arms and the neckline plunged to a simple knotted belt at the waist. As accessories, Jill had chosen a gold-banded bracelet and a pair of tiny gold earrings. To complete the style, she slid her feet into a pair of elegant gilt slippers. Necessity demanded that she wear a lightweight coat, and luckily, she just happened to have a stylish raincoat in the backseat.

Jill was rewarded with an exclamation of approval as Aggie opened her door.

"My, my! You're going to be the belle of the ball in that outfit!"

Giggling at the woman's playfulness, Jill felt the mounting excitement begin to churn in her stomach as they drove into Mill Valley. For some reason, Jill had pictured their destination as an imposing art gallery located somewhere in the middle of town. What she was greeted with was a rather ostentatious building that appeared to be someone's home. The outside of the house reminded Jill of the gothic romances she used to read as a teenager. The architecture even boasted a turret room, and Jill looked up at the dimly lit windows, half expecting to see Jane Eyre staring down at her. It was soon evident in which direction they should head, for the sound of scores of voices drifted across the lawn from a set of opened French doors.

"Sounds like Stacey has gotten the whole town to show up!" Aggie remarked cheerfully.

Following Aggie's lead, Jill was unprepared for the pressing crush of people. Everyone seemed to be milling about aimlessly; only a selected group of guests were examining the array of artwork that had been cleverly arranged against one wall. Looking around for Logan, Jill nudged Aggie as she saw Stacey Phillips bearing down on them, her face struggling against a sneer.

"Mrs. Beaumont," she cooed as she relieved Jill and her companion of their wraps, "I'm so glad you were able to join us. Logan has already sold three of his paintings, and a second dealer from Paris is trying to convince him to accept a contract for a showing at his gallery!"

"You sound surprised, Miss Phillips," Aggie said as she twisted her hand out of the woman's grasp. "I knew all along that Logan would be a success."

"Yes," Stacey said contritely, eyeing Jill for the first time. "And who do we have here?"

"You've met Jill before, Miss Phillips. She's the young writer who's been staying in Wynde Cottage."

"That's right," Stacey answered, her eyes narrowing into catlike slits. "I just suppose I'm used to seeing you in those faded blue jeans while you scrub toilets."

Disregarding Stacey's barb, Jill pretended to see someone she knew and headed for a corner of the room where she could search the crowd for a glimpse of Logan. Aggie trailed after her, only to be grabbed by the arm and asked to assess Logan's latest work by a short little man in wire glasses. Jill laughed as the woman reeled off praise after praise, her body quivering with enthusiasm as she realized that she had latched on to an eager listener.

Out of the corner of her eye, Jill saw Logan come into the room from what looked to be an adjoining study. A tall man stood beside him, and as they shook hands and parted company Logan's face flashed a charming smile. Undoubtedly, he had just closed the deal with the man from Paris.

"There he is, Arlene! That's Logan Matthews!"

Startled from her clandestine observation, Jill accepted a glass of champagne from a waiter who was roaming the crowd. Two girls were seated on a small divan, their attention riveted on Logan.

"I'm telling you, Arlene," one of them whispered, pulling her friend closer as she noticed Jill standing nearby, "he's the most gorgeous man I've ever seen!"

The other girl snorted, obviously not convinced. "So what if he is? Not one woman in this room would have a chance with him. Stacey Phillips has her claws in him, and she's not one to let go."

"I suppose you're right," the girl finally relented. "She does hang over him, and he, evidently, doesn't mind. Still, it's a shame...a shame and a waste."

Jill sipped the champagne in a vain effort to dull the agony she felt as she looked across the room and saw Stacey slip her arm through Logan's. She should never have let Aggie talk her into coming. Logan was so absorbed in accepting praises that he didn't even know she was there. Even Aggie had sought out a comfortable chair, her head nodding in an unmistakable doze.

Jill walked around the small, crowded gallery, looking at one angry seascape after another. She was stunned when she came upon a small canvas, exquisitely framed in gold, of a calm sea. She stood back to admire the brush strokes. How unlike Logan this painting was; the giant frothy swells were absent and in their place was an expanse of placid water stained with the colors of sunset and the sky a dusky sapphire blue. The brush strokes were lighter, more delicate, the shading more subdued. Yet off in the distance could be seen an approaching storm, threatening the calm in the foreground. How strange she hadn't noticed it before. It was a painting of that particular spot on the beach where she had first seen Logan.

Jill moved on to the next painting. Again it was spectacularly framed. There was something disconcerting about it. The painting was a continuation of the calm sea, but the shading was darker, the brush strokes heavy and predominant, and the sea was a roiling brew of tumultuous surf. Spindrift dotted the canvas, and Jill could almost feel it spraying her cheeks, she could almost smell the tangy kelp depicted in the foreground and hear the salt sea crashing against the ominously black rocks. Andrew Wyeth, move over, you've just met your match, she muttered beneath her breath.

Stacey Phillips narrowed her eyes as she watched Jill gasp when she came upon the second of the paintings.

A soft hiss escaped her lips. Deftly, she captured two cocktails from a passing waiter. "It's breathtaking, isn't it?" she said to Jill as she offered the champagne glass.

"Yes, it is," Jill agreed softly as she accepted the drink.

"Things seem to be under control here," Stacey told her. "Why don't we go out to the veranda and get away from some of this smoke? The noise and chatter is a bit much. Besides, I think it's time you and I became better acquainted."

It *was* stuffy in the gallery and a breath of air would feel good, Jill thought as she followed Stacey through the wide French doors. She felt uneasy about talking with Stacey, but she squared her shoulders and told herself that she could hold up her end of the conversation—unless, of course, it concerned Logan, and then she might have a problem. Safe topics of conversation would be called for.

Stacey set her drink down on a wrought-iron table and then leaned her elbows on the railing of the veranda. "Autumn is my favorite time of year. I first met Logan several years ago around this time. I'm very fond of him. I guess you know that, don't you?" She swung around suddenly, startling Jill.

Jill searched for the correct response. She had the distinct feeling she wasn't going to like the turn this conversation was going to take. "I…I think that most people who know Logan are fond of him. I haven't known him that long but I like him…."

"Yes, I know. Too much, it would seem. That's why I wanted to have this little talk. I suspect you have some sort of infatuation for him, and my suspicions were confirmed when I saw your reaction to his paintings. More than just a passing interest, wouldn't you say? Is it possible you're in love with him?" Stacey asked softly, her eyes glitteringly hard in the dim light.

Jill swallowed hard. The question was so soft, barely a whisper, that she felt she must have misunderstood. But the calculating look in Stacey's eyes told her she had heard right the first time.

"I don't think what I feel or don't feel for Logan is important, and it certainly isn't something I want to discuss in idle cocktail chatter," Jill answered coolly.

"You're right. It isn't important to me, but it could be to you. If you do love Logan, that is. You see, my dear, I'm going to marry Logan in Paris. Look," she said, opening the slim purse she had set down beside her glass and withdrawing an envelope. "Two plane tickets to Paris. One for Logan and one for me. Now you see why it's important for you not to be infatuated with him. Nothing can come of it. Logan belongs to me. He always has. Oh, I grant you I gave him a bit of a hard time last year when I thought…never mind. That's not important either. Fortunately, for Logan and myself, I came to my senses in time. We were meant for each other. We have so much in common. His work, my gallery, the whole art world for that matter. You don't fit in, darling. It's as simple as that. In more plain terms, you're out of your league, little girl."

Jill felt as though the breath had been driven from her body with a resounding blow. It couldn't be! Stacey must be lying. Logan asked her to marry him! Logan and Stacey! Yet she had seen the plane tickets. And she couldn't believe Stacey would lie about something so important. Jill groped for words. She had to say something, anything, to get away from the smiling woman with the narrowed eyes. Stacey was enjoying herself at Jill's expense. "Congratulations," she managed quietly.

Get away from here, her mind shrieked, get away from here, go somewhere quiet where you can be alone. You can't let her see how this has stunned you. That's what she wants. "I think it's time for me to leave now." Amazing. Did that calm voice really belong to her?

"Darling. I've upset you. That wasn't my intention," Stacey cooed. "It was just that I could see the direction you were heading, and I don't want to see you hurt. He's like the sea he paints. Parts of him are channeled and controlled and then he's whipped into a powerful and masterful force. I call him angry god of the sea."

Jill was furious. The last statement was uncalled for; there was no need to rub salt in the wound. Her own eyes narrowed as she turned to face Stacey. "I'm certain you and Logan will be very happy and I wish you well. Now, if you'll excuse me, I think it's time I was getting back to the compound."

"That would probably be best," Stacey said, following Jill back inside the crowded room. "I enjoyed our little talk. I find it pays to get things out into the open. This way there's no room for misunderstanding."

"You're absolutely right." Without another word Jill weaved her way through the crowd and down the steps to the small parking lot. She had to be alone, if even for a moment, before she went back for Aggie.

Logan was going to marry Stacey Phillips. Logan was going to... Over and over the words ricocheted through her brain. How could she have been so blind? How could she have thought she had a chance with him?

It was time to leave Mill Valley. Time to go back where she belonged. The question was, should she leave before Logan and Stacey left for Paris or should she leave immediately? Tomorrow was another day, she thought wearily. She would make her decision in the bright light of day, not in the dark that was as confused as her jumbled thoughts.

JILL SQUEEZED HER EYES shut against the darkness in her cottage, trying desperately to welcome sleep. Her body ached, crying out in loud refusal to her efforts to relax. The ride back to Mill Valley had been a quiet one, punctuated only by Aggie's snoring, confirming Jill's decision to take the wheel. She had been thankful the woman had napped soundly beside her, for she knew her weak rein on her tears would be broken if Aggie had asked her about her evening.

Damn Logan Matthews! Her hasty retreat from the showing had been the only thing that had caught his observance. Jill had helped Aggie into her coat only to look up and see Logan advancing on them through the crowd. He had looked so triumphant, so happy. How could he be so hypocritical? Why did she feel so betrayed?

The roar of an engine whizzed past Jill's cottage, pulling her from the bed to investigate. Even before she parted the curtains, she knew what she would see. Stacey's Porsche had come to a halt in front of Logan's house. Jill turned her back on the scene, certain she had spared herself the torture of seeing them both get out of the car and walk inside.

Unable to stand it, Jill jumped back into bed, pulling the covers over her head, needing to hide from the hurt of losing something she had never really had.

CHAPTER SEVEN

THE DIM GRAY LIGHT of dawn pierced through the curtains of Jill's window and found her still awake. The sheets were twisted around her legs. The pillows had suffered the torture of weary poundings and the coverlets had spilled onto the floor. Sleep had been impossible; thoughts of Logan and Stacey Phillips's cooing voice had haunted her. Whatever she had hoped for, whatever she had dreamed, had come to an end.

Throwing her legs over the side of the bed, Jill walked around the cottage, pulling on her jeans and a sweater. Glancing back at the bed, she frowned, "The princess and the pea," she muttered, kicking the covers out of her way. "Only I'll bet my last two bucks it wasn't a pea that kept her awake. It must have been a man!"

In the shadowy darkness of daybreak, she stumbled into her sandals, knowing her feet were going to be frozen. If she couldn't sleep, then she would walk. Walk and walk. Walk from here to Timbuktu, wherever that was, if she had to. She only knew she couldn't bear another minute of cloistering herself in this cottage.

When she opened the door, the slightest of breezes that accompanies dawn pushed billows of fog into the room. It was a low fog, reaching out and embracing the earth, swirling around her knees and making her sandaled feet damp and cold. Impervious to the discomfort, she placed one foot in front of the other and marched toward the beach.

The sound of the breakers came to her before she could see them. The rising sun had not dissipated the fog, although there were indications that it would burn off later in the day. Jill's long golden hair was loose, and now it was damp, almost wet. The thick, heavy sweater was sticking to her uncomfortably, but it was too chilly to remove it. These early-morning hours were as miserable as she felt.

Leaving the road, her foot touched sand. The sound of the surf was closer, but all she could see ahead was vast grayness. The same vague grayness her own future held—a future without Logan Matthews.

Down at the water's edge the hypnotic flowing and ebbing of the tide waves held her mesmerized. The sky was becoming lighter now as her thoughts became darker, ebbing into night and beyond. *Desolate, alone*—words that could frighten her dominated her thoughts. *Lost, forgotten*—words that damned were the curse of her destiny.

Her arms wrapped around her, and she hunched her shoulders, seeking warmth, pleading easement from this abandonment. The tears ran down her cheeks, blending with the salt spray as she turned her steps to the beach, to the far outcrop of rocks from which she had watched Logan that first day, eternities ago.

Inwardly, she scolded herself, berating her foolishness. A midnight visit to her cottage and unexplored passions did not make a relationship. There were no commitments, no vows, no words of love. There was nothing and there would be nothing. She had managed to pull herself up by her bootstraps once when she was jilted by

Deke, and she would again. Although somehow the end of the relationship with Deke hadn't wounded her the way the thought of Logan belonging to someone else did.

Prophetically, a thin golden shaft of sunlight pierced the wispy fog. It was possible now to discern the far horizon. Throwing back her shoulders and lifting her chin, Jill walked along the shore, her feet keeping time to a rhythmic drumming in her head.

It was then that she saw him, leaning against the rocks, looking off into the distance. His Irish woolen sweater enhanced his broad shoulders and defined his tapered waist. His long, denim-clad legs supported him in an easy balance. The wind had played through his night-dark hair, rippling it into stray curls and waves that fell over his brow and tumbled roguishly over his ears. Suddenly, as though sensing her presence, he turned and saw her.

Jill turned on her heels, gulping air, knowing only that she must get away from him, leave him. Otherwise she could never rebuild her life. Desperation lengthened her stride; rejection quickened her pace; hopelessness pounded in her breast.

"Jill!" Her name carried across the sand, losing itself in the fog. The sound of his voice held a command, an order that she halt.

She ran, her breath coming faster, her heart pounding louder. The loose sand rolled beneath her feet, slowing her pace. The light wind lifted her hair, pulling it back from her face, exposing it to the misty vapor surrounding her.

She knew he was close behind her. She imagined she could hear the deep breaths he was taking, and then she heard him call her name once again. "Jill!"

Gone was the command, the order. In its place was

a plea, a hope. Still, she ran. There was no hope, no survival if she stayed. Jill ran, ran for her life.

"Jill!"

His voice was closer now, stronger, coming to her through the air, blown to her on the breeze. Her steps faltered; she struggled to keep balance, determined to keep running.

His hand came from behind her, staggering her, spinning her around. "Let go of me!" She struggled desperately, fighting.

He was trying to say something, tell her something, but the panic was erasing all her senses, everything except the need to run. She kicked at his shins with her sandaled feet, twisting to escape like some trapped feline.

The edge of hysteria was evident in her voice. As if he sensed it, he seized her shoulders and shook her violently until she thought her neck would snap.

"Let me go!" she demanded again when he had stopped shaking her. She still struggled to free herself of him.

His hold tightened, biting into her flesh beneath the thick sweater, refusing to set her free, holding her firm.

"I hate you! I hate you! Let me go!"

His eyes blazed down at her, singeing her with their fury. His mouth tightened grimly, a mask of rage. A muscle convulsed in his jaw, giving proof of his furor. Before she could protest further, he captured her hands and held her arms behind her back, and she was crushed against him, trapped, imprisoned, cornered.

The salty scent of the ocean was in his sweater, but beneath it was the male scent of him, heady and potent. Her senses were sharp, alert, watchful. Driven by her desperation to escape, she struggled again, writhing against him, her pulses pounding.

The broadness of his shoulders became her pummeling posts, as she beat against him, bending backward, forcing him to follow.

Together, they dropped to the sand, tumbling over and over, grappling for supremacy. Logan's power intensified, the sheer brawn of him making her conflict strenuous and labored. Choking tears tore her throat, heaving sobs stifled her breath. Wordlessly, he gripped both sides of her head, forcing her to be still, freezing her into immobility. She was helpless, conquered, and cold fear stabbed her when she at last lifted her eyes to his.

The bruising possession of his mouth was an assault. His anger stiffened his body against hers, holding her firm, denying her escape. Her cold fear was replaced by his fire, licking up and down her spine. Still she fought, as though for her very life. Stronger now, fortified by obstinacy, she used her arms to wedge a space between them, frustrating his efforts to crush her again in his unyielding arms.

His hands circled her throat, forcing her chin up, making her mouth vulnerable to his. His lips held her captive, covering hers firmly, warmly. Stubbornly she tried to pull away, but he tightened his hold on her neck. His kiss deepened searchingly; hot flames touched her toes and flickered up her legs, centering somewhere in the center of her being.

Her small cries of surrender were conceived in her throat and born on her lips. His name began as a curse and became a prayer as he held her, pressed her into the sand, covering her with the length of him.

She was without will as his hands touched her. Her resolve became a vapor as his lips traveled the slim column of her neck, finding their reward in the throbbing pulse he found below her ear. When his hands cupped her breasts, a flaming desire ignited within her to know the fullness of his possession.

Her arms circled his neck, capturing him in her embrace. Her lips were her offering; her body was created to please him. Low sounds rumbled in his chest, heightening her awareness of him, delighting her senses.

The wings of trapped birds fluttered in her breast when resistance reasserted itself. His mouth opened over hers, parting her lips, tasting the sweetness he found there. The ocean roared in her head, pounding, eroding her will.

Logan lifted his head, looking down into her upturned face. He gazed at her for a moment, his eyes alive with a vibrant passion she had never seen in another man's eyes. Jill reached up to touch his face, caressing his jaw. He buried his face in her neck, his mouth stirring a twin desire in her. His caresses traveled the length of her, leaving her breathless, her heart nearly bursting as she exulted in his touch.

"Logan, Logan, I love you," she breathed, her murmurs a confession of the feelings she could deny no longer.

Logan's body stiffened, pulling away in abrupt denial, leaving her confused and abandoned. Pulling himself upright, he sat gazing out at the sea for a long moment. She lay still, watching him, seeing his turmoil in the wrinkling of his brow and the grim set of his mouth.

What had she done? Why had he pulled away from her? Was he still playing games? Awakening her one moment and rejecting her the next. She should hate him! Hate him with every fiber of her body. But somehow it was impossible to hate Logan Matthews.

Every instinct told her he had been sincere each time he had pressed his lips to hers. She had felt it in his touch, in the urgency of his passion, in the tenderness of his lovemaking.

At last he turned to her, looking down at her, touching her hair with his fingertips.

"Jill, you're so young. I'm not certain you know what love is all about."

Logan's voice was soft, almost a whisper.

"I can learn, Logan," she heard herself say, but when she looked up it was to find him gone. He was walking down the beach, away from her.

TODAY WAS TO BE Aggie's last day before leaving for Seattle. She was "packed and rarin' to go," as she had put it to Jill. Today, she had said, was going to be like any other day until the dinner hour was over. Then and only then would she leave. Logan was taking her to the airport. In other words, it was business as usual, she had said succinctly.

Jill felt as though she had lead weights tied to her feet as she went about her chores. The sun had burned off the fog but she didn't want to face the day or Logan Matthews. Facing herself in the tiny bedroom mirror, her cheeks blotched with tears, was all the facing up she was going to do for a long time to come. She should leave, she told herself, but something was holding her back. Hope? Fool, she told herself. Men like Logan Matthews killed hope. They set about their orderly lives, and if you were included, you could count yourself lucky. If not, you could consider yourself hopeless.

A feeling of impending doom seemed to be settling over her. The feeling was so strong she shivered. What else could go wrong that would or could possibly matter to her? It wasn't that she was going to be in charge of the kitchen chores. Aggie had said that her new friend, Pat the journalist, and Jack were to be her new helpers. No, she could manage the chores. It was something else. She tried to shake the feeling, but it stayed with her while she cleaned the bathrooms, and it was still with her when she walked forlornly to the dining hall.

Doozey ran toward her just as she reached the front door.

"Hi ya, Doozey. How have you been? Haven't seen you for a while," Jill said, scratching the setter behind the ears.

"He's been punished for digging in the garbage," a voice said behind her.

Jill ignored Logan Matthews and walked into the dining hall. She walked as quickly as she could to the opposite side of the room and sat down. She couldn't face him, didn't want to face him, not after he had left her alone on the beach wearing her heart on her sleeve.

"Mind if I sit down?"

"And if I did, would you leave? It's your dining hall, Mr. Matthews, sit anywhere you please."

"Testy this morning, aren't we?"

"That's as good a word as any I could come up with," Jill snapped.

"I thought you would like the word. After all, words are your business. I'm just a lowly painter. You writers seem to have the world cornered as far as emotional words are concerned. By the way, how are your memoirs coming?"

Jill fidgeted. She hated it when he brought up the lie she had told him. She squirmed in her seat and shrugged. "I'm far from a professional" was all she could manage.

"It must be tedious work, trying to remember all the details of your life."

It sounded to Jill like a statement of fact that required no answer. She shrugged again, wishing the waiters would get on with serving breakfast. Where was Stacey Phillips? Now, that was a loaded question, and she would dearly love a loaded answer.

"What are you serving for my going-away party?"

"I wasn't aware that you were going away, much less having a party," Jill fibbed. "Nothing was said to me about having extra duties. I have my hands full as it is."

"It's not an order," Logan replied just as coolly. "What we usually do is have cake and coffee the night before one of the guests is due to leave. Very simple fare."

"Guess that lets me out, then. I can't bake," Jill said, watching the door carefully for some sign of Stacey.

Logan got to his feet and stood towering over her. Gone was his playfulness and humor. His eyes were narrowed to slits as he stared down at her. For a moment Jill remembered the odd feeling of impending doom she had experienced on awakening.

"By the way, a call came in for you this morning, quite early, as a matter of fact. I took the message and left it on the desk in the office. Someone by the name of Deke called."

Jill swallowed hard. Impending doom was too tame a phrase. She felt all the color drain from her face. Unconsciously, she grasped the edge of the table, her knuckles white against the burnished maple.

"He sounded like an anxious husband to me," Logan said coldly. "I know I must be mistaken because you said you weren't married when you registered."

Jill was stunned. It was impossible! There was no

way, absolutely no way, for Deke to find her. By rights, she should be as safe in Mill Valley as she was if she were on the moon. How had Deke found her? And, more important, what did he want? Wasn't he satisfied that he had left her standing at the altar? Wasn't her humiliation enough?

Jill felt numb as she stared at Logan, willing words to her tongue.

"I am not married."

That was all. There was nothing more to say. The steely eyes penetrated her being. The anger on his face that first day on the beach had been nothing compared to what she was seeing now.

Jill was silent a moment longer and then turned and left the dining hall. Her voice had been cool, almost impersonal. Amazing. She was dying on the inside, and she could be as cool as the proverbial cucumber on the outside. Her shoulders slumped the moment she was outdoors. How could Deke have found her? Her mind raced frantically, trying to reconstruct an answer to the riddle. Unless someone had searched her belongings, there was no way that she could be connected to Deke Atkins. She hadn't mailed the postcards to Nancy and the girls.

Jill raced back to her cottage and looked in her handbag. All was as it should be. The postcards. She turned, expecting to see them on the dresser. No, that had been in Briar Cottage. Before Stacey took it over!

"Oh, no!" she wailed. Aggie, when she straightened the cottage for Stacey, or Stacey herself must have mailed them, thinking that was what Jill wanted.

Call Deke, she told herself. She turned in the direction of the door and then suddenly sat down on the bed. No. She didn't want to talk to him. She couldn't face that today. It would be an ugly scene because she felt ugly inside.

Pack and leave! her mind ordered. "I can't," she whispered. "If I leave now, I'll never see Logan again, and I don't want to remember him with that anger in his eyes. After the party."

A going-away party for Logan! How in the world was she going to handle that? Perhaps if he had just made some mention of his impending marriage to Stacey it would have cleared the air between them.

A party. Colorful party plates, balloons, streamers…all the trimmings. Was she expected to go all out for this bon voyage affair? Cake and coffee sounded simple enough. But a party wasn't really a party without the festive accoutrements, and with Aggie in Seattle this was more than she felt she could handle.

Somewhere in the laundry area she recalled seeing a box with a handmade label stating simply Party Decorations. Undoubtedly, Aggie had a varied assortment of trimmings. She promised she would check it out as soon as she checked the larder to be certain all the ingredients were on hand to bake the cake. It shouldn't be too difficult, not with Aggie's own handwritten recipes in the little tin box by the stove.

Jill determined this was not going to be a bland affair. She would outdo herself. No one, not ever, would know what this effort would cost her. If she was lucky, she might even be able to choke down some cake and swallow the coffee.

Facing Logan and pretending happiness for him would be so hard. Could she do it? Of course, she had no other choice. Stacey Phillips would get Logan, and she, Jill, would salvage her pride. A very poor comparison no matter how she looked at it. But a necessary one.

Selecting a recipe for Black Forest Cake, Jill rummaged in Aggie's cabinets till she found a suitable bowl for mixing a double batch of batter. The heavy ceramic bowl was cheerful, with a clever pattern of Indian design around the sides and trailing to the bottom of the bowl. For some reason it cheered Jill as she measured and then sifted the flour into the huge cavity.

Her preparations were well under way and the oven was heating when Jill was aware of a presence in the room. She stopped greasing the cake tins and looked around. It was quiet. Just the soft music coming from the radio perched on top of the refrigerator. She looked around again, an uneasy feeling creeping between her shoulders.

"Anyone there?" she called in the direction of the laundry room. There was no response. The strange feeling stayed with her until she slid the cake pans into the oven. She quickly set the small timer on the stove and just as quickly strode into the laundry room. It was empty. No sound at all came from the small area. Her eyes went to the screen door. Latched. She shrugged; it must be her imagination. She was on edge, there was no doubt about it. If she didn't watch it, she would get the heebie-jeebies, seeing and hearing strange noises that didn't exist. Actually, it wasn't anything that could be seen or heard. Only a dreadful feeling.

The alien feeling stayed with her while she sorted through the party box. Everything was there—paper plates with matching napkins; multicolored streamers and a fresh package of balloons. There was even an assortment of noisemakers. She would take them over to the dining hall as soon as the cakes came out of the oven. Just before the party, she would blow up the balloons and string them along the beams. Logan would appreciate the pains she had taken for his party. He might even thank her. But she didn't want thanks. She wanted Logan.

Jill shook her head. She had no right thinking such thoughts. Not now, since Stacey Phillips had confided their plans. She had to keep busy so she wouldn't think.

A glance through the glass window on the oven door told her the cakes were rising evenly, so she set about washing up the utensils she had used. Next, she readied the fruit and mixed the frosting. When she was finished, she still felt jittery and out of control. The feeling of impending doom stayed with her while she made herself a cup of coffee, and it was still with her when she removed the cakes from the hot oven thirty minutes later.

While she sipped her coffee she mentally ran over the dinner menu in her mind. Spaghetti and meatballs. All she had to do was heat the frozen sauce and meat that Aggie had left in the freezer. The spaghetti would cook at the last minute, so her time for the most part was all right. She would even have time for a bath while the sauce heated and the water boiled. She grimaced as she wondered what she would do if she really were a writer. With all she had to do she would have had to forgo sleep in order to accomplish anything at all. Still, she wouldn't have missed this experience for anything. Meeting Aggie and having her for a friend was one good thing that had come of it.

If only things had worked out differently it would have been a memorable experience, one that would have lasted a lifetime, an experience that she and Logan could have shared together. Now he was going to share it with Stacey Phillips.

Jill straightened her shoulders. She couldn't think about this now, she warned herself, or soon the tears would start to flow and she would end up feeling sorry for herself all over again.

IT WAS HARD TO TELL from Logan's expression if he was pleased with the party decor or not. He seemed preoccupied, almost in another world. Stacey spoke to him several times before she could gain his attention. Jill watched, a puzzled expression on her face, as she sliced through the thick frosting, down through the layered fruit and fluffy cake until her knife touched the plate.

There were oohs and aahs as the guests stared at the mouthwatering dessert. Even Logan favored her with a smile. "I thought you said you couldn't bake," he teased lightly.

Jill's tongue felt thick, rendering her speechless. She could only stare at him for a moment before she handed him his plate and fork. Logan's eyes were dark and unreadable as he matched her gaze.

Stacey shouldered her way between the two chairs, literally pushing Jill from Logan's side. "Let me see this confectionery delight," she demanded. Then, more shrilly: "Darling, I couldn't possibly eat this. It would add twenty pounds immediately. For shame, Jill! Didn't you give any thought to us girls when you baked this cake?"

"Then don't eat it," Jill snapped as she headed back to the far end of the table, where she left the cake for quick disposal by the rest of the little group.

Forcing herself to take part in the festivities, Jill joined in a toast to Logan. "To good friends," Aaron said happily. "Here's hoping you have a safe and profitable journey, Logan." The others joined in as they attacked the rich dessert.

Jill was tasting the cake, her fork poised in midair,

when the door to the dining hall opened and a voice called out, "Hello!"

Logan rose from the table and the others quieted, a hush falling over the room. A stranger in the compound at this hour of the evening was a rarity.

Jill froze as the man walked farther into the center of light. Deke!

"I'm looking for Jill. I'm Deke Atkins," he said, holding out his hand to Logan. The men shook hands briefly as Logan turned to look for Jill.

"There's someone here to see you, Jill. Sit down, Mr. Atkins. Have a cup of coffee and a piece of cake."

Jill clenched her teeth as she made her way over to the table. The easy camaraderie was broken with Deke's arrival. The men finished their cake and Pat started to clear the table. Stacey remained quiet, her eyes narrowed and watchful. Neither Logan nor Stacey looked as though they were going to move or say anything.

"Deke" was all Jill could manage to say. Why had he come here? After his phone call to her she should have followed her instincts and called him back. Told him to stay away from her, that she never wanted to see him again. But she hadn't. She had run away from an unpleasant situation and buried her head in the sand, hoping it would go away. And now he was here, in the flesh, and what might have been unpleasant on the phone was going to be a face-to-face confrontation.

"I had a devil of a time finding you, Jill. Look, is there somewhere we could go and talk? I have a lot of things to tell you. I'm not interrupting anything, am I?" he asked, finally noticing the silence.

"Not at all, Atkins. It's just a small going-away party with a few friends. Jill was good enough to bake the cake and serve it. Sure there isn't anything we can get you after your long drive? Jill has a few things to do, and then she'll be right with you."

Why was Logan speaking for her as if she were a child? She could answer for herself. She steeled her resolve. Just because Deke had arrived on the spot didn't mean a thing. She could send him on his way with a few choice words, either in public or in private. She owed him nothing. She had burned her bridges when she left New Jersey.

"If you'll wait a few minutes, Deke, I'll be glad to listen to anything you have to say." Before I send you packing, she added under her breath. Busily, she stacked the dishes and set about clearing the table.

Jill worked feverishly tidying up the service area. Out of the corner of her eye she watched Logan and Stacey eye her with speculation. Deke toyed with a cup of coffee, saying nothing, not even bothering to try to make simple conversation. She placed the dish towel on the rack just as Deke stood up.

"Ready?" he called.

Jill nodded to Stacey and Logan and followed Deke outside into the crisp autumn night.

"You look well, Jill."

"I'm wonderful," she told him, realizing with a sense of amazement that it was really true. She was wonderful. Regardless of her disappointment over Logan, she was wonderful. A sense of security in her own worth was something she had only recently found and would never relinquish. "Why are you here, Deke? What do you want? If memory serves me correctly, you left me standing at the altar. Offhand, I would say that finishes things between us. I simply cannot imagine why you're here now. You left me, remember? No phone call, nothing. You just didn't show up." Her voice was heated now, hard with anger. Not because she had been left standing at the altar but because he was here, trying to walk back into her life.

"Jill, I know what I did was unforgivable. I have no excuse. I got cold feet, it's as simple as that. I came here to see if just maybe you might find it in your heart to forgive me. I know I have no right to ask anything of you after what I did to you, but I had to try. All I can say is I'm sorry."

"I'm sorry too, Deke. It's too late."

"Can we at least be friends? After all, we're going to be working in the same office when you get back. I'd like to give it a try if you're willing. We really did have some good times together if you stop and think about it."

"I don't know, Deke, about us being friends. I don't think it would work. It's true that I'm going to be going back to the office, but only on a temporary basis. I plan to give my notice and then I'll wait until they replace me so I don't leave them shorthanded. I really don't think there's a future for either of us."

"There must be something left," Deke pleaded. "I expected you to be angry and throw me out on my ear. We're talking calmly like adults, so you can't be all that upset with me."

"I've had a lot of time to think since I got here, Deke. What happened was for the best. At first I was angry and humiliated, but I'm over that now. We all have to grow up sometime. Perhaps if you had been decent about it and called me to tell me you didn't want to marry me, things would be different. I'm not saying for sure that I would forgive and forget and take you back, but I might at least have some respect for you. It's over, Deke. By the way, when did you get here? Were you anywhere near the kitchen this afternoon? I had the feeling someone was watching me."

"Yes, it was me," Deke said glumly. "After I got here I sort of walked around for a while looking for you. I just wanted to see what you could be doing in a place like this. And I wanted to see if you were happy. I told myself if you were happy I would leave and go back to New York and not even bother letting you know I was here. But you looked so forlorn and miserable as I stood outside the window watching you. It took me a long time to get my nerve up to go over to the dining hall. I know you find this hard to believe, but I really do want to marry you. Jill, why couldn't you have waited instead of taking off the way you did? If you had been just a little patient, a little more understanding, we could be married and honeymooning in Hawaii. I knew by the next day that I had made a mistake, so it's just as much your fault as it is mine."

Jill grinned. "I *was* a jilted bride. You must be more of a fool than I thought if you think you can come here and expect to pick up where we left off—rather, where *you* left off."

"You must really hate me."

Jill's face grew serious. "No, Deke, I don't hate you. I even understand and I'm sorry that you made the trip up here for nothing. I'm leaving here in a little while myself. Why don't we say goodbye now and forget everything that's happened? You get on with your life and I'll get on with mine."

"I know that you're going to regret this someday, Jill. Someday you'll wish you hadn't been so hasty and foolish."

But Jill knew now that she was free, free of Deke

by her own choice, free of Logan even, but not by her own choice.

"Goodbye, Deke," Jill said, holding out her hand.

Deke stared at Jill a moment and then lowered his eyes to her hand. Without a word he turned and walked toward his car.

While Jill threw her clothes into her bag she could hear Deke's engine cough and sputter. She grinned to herself. All the money he had paid for his sports car and he couldn't get it started. It would be just her luck to have to give him a ride, or worse yet, tow him to a garage. Her eyes widened. He wouldn't, he couldn't, be doing it on purpose. He could just sit there till it snowed before she would give him a lift anywhere.

"Doozey, come back here with my handbag!" Jill shouted as she closed the last of her cases. Where had the setter come from? He must have been sleeping under her bed all this time. "Doozey! Come back here. Doozey!" The setter ran across the compound, the contents of her purse spilling as he raced toward Stacey and Logan, who were talking to Deke.

By the time Jill reached the middle of the compound, Logan was bending over, gathering up the spilled contents. He spoke sternly to Doozey, who rolled over on his back to show he was sorry.

"I think that's all of it," Logan said, holding out the oversize purse. "My apologies. Doozey must have thought there was candy in your bag." She couldn't miss the strange coldness that permeated his voice.

Jill reached out to take her bag. "Thank you," she said quietly as she headed back to the cottage. One by one she carried her cases to the car and unceremoniously dumped them in the backseat. She turned the key and was rewarded with a low, throaty engine roar.

Suddenly, in her rearview mirror, she saw Deke's car come to life and his oversize wheels kick up dust as he zoomed out of the compound.

Sighing, Jill steered her car in his wake, only to stop quickly when Stacey's arms flew up, signaling. "What is it?" Jill asked, alarmed.

"Wait, you forgot something!" Stacey said sweetly. "I'll get it for you. I won't be a second."

As Stacey dashed off Logan turned to face Jill. "It would have been nice if you had told someone you were leaving. It is usual practice to give one's notice."

This was almost more than Jill could take. It would have been nice if he cared that she was leaving instead of only worrying about who was going to scrub the bathrooms. "Look, Mr. Matthews. I really don't owe you anything. Notice or otherwise. I worked my fingers to the bone around here. I did more than my share. That makes us even in my eyes. And I didn't know notice was required. I find that I have pressing business at home that I must attend to. I want to thank you for allowing me to stay here. Please say goodbye to the others for me, especially Aggie." In spite of herself, Jill found that her voice had softened and lost its edge.

"And would that pressing business happen to be Deke Atkins? You're not on his trail, are you?" There was a strange glint in Logan's eyes—anger, hostility, disappointment?

"Is that what you and Deke were talking about?" she asked. She wouldn't have put it past Deke to tell Logan an outright lie. Deke had pride; it would be too much for him to admit that he had driven all the way from New Jersey to be turned down by Jill.

Before Logan could answer, Stacey Phillips came down the path holding out a cloud of billowing white froth—Jill's wedding gown that she had discarded in the closet of the cottage that Stacey now occupied. "Darling, here. You certainly can't leave this behind. I know you'll be needing it."

All Jill could see were Logan's cold, chiseled features. In that one split second his eyes accused, judged and convicted. "You keep it. You'll need it long before I will," Jill said hoarsely.

Stacey's tinkling laugh followed her all the way to the gates. Logan's dark, unreadable eyes would haunt her for days to come. Would she ever be able to erase that memory of his face from her mind? He thought she had lied to him, lied to him all along. Tears pricked and stung her eyelids. She loved Logan and she could no more erase him from her mind or heart than she could stop breathing.

Jill drove down the highway and doubled back for the strip of beach where she had spent those few moments of unleashed passion with Logan. She knew it was a mistake to get out of the car to walk the sands at this time of night, but she felt a searing need to be near the water that Logan loved to paint. All she wanted was one last walk, one last look.

Jill kicked off her shoes and set them on her car hood. The sand felt cool to her tired feet. She walked to the water's edge and tested it with her toe. It was as cold as the depths of Logan's eyes.

She walked back to one of the dunes and sat down. Intently, she stared out at the water, willing something to ease the ache in her heart. Several long quiet minutes were suddenly broken by Doozey, toppling her backward, licking her face.

"Doozey! What are you doing here? Of course I know you love to run the beach at night, but this is pretty far from home for you. You'd better get back before Logan starts to look for you."

Banishing Doozey to home, Jill went back to her car. Within a few minutes the highway was beneath her wheels. The window near her left shoulder was open and the crisp autumn air blew against her cheeks.

The white line on the road blurred in her vision. She was tired, too tired to drive all night long as had been her plan. Making a left at the turnoff that led into town, she changed her plans and decided to spend the night in the local motel. Besides, Aggie was returning home tomorrow morning and Stacey and Logan would be leaving. By early afternoon Aggie should be home and it would be safe to go back and say her goodbyes in person. Jill had come to love Aggie and could almost feel the older woman's strong, comforting arms around her.

Jill whispered Logan's name, the sound of it stolen away by the wind passing her window. She wouldn't cry; she had cried her tears for him. Now she was going to try to banish him from her soul. She made a silent resolution to convince herself that the man she dreamed of, the man she loved, had never really existed at all.

CHAPTER EIGHT

A LOW, ANGRY WIND raced around Logan's house as Jill knocked on the back door to see Aggie.

"I've seen some tired-looking people in my day, but you sure beat them all," Aggie Beaumont said as she held the kitchen door open for Jill. "You been crying too, I can tell," she added matter-of-factly. "Come on in. I'll make us both a cup of tea. Tea fixes everything," she said, a note of authority in her voice.

The minute Jill sat down at the table, she reached for Aggie, longing to feel those comforting arms around her. Bit by bit, fighting back tears, dry-eyed, she told Aggie her entire story. She left nothing out.

"I feel so helpless, Jill. I've known Logan all his life. Once that man makes up his mind the heavens themselves can't make him change it. I know that's not what you want to hear, but it's true. I think you were wrong to leave. You should have tried to explain. I know, I know, there didn't seem much point after what Stacey told you about her and Logan getting married. Land, child! You should have told me right away. I still can't believe it! If you'd told me I could have asked Logan myself."

Round and round the conversation went until Jill stood, ready to leave, feeling much much better for having talked with her friend.

"Better get moving, Jill," Aggie told her with a re-morseful note in her voice, sorry to see Jill leave. She had really come to love the girl as her own. "Some of these roads are bad after dark. You leave me your address, and I'll get in touch with you as soon as I can."

Jill dried her tears. "You believe me, don't you, Aggie?"

"'Course I believe you. Any woman would believe you. It's just men, Logan in particular, that don't believe." She grimaced. "I know it has something to do with being creative, him painting and all. I told you he sees what he sees and he hears what he hears. He wasn't always like this, but he's been hurt, and from the looks of things, he's gonna get hurt again. It's a sad fact of life, but it happens to be true."

Jill accepted a paper sack full of peanut butter cookies along with a thermos full of coffee. Tears blurring her vision, she embraced the older woman and was not surprised to see the faded blue eyes brim over.

"You drive carefully, you hear?"

Jill nodded as she climbed into the car. Doozey whined pitifully as he watched Jill pull out of the compound.

A WEEK LATER, her honeymoon luggage stored in the basement, her honeymoon clothes sealed in plastic bags, Jill went back to the office. She was only working on a temporary basis, she reminded herself, until she could find another job. She knew she would see Deke and was prepared to handle it in the best way she could.

Jill felt her stomach heave with apprehension as she pressed the interoffice intercom and buzzed Deke's office. It had been easy to dodge him since her return, although tedious, for his working hours had become routine. It was only when Nancy had dropped off the claims marked for immediate attention that Jill admitted to herself that her game of hide-and-seek was only temporary.

"Mr. Atkins," she announced to the button-studded terminal on her desk, "there are some claims here that need your signature before they can be approved. Would you like me to bring them in now?"

"Jill? Jill, is that you?"

"Would you like me to bring in the claims now, Mr. Atkins?"

"Yes," Deke snapped, obviously stung by her cool behavior, "right away."

Deke's office was down the hall from Jill's desk and she walked toward it slowly, pacing each step as though she were walking to an early-morning execution.

Giving the door an announcing knock, Jill strode into the room, her demeanor hinting at a confidence she didn't really feel. Placing the papers on Deke's desk without a word, she turned to go but stopped short as he reached out and grabbed her by the wrist.

"Please, Jill," Deke whispered, his eyes begging, "sit down and let's talk."

"Deke, there's nothing to say."

Deke shook his head, pulling out a chair for Jill before he sat perched on the corner of his desk. "Perhaps you have nothing to say to me, Jill. I can understand that after everything that's happened. It's only that I was half out of my mind with worry. When you ran away, I thought that it would all work itself out if I didn't press you. I honestly tried to keep away from you."

"We were both wrong," Jill said quietly.

The statement somehow appeased Deke, for his face relaxed and he reached out to pull Jill to her feet. Embracing her, he looked down into her face.

"Knowing that, can't we try to start over again?"

Without a struggle, Jill let herself be led into a kiss, her mouth bruised as Deke pressed his lips against hers with a moan. She clung to him desperately, willing herself to respond. Instead, her mind conjured up Logan and the way her body had melted into his.

"You're crying," Deke observed, his fingers wiping the traitorous moisture from Jill's cheeks.

"We'll take things slowly," Deke promised. "There's no need to discuss our future together right now. We'll take it one day at a time…get to know each other again."

DEKE HELD FAST to his word. The weeks passed swiftly, each day bringing a new surprise as Deke stepped up his campaign to enchant Jill. A bouquet of flowers appeared at her door every day, sometimes accompanied by enormous boxes of candy, which remained stacked in Jill's refrigerator for the time when she felt compelled to binge. It was a time of wine, French restaurants and sojourns in Chinatown, a time to forget dreams of watching the sea by moonlight and tumbling passionately in the sand.

It was Saturday, and Jill awoke early, roused by a pounding at her door.

"Awaken, my lass!" Deke laughed as he leaned on her doorstep waiting to be invited in. "Your carriage awaits!"

Jill giggled. "Where are we going today?"

"You think I'm going to let the cat out of the bag?" Deke teased. "Get dressed and we'll see if you deserve to find out."

Deke drove for hours and Jill began to think that he was traveling in circles. When at last the car pulled to a stop, Jill considered herself completely lost.

Taking her by the hand, Deke led the way up a flight of enormous stone steps. The building that seemed to be his goal reminded Jill of the oversize library where she had spent many an hour during her childhood. The brick exterior was covered with trailing clumps of ivy, a square chunk of it kept trimmed beside the double glass doors at the front of the building to reveal a bronze plaque. Jill felt confused as she got close enough to read it. Barth Art Gallery.

From the interior of the building it was evident that the reputation of the gallery had once been very prestigious. Jill marveled that she had never heard of it before.

"How did you find this place, Deke?"

Deke pressed his finger to his lips, shaking his head as though sworn to secrecy.

It was the room reserved for the newest pieces into which Jill found herself being led. Most of the displays were sculptures, a few black and white etchings, and even some still photography. Jill was turning to Deke to demand an explanation when her eyes were caught by a solitary oil painting that had been given the honor of gracing one blank wall. She moved closer to it, her heart in her throat as she recognized Logan's style.

"I read about it in the papers this morning," Deke said from somewhere behind her. "It's that artist from Mill Valley. They had a whole write-up on him in the art section of the newspaper. He's had a big success in Paris, and he donated this painting to the curator of this gallery because the guy gave him one of his first breaks when he was starting out."

"I never mentioned Logan Matthews to you, Deke," Jill said, her insides aching as she felt all her longings for Logan renewed.

Deke flushed but didn't answer.

"You checked up on me?" Jill accused hotly.

"Of course I did!" Deke admitted. "How the hell was I supposed to know what was going on?"

Suddenly, it was all very clear, the truth drowning Jill in a whirlpool of resignation. Deke hadn't changed; he had only sat down and plotted out an intricate plan to wheedle his way back into her life.

"Take me home," Jill said calmly as she walked away from Logan's painting. "Take me home, Deke, and promise me that I'll never have to see you again."

"YOU'LL CHANGE YOUR MIND, Jill," Deke warned as he dropped her off in front of her apartment. "You'll change your mind, and this time I won't be there."

Not looking back to answer, Jill walked up the stone path that led to her door and automatically took the mail from the box beside it before turning the key in the lock. Pressing her back against the solid support of the carved wood, she summarily sorted through the selection of bills and advertisements. Sticking out from the ordinary was an oversize pink envelope, Mrs. Beaumont's familiar scrawl taking up one whole side. Crossing to the couch, Jill sat down, propping her feet up on the coffee table. She managed a laugh as she pulled the letter out and smoothed it with the palm of her hand. It was written in pencil on the back of a sheet of cross-word puzzles that Aggie had completed with great difficulty, evidenced by the smears of a soiled pencil eraser.

Dear Jill,

I've been meaning to write for some time, but as you know, it's time to close up the cottages for the winter and I've been busier than a spaniel with new pups. I got your letter and I am very happy that you're doing well and making a go of things. Every so often Doozey goes by the cottage and whines and yaps outside the door. I know he's looking for you. Logan is back in Boston. I'm sure, by now, you must have read about his success in Paris. It was in all the papers and one night he was on television. I was so proud I thought I would burst. Miss Phillips was married in New York. Logan gave her a painting for a wedding present. Logan didn't seem at all surprised or even hurt. He was real mad, though, that day you left. He mumbled something that sounded to me like "impatience of youth." He did ask me for your address before he went back to Boston.

Take good care of yourself, Jill. Think about me and Doozey out here walking the beach with the wind whipping about us. Both of us miss you. Have a nice Thanksgiving and a happy holiday season. Love from me and wet kisses from Doozey.

Aggie

Jill stared at the letter for a long time, rereading it until her tears made the words illegible. What had she done? Logan hadn't taken Stacey to Paris with him. Then why had he needed to book two seats on the airline? Could it have been for the dealer who had drawn up the contract at the showing that night? Jill sobbed, knowing that the details didn't matter. All she knew was that she loved Logan and she had allowed herself to walk away from him. Her life was crumbling around her, falling to pieces before her very eyes. It was as though her entire future flickered in the flame of a candle and she had been the one that had snuffed it out, pitching herself headfirst into darkness.

A WEEK BEFORE Christmas, Jill made her decision. The arrangements had been so easy to make once she had made up her mind. She knew she could never return to the office as long as it held the certainty of daily confrontations with Deke. Her prospects appeared bright as she faced two interviews in the coming week. The packing had been the hardest. Her possessions had seemed so familiar in her apartment, and Jill wondered if they would ever fit another environment.

She had one last week to tie up all the loose ends. Her lunch on that day was a primitive one as she awaited the arrival of the moving van. Surrounded by all the packing crates, Jill was overcome with a mixture of emotions. She was positive that her entire life lay before her ready to be discovered. She felt sad as well, regretting that her past still haunted her.

When the movers called to report an emergency that would prevent them from coming today, Jill decided that she couldn't sit here in the apartment a moment longer. "'Tis the season to be jolly," she hiccuped as she put on her coat. A trip into New York and a little Christmas shopping would perk up her mood. She was sure of it. Perhaps she could find a Christmas present for Aggie and have it sent. If there was a doubt that it would get to Mill Valley before Christmas, she would take the gift home with her and send it out with a belated card as soon as the holiday season was over.

Tramping and jostling her way through the holiday shoppers, Jill managed to lose herself in the spirit of the season. With gay abandon she purchased several bril-

liant bows and a sparkling gift wrap for the nonsensi-
cal little trinkets she had previously picked up for her
friends. A few shining ornaments were bought with
thoughtful consideration and wrapped in tissue paper.
Each purchase was placed carefully in an oversize
shopping bag with a brilliant Santa on the side.

How marvelous if the spirit of Christmas could be
extended to take in the entire year! Goodwill and the
cheer of the holiday season were contagious as Jill
smiled and nodded to the harried shoppers.

Jill had one bad moment as she stood on the escala-
tor in Macy's. She turned to admire the overhead decorations and the brilliant evergreen that looked so
stunning from on high. She let her eyes fall to the
milling shoppers and felt her heart lurch. Logan. Logan
was standing in the sporting-goods department. It was
Logan, she was sure of it. Jill stepped off the moving
stairway and raced around to the other side, and actually
walked down the steps in her eagerness to get to the
bottom. Jostling and shouldering people out of her way,
she ran past the tobacco shop and a display of wicker
to the sporting-goods section. Her eyes searched frantically for some sign of Logan in his shearling jacket.
He was nowhere in sight. She couldn't have been
wrong. He had looked just like Logan. Surely, she
hadn't been mistaken. She shook her head. She could
never have mistaken someone else for him. There was
only one Logan Matthews in the whole world, and she
had just lost him for the second time.

Weary to the point of exhaustion, Jill made her way
to a small snack bar. She waited patiently, her eyes
searching the crowds as they flocked through the thriving
department store. When she was finally ushered to a

booth at the rear, she felt like crying. She had lost him again.

She gave her order of a Waldorf salad and black coffee to the waitress. Her shoulders slumped wearily. It was just the season for hope, she told herself. She wanted to see Logan, so somehow her mind conjured him up at just the right moment. If only Logan were with her it would be the perfect Christmas. She couldn't think of anything more blessed and peaceful than being in his arms. Holiday season or not, this dream was not meant to be.

Her mind was playing tricks on her again. Aggie had said Logan had asked for her address. Panic gripped her. If she moved from her tiny apartment, he would never find her. Visions of the packing cartons and the order form for the movers flashed before her. She couldn't move.

As she chewed her way through the crisp salad she first contemplated moving and then not moving. Logan. Aggie hadn't said when she gave Logan her address. Certainly, he had had plenty of time to get in touch with her if he had wanted to.

Boston was his home base. What could he possibly be doing here in New York at this time of year? Since he was a lawyer, it was logical to assume that he was on business for a client or even that the client resided here. If that was so, her mind questioned, what was he doing in the Macy's sporting-goods department wearing a shearling jacket?

She didn't have the answers. Jill pushed the salad plate away and picked up her coffee cup. She couldn't keep on torturing herself with maybes and what-ifs or might have beens. She still had to find a suitable present for Aggie. She knew that if she really wanted more information concerning Logan, all she had to do was pick up the phone and call Aggie. Aggie would tell her whatever she knew.

Jill paid her check and walked back into the crowded mall, her thoughts concerned only with steering a straight course to the blanket department. She would get one of those new fashionable comforters so Aggie could toast herself in front of the fire, and, of course, a new superdeluxe bone for Doozey, or perhaps a new collar.

The salesgirl laughed mirthlessly when Jill asked if there was any way for the gift to arrive in time for Christmas. "What year?" she demanded.

BACK IN HER APARTMENT Jill looked around at the packing crates and felt sad. For the most part she had been happy in this apartment. What good was moving going to do? It seemed lately that all she did was run away.

Maybe what she should do was sit down and write Aggie a letter. No, it would be simpler to pick up the phone and call. On the other hand, she could pack a bag and drive to Rhode Island. She had no job now to worry about. Her rent was paid till the fifteenth of January. The tropical fish had long since found a new home with the elderly woman down the hall. There was nothing to keep her here. How she longed for Aggie's comforting presence and Doozey's jubilant affection. Why not? She would surprise both of them. Aggie would let her stay in her room with the twin beds.

Before she could change her mind, she wrapped Aggie's comforter and the dog collar for Doozey.

The first thing in the morning she would pack a small bag and leave. If she drove all day, she could make it by late evening.

Before she could change her mind, she called the movers and canceled her order to transport her furnishings and belongings to storage.

She felt better just knowing she was going to see Aggie and that the older woman would have some news of Logan. Just words. That was all she needed to help her get through the holiday season.

Before she could change her mind, she called the
movers and handed the order to them just for the furniture and belongings to storage.
She felt relieved that knowing she was going to see
Aggie soothed the transition which took all the guilt
out on Jill's widely. There was all the way home to do
her own thing.

CHAPTER NINE

IT WAS CRISP AND COLD with more than a hint of snow
in the air as Jill started out for Rhode Island. She felt
exhilarated as her car sped along the open highway. She
felt as though she were going home for Christmas. The
feeling was so intoxicating that she started to sing under
her breath. "Jingle bells, jingle bells," over and over.

Would Aggie have a Christmas tree? Was she the
kind of person who baked and decorated the house for
the holidays? If by some chance she didn't want to
bother because she was alone, she, Jill, would do it for
her. They would festoon the kitchen with evergreens
and light big fires in the old stone fireplace. Aggie
would wear her wrap comforter and Doozey would
snooze in his new collar on the hearth. And Jill would
putter around making both of them comfortable by
making hot rum toddies.

She stopped once for a quick sandwich to take with
her. She ate as she drove, not wanting to waste a minute.

It was shortly before dusk when the first snow started
to fall. Jill cried out in excitement. There was nothing
she loved more than a white Christmas. If only Logan
were with her to share it! For now, thinking about him
was almost as good as being with him.

By six o'clock the snow was falling heavily and the
roads were becoming slippery. Jill slowed the car and

made her way carefully. Another hour of cautious driving should get her into Mill Valley only an hour behind schedule. Lord, she was tired; her shoulders ached and her eyes were starting to burn with the close attention she was paying to the highway.

She skidded once and her heart leaped into her throat. To have come so far and have an accident now was unthinkable. She shifted the car into first and felt the wheels grab. That was better. She literally crawled as she made her way off the open highway onto one of the secondary roads that would lead her to Mill Valley and Logan Matthews's artists' colony.

The snow was coming down so fast she had to inch her way down the road. She peered out the open window for signs that she would remember. Her face and hair were soaked, but she could no longer see through the windshield.

The white sign with black lettering stood sentinel as Jill guided the car down the old road. Her tires made coarse tracks in the new-fallen snow. It was tricky going, but at least she knew she would meet no other vehicles on the road. The worst thing that could happen was that she would skid and careen into one of the ancient evergreens that lined the road.

Her first sight of the cottages and Logan's house sent a chill over her. She was home. This was where she wanted to be, where she needed to be—at least for the time being.

She was in the open compound now and driving carefully toward Logan's house. She parked in front, not sure exactly where the driveway was in the swirling snow. A faint yellow glow shone on one of the evergreens from Aggie's kitchen. Was she mistaken, or was that a bark? Could Doozey sense that she was back?

Jill cut the engine and pocketed the key. She struggled to get out of the compact car. How cramped and tired she was, yet she felt buoyed somehow. She was home; that must be it. She had just closed the front door and opened the door in the back to take out her bag when eighty pounds of dog leaped on her back, sending her sprawling onto the backseat.

Laughing and howling with happiness, Jill let the dog lick her face and her hair. "You aren't going to believe this, you dumb dog, but I've never been so happy to see anyone in my life. What have you been up to?"

Doozey cavorted in the snow, rolling and jumping like a puppy to show his delight with his new visitor. "Shh. I want to surprise Aggie. Come on, now; quiet is the name of the game." Jill could only assume the setter understood because he walked alongside her, licking her gloved hand.

Quietly, Jill opened the door and stared around the kitchen. Aggie was standing next to the stove, popping corn. She turned quickly, a look of alarm on her face, when she felt the cold draft from the open door. She pushed the popper to the back of the stove and grinned from ear to ear. "Well, I never," was all she said as she gathered Jill into a bone-crushing hug. "If you ain't just the best thing these old eyes could ever want to see. What are you doing here, child?"

"I came to spend Christmas with you. That's if it's okay with you."

"It's more than okay. But why would you want to lock yourself away here in the country with an old lady like me? Ain't nobody here but me and the dog."

"That's why I came. I was alone and knew you would be too. I figured two loners should be together.

Besides—" she giggled "—they said there was no way your present would get here in time so I brung it."

"You *brung* it, huh? Is that any way for a writer to talk?" Aggie laughed.

"It's okay for pretend writers who don't know any better. I'm hungry, Aggie."

"I expect you are. Take off those wet things and I'll fix you something. Here's a towel. Wrap your hair in it before you catch your death of cold and sit there by the fire."

"Are you going to have a Christmas tree, Aggie?"

"Wasn't planning on it, but I can see where I just changed my mind. There's boxes of decorations in the attic."

"Can we pop corn and string it on the tree?"

"You bet we can. I was just popping some now to put out for the birds tomorrow." Aggie gurgled with happiness. "Lord, child, you are a sight for sore eyes. Christmas always gets to me. Logan asks me each year to come to Boston to spend the holidays with him, but I don't belong there. I belong here, and here is where I stay. Me and Doozey make out fine. We get a little melancholy, but we manage."

Within minutes Aggie had a tray filled and settled it on a small table near the fire. Jill had never smelled anything as good as the big bowl of thick vegetable soup. A wedge of French bread spread lavishly with butter made her hungry just looking at it. A generous helping of peach cobbler, along with a glass of creamy milk, completed her dinner. Jill devoured each morsel, savoring it. No one in the whole world could cook like Aggie.

"You look tuckered out. Why don't you sleep now and we'll talk tomorrow."

"Good idea, Aggie." Jill yawned. "But first you must

tell me about Logan. Your letter said you gave him my address. Aggie, he never got in touch with me, not once." She hated the tremor in her voice and knew she was next to tears.

Aggie seemed to choose her words with care. "Honey, I told him everything you told me. I even called him a fool, a privilege he allows me from time to time. Logan, as I told you, he is not like most men. I don't ever remember Logan being in a position quite like this before. It's my opinion that he couldn't handle it, along with all of his successes in Paris. He knows he should have given you the chance to explain. But then you turned tail and ran. That was what made him think you lied to him. He was going to talk to you when he got back that day, but you were gone. Jill, in all fairness to Logan, you did lie to him. Logan never operates on a double standard. Seems to me both of you are at fault."

Jill nodded miserably.

"How is he, Aggie? A day didn't go by that I didn't think of him. Yesterday, I thought I saw him in Macy's. Does he have a shearling jacket, Aggie?"

"Yep, and a gorgeous thing it is. It probably was him you saw. He's in New York and has been for a week. I thought for sure he would have gotten in touch with you by now. Be patient, Jill."

"I love him," Jill said simply.

Aggie said nothing, but her eyes misted at the miserable look on Jill's face.

"You go along to bed now, and I'll clean up here. We have a lot of days ahead of us to talk."

"You're right, Aggie. I'll see you in the morning."

Long after the bedroom door closed, Aggie called for Doozey. Together they walked across the compound to the office. With the aid of a flashlight she picked up the phone and asked for the long-distance operator. Doozey barked his delight when he heard the tone of Aggie's voice.

By morning the deep tracks leading back and forth to the small office were obliterated by an additional ten inches of snow.

THE FOLLOWING DAYS were spent tramping through the woods looking for the perfect Christmas tree. Together Aggie and Jill chopped and sawed until the monstrous evergreen thundered to the ground. Heaving and struggling, they managed to slide the monster onto the sled they had brought along.

"Are we going to put it up in the kitchen next to the fireplace?" Jill asked, a note of hope in her voice.

"Of course. And we're going to string garlands all over the kitchen. I don't spend any time in the other part of the house and keep the heat down mostly to the kitchen, so that's the place for this beauty. Do you want to put it up tonight or wait till Christmas Eve?"

"Let's put it up but wait till Christmas Eve to decorate it. That's what we used to do when I was little."

"Then that's exactly what we'll do." Aggie laughed. "Remember, now, we have to bake a rum cake, a fruit cake and some cookies cut into Christmas shapes. I think I still have the old cookie cutters. I have a big turkey in the freezer, and I'm going to stuff it for our dinner. Tomorrow, we make the plum pudding and mince pie. A real old-fashioned Christmas. I'm real glad you came, Jill, and I'm just itching to see what's in that box you brought for me."

Jill laughed as she tugged at the heavy rope handles pulling the sled.

"I know you can't wait. No, you can't open it till Christmas Eve when we have our eggnog. Promise that you won't peek."

Aggie grinned. "I'm probably the oldest kid in these parts. If there's one thing I dearly love, it's to get a present. Always did love presents. Didn't matter what it was as long as it was wrapped up."

"Me too. I can't believe we really chopped down this tree," Jill said in amazement as she stared at the giant tree. "I think it's too big for the kitchen. We'll have to cut from the bottom."

With Aggie's New England practicality, they tied the branches together and were able to squeeze the tree through the back door. Huffing and puffing, together they managed to place it in the stand. The pine filled the kitchen with its scent, bringing the magic of Christmas indoors. Against the stolid background of field-stone and brick, nature's greenery was set off to perfection.

"Oh, Aggie, it's beautiful," Jill whispered, the spirit of the holidays glowing in her eyes.

"Aye, it is that." Aggie beamed in approval. "Now for a nice hot cup of tea and we can begin making Logan's favorite gingerbread cookies."

At the sound of his name, Jill's eyes widened. "Logan?"

Aggie seemed to recover herself. "Er...yes. Logan's favorite. 'Course, they just happen to be a favorite of mine, too," she explained. "Now get the kettle on and I'll get the teacups."

AFTER A DAY OF BAKING and cleaning up, the wind seemed to have gone out of Aggie. "This is too much for you, Aggie. Maybe I never should have come."

"Don't say that, child. Christmas can be a lonely time for an old woman who has nothing to warm the holidays 'cept wood that she's chopped for herself and lots of old memories. Glad I am that you cared enough to come visit an old woman. As for being tired, you don't look so peppy yourself. I'm going to lie down and grab a few winks, and you should do the same."

Jill smiled, glad to be here with Aggie. "I will, I promise. But first you go. I'll finish out here, and then I want to write a few Christmas cards. Okay?"

"All right, but don't tire yourself out." Aggie's carpet slippers hardly made a sound on the linoleum floor as she made her way to her room.

As she had said, Jill finished washing the dishes and pans in the sink and put them away as she dried them. Every so often her eye was caught by the sight of the tree, and a little stab of melancholy made her brush a tear from her eye. Christmas, good cheer, peace on earth—would she ever find peace in a world without Logan?

Pushing away the thought of a lonely future, she snapped on the radio, playing it softly so as not to disturb Aggie. "...through the years we all will be together, if the fates allow..." The little stab of melancholy became an unexpected pang of sorrow, deep and profound. What she wanted most in the world was to share the holidays through the years with Logan. Sharing love, warmth— Stop it! she warned herself. Otherwise, you'll be a blubbering idiot and spoil Aggie's Christmas!

Sitting at the kitchen table, Jill finished her list of cards, signing each and every one of them "Love, Jill."

The teakettle whistled again, calling to her. Hurriedly, she jumped from her place at the table and went to the stove, nearly tripping on Doozey. "Doozey, love, you do have a way of getting underfoot."

Dunking her tea ball in and out of the tiny porcelain cup, Aggie's pride and joy, Jill stood near the window and gazed out at the winter wonderland. The snow was falling in big, fat flakes, but the sky was becoming brighter even for the late-afternoon hour. The storm would come to an end soon, and that special quiet would blanket the earth. Sighing deeply, she went back to the table to finish her cards. With the end of the storm, mail delivery would begin again as soon as the roads were cleared, which, Aggie assured her, would begin almost immediately. Here in New England, know-how and persistence were needed to keep the roads open in winter.

Sorting through the cards, Jill searched for her pen. A crunching noise caught her attention. "Doozey!" she scolded. "What have you done to my fifty-nine-cent ballpoint? Naughty dog!"

A search through her handbag was disappointing. No other pen. A look through the kitchen drawers turned up a pencil. Eager to finish her cards, Jill pushed through the kitchen door into Logan's study. Surely, there must be a pen on the desk.

With Doozey in close pursuit, she entered Logan's inner sanctum. The large, square room was full of the artist. Shelves of books lined two walls. A bay of windows looked out onto the drive and beyond, letting the wintry landscape into the house. Paintings, Logan's of course, filled the other wall. Here was the heart of the man—a slightly disordered desk that defied Aggie's attention, deep leather chairs and, most wonderful of all, a window seat nestled into the bay of glass. A carelessly tossed afghan supplied a splash of color against the dark shutters. Unable to resist temptation, Jill opened the shutters and was spellbound by the view. Hurrying back to the kitchen for her tea, she quickly re-entered Logan's study and crawled up on the window seat, resting against the wall, feet tucked under the knitted shawl. The sky had become faintly gold, promising a beautiful sunset. She was determined to sit here and watch it, warmed by Aggie's tea and Doozey's presence beside her.

It was then that something caught her eye. Peeking from behind the sofa was the gilt corner edge of a picture frame. Curious that Logan should hide away a piece of his work, Jill was drawn to it.

The old sheeting that covered and protected it slipped away in her hands, and she gasped when she saw herself looking back from the canvas.

The sky outside brightened, illuminating the painting, bringing life to the colors Logan had placed there. Against the blue seashore, beside the familiar outcropping of rocks, pranced a white unicorn, and on his back was a slim, ivory-skinned girl whose long golden hair draped to her waist. And in the sky was the shimmering arc of a rainbow.

Jill sank to her knees. Logan had meant this painting to represent her. But when? The figure on the unicorn was vibrant with life. He must have painted it from memory; but how? Had she seemed so alive to him, so real? Had his fingers memorized her face? Had his hands chartered his memory with every curve and line of her body? Why?

Propping the painting against the sofa, Jill took her place on the window seat. Again and again her eyes were drawn to it, looking, searching for the inner woman that Logan had seen and rejected.

CHAPTER TEN

CHRISTMAS EVE WAS COLD and bitterly crisp. The wind lifted the powdery snow and caused it to drift into patterns and shapes, disguising everyday objects beneath its whiteness.

Aggie was already busy in the kitchen when Jill crawled from beneath the covers, hurriedly dressing, eager to be in the warm kitchen. Delicious aromas surrounded her—spices, gingerbread, chocolate chip cookies, homemade breads and the beginnings of the turkey stuffing, tangy with sausages and chestnuts.

"Aggie? You must have been up for hours? Why didn't you waken me?"

"Have yourself a cup of coffee, Jill. I heard you prowling around most of the night and I know you didn't sleep well. It didn't seem right to get you up so early just because an old woman doesn't need as much sleep as some young person. Besides, you have a full day ahead of you, I promise you that," she added in a cryptic tone.

"And what's that supposed to mean?" Jill asked, pouring herself a mug of Aggie's fragrant brew.

"Oh, just that it's Christmas Eve and there's the tree to trim and food to prepare...."

Looking around, Jill gasped. "Aggie, are you expecting the Army's Fourth Infantry? There's enough food here to feed them. I thought there was just going to be you and me."

"Well, there is...actually, sometimes the neighbors stop by and carolers..."

"Aggie—" Jill lifted a suspicious eyebrow "—carolers all the way out here from town when they know there isn't anybody here except you?"

"Well, child, some folks out this way are real neighborly, and, besides, maybe some people from church will stop out here on their way home. Didn't I tell you we go to Christmas services...?"

Aggie continued to chat, her words and tone sounding nervous to Jill's ears. But soon she was lost in the preparations for tomorrow's dinner, peeling and slicing potatoes and mixing the ingredients for the Christmas pudding.

After stuffing pitted dates with walnuts and rolling them in sugar, Jill dusted her hands, surprised to see that it was nearly noontime. "Time to get the tree trimmings out of the attic."

"Now, wear your sweater," Aggie admonished. "Gets to be pretty cold up there. And be careful. I don't want you coming through the ceiling and breaking your leg."

All that afternoon, Aggie and Jill worked, humming along with carols played on the radio. Lemons and oranges, studded with cloves, were hung from the rafters, emitting their sweet smell. Yards and yards of popcorn draped the tree along with shiny balls and tinsel. Doozey, throwing himself into the holiday mood, sniffed the sweet, pungent air and begged for puffs of corn.

"This was an ornament from Logan's first Christmas tree," Aggie said proudly, holding up a fragile blown-glass clown whose colors had faded to soft pastels. "And here's another. I remember when me and my husband bought him his first tricycle. That child!" She laughed. "He'd whiz around this kitchen on that bike and my husband used to say he was hell on wheels. I was happy when spring came so he could ride it outside, I'll tell you."

The old memories clouded Aggie's face. "And see this one, Jill? It's a little gingerbread house. That was the year Logan was abed with the chicken pox. He sure was one sick little fella. Gave us some worry. He was six, that year."

As Jill tinkered with the ancient set of lights Aggie told her stories of Logan as a child. The memories softened the old woman's features, clouding her eyes. But her words were vivid, sharp with detail, and Jill imagined she could actually see little Logan pedaling his trike around the huge kitchen and praying for spring when he could take it outside and seek adventure. In those few short hours she learned more about the man she loved than any book could tell her.

When Aggie and Jill had finished putting away the last box, they stood back to admire their work. The kitchen had been transformed. Boughs of evergreen draped the exposed beams and the door lintels. Bright red ribbons added a gay note, and a myriad of candles stood waiting to be lighted. Everything was polished and gleaming, ready for the Night Before Christmas.

Aggie went about her last-minute chores humming "I'll Be Home for Christmas" and then switched to "I Wish You a Merry Christmas" when they went off to their bedrooms to dress for the church service.

Jill chose to wear a bright red woolen dress that hugged her waist and fell in soft gathers over her hips. The little shirtfront with its button-down collar and short sleeves enhanced her diminutive figure. A simple addition of a gold chain and bracelet accompanied by tiny gold hoops in her ears were her only jewelry. Her shining, long blond hair was sleeked back and lifted onto the top of her head, its soft tendrils escaping and falling on her cheeks and the nape of her neck. The tall black boots gleamed in the lamplight.

A new beige cashmere coat, her only luxury in years, was belted at the waist. When she finally put on her bright red muffler and red gloves, she was ready.

"Coming, Aggie? I'm all set. What should I do with Doozey? He's not safe to leave alone in the kitchen. I'm convinced he can open the refrigerator door, and that would be the end of our Christmas dinner."

Aggie laughed. "Not to mention all the cookies and candies we baked. Better put him downstairs here in the bedroom where he can't do much damage."

Aggie looked lovely, her gray hair covered with a close-fitting fur hat and a black woolen coat. The galoshes on her feet did nothing to detract from her glowing face and sparkling eyes. On impulse, Jill snapped a tip from the Christmas tree and tied a red ribbon and two tiny Christmas balls to it. With the help of a safety pin, she placed the corsage on Aggie's collar.

"Now you're perfect, you really are, Aggie." Her voice was soft, on the edge of tears. "I want you to know that you've made this one of the happiest holidays I've ever known. I love you, Aggie."

"Pshaw, child, I knew that." Aggie wiped a tear from her eyes and hugged Jill tightly. "I feel as though you're my own child, and I only want the best for you. Sometimes I'm interfering and…and I just want you to know that whatever I do, it's because you mean the world to me. Come on now, or we'll be late."

The little yellow car hugged the road admirably, taking them the five miles to church. The black winter night sky was studded with stars, and in town colored Christmas lights dazzled the eye. The tall, steepled church was alive with light and humanity. People greeted one another and shook hands, wishing the best of the holidays. There was a peacefulness in the air, a reverence that shone from their eyes.

Inside was the scent of evergreens adorning the pulpit. Tiny candles glowed, and the choir stood at easy attention in their cranberry-colored robes. A nativity scene had been erected at the front of the church, and all eyes were turned to the empty manger that awaited the placement of the Christ-child figure at the stroke of twelve.

Aggie led the way into the pew, Jill right behind her. Although the church was crowded and every seat was needed, Aggie ignored Jill's proddings to push over instead of leaving room between herself and the last man on the long bench. The church filled rapidly, and several times someone came down the aisle expectantly waiting for Aggie to push in. Each time she refused.

The organ resounded from the rafters, filling the small interior of the church with music and voices. A hush fell over the congregation as the preacher took his place at the pulpit to recite the story of Christmas.

Jill's eyes touched on the people surrounding her. Husbands and wives, mothers and fathers...everyone seemed to have someone. Everyone but herself. Instinctively, she nestled closer to Aggie, appreciating the woman's presence and taking comfort from it. Everyone had someone and so did she. She had Aggie.

The minister instructed the congregation to all rise and open their hymnbooks to 139—"Silent Night." Together, they lifted their voices in song, filling the small church with sound: "Silent night, holy night, all is calm, all is bright…"

A jostling at her elbow insisted that Jill move over. Remarkably, Aggie had slid over, making room, allowing Jill to admit the stranger beside her into the pew. Without looking up from her hymnbook, following the words to the carol's obscure second stanza, Jill continued to sing, lifting her voice along with the congregation's.

A bold hand took one side of her hymnbook, sharing it with her, and a deep, masculine voice joined hers in song. Jill turned, looking up, her knees nearly buckling under her. Logan.

His eyes smiled down at her.

Throughout the remainder of the service Jill's heart thumped madly in her chest. Logan! What was he doing here? Had he come expecting to find Aggie? Wasn't he supposed to be in Boston, New York, somewhere? Anywhere besides Mill Valley?

Toward the end of the service, when the choir's voices rang out the moving melody of "Ave Maria," Logan took her trembling hand in his. His fingers pressed an unspoken message into hers, and when Jill glanced at Aggie, the old woman had tears in her eyes and a smile on her face. She looked up at Jill, seeming to tell her that Logan's presence was Aggie's Christmas present to her.

Outside the church, Logan and Aggie renewed acquaintances, inviting people over to the house for eggnog and cookies. Logan introduced several of his friends to Jill, all the while draping his arm possessively around her shoulder.

During the trip back to the house Jill drove cautiously. Aggie was perched on the cramped backseat while Logan stretched his long legs beneath the dashboard. There were questions, so many questions, but somehow they would not come to her lips. She didn't want anything to spoil this night. Aggie kept the conversation alive by regaling Logan with stories of how she and Jill had found the perfect tree and decorated it, of all the cookies they had baked and of how Jill was fast becoming a first-rate cook. All the while Jill could feel Logan's eyes on her, watching her, smiling at her.

Before they could walk across the shoveled path to the back door, several cars had joined hers in the yard. People spilled forth, issuing glad tidings and good wishes. Inside, it was cozy and warm, and Aggie immediately lighted the many candles while Jill touched a taper to the firewood that had been laid. Logan greeted their guests and spoke of Christmases past while Jill and Aggie served eggnog and the various delicacies they had made with pride. Every so often when Jill turned, she would find Logan looking at her again, a strange light in his eyes.

Over the merry conversation in the expansive kitchen, voices were heard outside: "…We wish you a merry Christmas, we wish you…" Carolers! Someone exclaimed and they all rushed to the door to stand outside, shivering from the cold, to listen to the joyful sounds.

Jill pressed behind the crowd, and Aggie, in a flutter of motion, began bringing out more glasses and another tray of cookies for their songful visitors. An arm wrapped around Jill, warding off the cold. Logan. Always Logan.

As she gazed up at him she realized he was leading her back inside the house, through the kitchen and beyond the door, into his study.

Closing the door behind him, shutting out the intrusive sounds, he took her in his arms and pressed his face into her hair. "Umm, you smell so good. All soap and water. Kiss me, Jill." His finger lifted her chin, bringing her face up to his as he covered her mouth with his own in the sweetest, most tender kiss that seemed to last and last. And when he moved his lips from hers and looked into her upturned face, she could still feel the imprint of his mouth on hers.

"Merry Christmas, Jill." His voice was husky, deep with emotion. "I went to New Jersey, looking for you, you know. It wasn't till I heard from Aggie that I knew where you were. I would have been here sooner except for the snowstorm...."

"Why?" she asked simply, her heart breaking with unanswered questions, questions which only Logan himself could answer.

Logan pulled her over to the window seat and sat down, holding her on his lap, nuzzling her neck. "Why did I leave you?" he asked.

Jill nodded, unable to speak, unable to break through the barrier of pain that had been with her since the last time she had seen him.

"Jill," he began softly, so softly, "I knew you were running away from something, someone. I was becoming too involved with you. That early morning on the beach I realized I loved you, with all my heart. I didn't want you to turn to me on the rebound. But when you answered my kisses, responded to my lovemaking, I lost myself in you. And heaven help me, that was what I had wanted and waited for all along. You, Jill. Only you. Whatever had come into my life before you was only a shadow, a cruel nightmare. I'd loved and lost once before, but never the way I knew I loved you."

"But you left me, Logan," she choked, whispering because she did not trust her voice.

"I told you then that you didn't know what love was all about. I was wrong. I even told myself I was wrong when I left you on the beach. I even went back looking for you, but you were gone. The next I saw you was here, at breakfast. And then…the…"

"Then Stacey Phillips found my discarded wedding gown…."

"Yes. I cursed myself for being a fool. I believed you were looking for love on the rebound. I was hurt, Jill, so hurt…."

"But I wasn't, Logan. You drove Deke out of my heart. You showed me what love was, something I'd never experienced before…."

"And then I learned the story from Aggie. I thought it was too late. I went looking for you before I left for Paris. What I learned was that you were still seeing him. Then I learn you're here, with Aggie for Christmas…. Jill," he breathed solemnly, "don't ever leave me again, not ever. I won't let you."

Jill snuggled closer on his lap, wrapping her arms around him, determined never to let him go. For a long moment they held each other, conveying their love. Logan's eyes fell on the painting he had done of Jill riding a unicorn. "I see you found it, the painting I've done of you. That's what you've done for me, sweetheart. You've made me a romantic, believing in the power of love. You've shown me the world of whimsy through your eyes and made me believe in unicorns and rainbows."

"You've made the world for me, Logan, in here." She placed his hand over her heart. "You've made the rainbows, the light after the storm."

Reaching around his neck, she pulled his face down to hers, lifting her mouth for his kiss. "Paint me rainbows, Logan," she breathed before his mouth touched hers and a riot of colors flared in her heart.

* * * * *

WHISPER MY NAME

CHAPTER ONE

WASHINGTON, D.C., IN AUTUMN can be one of the most beautiful and exhilarating cities in the world, yet Samantha Blakely walked on lagging feet down Connecticut Avenue, oblivious to the bright gold and orange leaves that cast dappled shadows on the sidewalk. It was unseasonably warm and she felt itchy beneath her heavy sweater jacket, but she was too disheartened to remove it and carry it over her arm. Indian summer, she mused as she kicked at the dry, papery leaves. All Hallow's Eve was tomorrow, and tonight was Mischief Night, when all the neighborhood children would be out wreaking havoc.

Samantha grinned. How well she remembered her own youth and the bars of soap streaking windows and the eggs thrown with gay abandonment. It seemed so long ago, and everything had changed from those remembered nights in a New York neighborhood. Right now, she felt as old as Methuselah and as weary as Job.

She looked up and scanned the numbers on the row of houses and realized she was home at last—the basement apartment she rented from Gemini Delaney.

Samantha fished in her handbag for the bright gold key, which hung from a Gucci chain and had been a gift from Gemini, who said that every girl who had her first apartment deserved a Gucci key chain. For some reason the sparkling gold always gave her such a lift, like now, when she was depressed. Gemini always had the answers.

At first Samantha thought she was at the wrong brownstone when she saw a huge orange pumpkin, which leaned against a straw facsimile of a scarecrow that leaned beside her door. A giggle found its way to her lips. Gemini again. Gemini Delaney was the oldest little girl Samantha knew, getting her pleasures from the celebration of a second-rate holiday. Sam knew when she made her way to the old lady's door she would find a replica of her own decorations. Wonderful, thoughtful Gemini.

Sam's eye fell to the thin circlet on her wrist as she fit the key in the lock. She would have to hurry or Gemini would start to fret, and she shouldn't be upset, not with her precarious health. All Sam really needed was a quick splash of cold water on her face, a dab of perfume, and a fresh scarf around her neck, preferably one Gemini had given her, and she could skip next door and make it right on time.

Reverently, Sam placed her camera, a Hasselblad and her dearest possession, on the foyer table. Her cinnamon-colored eyes lingered for a moment on the worn case and a single tear formed in the corner of her eye. She wiped at it impatiently. The camera was all she had left of her father, who had been a photojournalist for CBS News. When he had been killed by terrorists while on an assignment, the camera had been sent along to her by one of his associates. It was all she had left of the man she called Father and who had taught her everything she knew about photography. She couldn't think about that now. Now she had to shift into third gear and get over to Gemini's.

As Sam smoothed the towel over her creamy complexion, she wondered how her feisty but lovable old neighbor had fared with her physician's visit that she knew had taken place early that afternoon. As she ran the brush through her short cropped hair, she realized she had come to love the old woman and would grieve sadly when she was gone.

Don't think about that now, she cautioned herself. Think about how happy Gemini is going to be when the portrait of her nephew, Christian Delaney, was finished. Sam's eyes lightened at the thought and her somber mood lifted. The portrait of Delaney was a piece of her finest work, and she knew it. Running a close second to her love for photography, painting in oils was her most gratifying work. Tonight, after she returned to her own apartment, she would work on the background for a few hours. She hadn't exactly sloughed off working on the portrait, but job hunting was no easy feat, and she was so tired when she returned home at night that all she wanted to do was sleep. Most of the headway she had made on the portrait, which she was copying from a photograph, was done on the weekends. And Gemini had been a real gem about the whole thing. Gemini understood; she always understood.

Sam rummaged on her cluttered dressing table and found the bottle of Chanel No. 5 that had also been a gift from Gemini. She lavishly dabbed on the potent scent. Sam giggled again when she remembered how she and Gemini had been watching television one evening when the commercial came on for the famous perfume. Gemini had laughed uproariously and called the advertisement an obscenity. The next day Neiman-Marcus had delivered the square, elegant box of Chanel to Sam's doorstep. "I will feel this way forever." Sam giggled again, recalling the husky, sensual voice of the model in the ad as she exited her apartment and locked the door. But only if the male model emerging from the water was someone like Christian Delaney. He was the stuff dreams were made of—impossible dreams.

Before she had a chance to lift the heavy bronze knocker, the door was opened by Gemini's house-keeper. "Miz Delaney is waiting for you and has your cocktail all ready. She's a bit upset because her doctor told her she couldn't have a sherry before dinner. Right now she's in there sipping the cats' gin-and-tonic. She don't listen to me, Miss Blakely. Maybe you can talk to her."

Sam's eyebrows shot upward in alarm. "Esther, maybe it's just tonic water she's drinking. Gemini wouldn't disobey the doctor's orders. Where is she?"

Esther snorted indignantly. "It's gin, all right, and you can just forget about that tonic water. Them cats are both drunk as two skunks. She's been giving them sips in their water dishes. And I can smell gin a mile away. Miz Delaney is well on her way to getting looped, and I know it." With another snort Esther bobbed her spikey gray head and departed for her own domain—a brick and copper kitchen aromatic with spices and herbs. Sam blinked. She had never seen anyone except Esther who could actually swish an apron the way a stripper tossed her tassels.

If Gemini was drinking, that meant the doctor's news was bad. Gemini could handle anything, even a good drunk. Squaring her shoulders and pasting a smile on her pretty face, Sam bounded into the room and headed straight for the Queen Anne chair where the old lady sat. "Gemini, you are something, do you know that? A pumpkin and a scarecrow. It's perfect. What made you think of it? I love it. How in the world did you get them here?" She knew she was babbling, but she was unable to stop herself. "And that pumpkin is a perfect round ball. When I was a kid, they were always sort of lopsided and… Oh, darn it, Gemini, what did the doctor say?" Sam blurted out as she dropped to her knees at the old woman's feet.

Gemini Delaney straightened her back and patted her blue-white hair, which was carefully arranged down to the last strand. "That doctor is nothing but a spring pup; he's not even dry behind the ears," Gemini said testily, ignoring Sam's question. "For the life of me, I don't know why I put up with him."

"You put up with him because he's the best cardiologist in Washington, D.C., that's why," Sam said softly. "Now, tell me, what did he say?"

"Among other things, he said I was a vicious, cantankerous old woman who should have been put out of her misery ten years ago. What do you think of that?"

Sam forced a smile to her lips. "Did he, now? Or did he say you were a spirited, beautiful lady who should know better than to ignore a doctor's orders?"

Gemini slouched slightly in the yellow velvet chair and muttered, "It might have been something like that, but I really can't remember. This gin robs your brain; you know that. Just look at those stupid cats lying in the fireplace," the old lady snapped.

Sam laughed. "I'd be lying in the fireplace, too, if I drank straight gin. What happened to the tonic water?" she asked, sniffing the glass that rested next to Gemini's chair.

"That fool doctor said if I didn't go into the hospital for his triple bypass I wouldn't last out the week; those were his exact words. That means I have exactly four days left. It's funny how I can remember those words so exactly. Don't you think that's funny, Sam?"

"Hilarious," Sam said past the sob in her throat.

"But there is some good news," the old lady said brightly. "Christian is on his way home. Speaking of Christian, how is the work going on the portrait?"

"Fine, just fine. When I go home tonight, I'm going to work on it. I think I landed a job today. They actually gave me a contract, and I wanted to talk to you about it. I don't know what to do. It's with *Daylight Magazine,* and I think the only reason they even considered me was because of my father."

"Don't be such an upstart that you can't accept help, Sam," Gemini said shortly. "You're an excellent photographer; I've seen your work. Almost as good as your father's. In time you'll be better. Take the job and prove your worth to them. Something else is bothering you. Tell me about it."

Anything to divert the old lady from her grim thoughts, Sam thought worriedly. "It seems to me this contract is tying me up pretty tight and the money they're paying isn't all that good. I know I can't demand or expect anything like the seasoned pros get, but this is barely a living wage. I thought *Daylight* paid well and...oh, Gemini, I don't know what I expected. Look, here's the contract; it's the last two paragraphs that concern me. What do you think?"

The pale, blue-veined hands that reached for the contract were steady, as were the bright, piercing blue eyes. Gemini scanned the printed words and then guffawed. "You're right, child, this contract—" she sought for just the right word and finally came up with it "—stinks! Now, this is what you do. You tell them to take out...get me a pencil over there on the desk. Good girl. Now, have them take out paragraph four altogether, demand that paragraph six give you better splits, delete paragraphs nine and ten and—" the pencil flew over the pages as Sam watched in awe "—and this is the figure you ask for, and you tell them you won't take a penny less. You tell them that photographs by Orion, that unisex name you insist on using, is one day going to put *Daylight Magazine* right up there with *Time*. You have to be tough and you can't backwater. Tomorrow you march right in there and stand up like your father did. This is what you want. Then you tell him to take it or leave it. Leave your portfolio. Who gave you this contract, anyway?"

"A Mr. Jebard in personnel. Gemini, I don't know if I can do that," Sam said hesitantly.

"Do you believe in yourself, Sam, and in your work?" Gemini said testily.

"Of course. You know I do."

"Then you can do it. I don't want to hear another word. Call me tomorrow after you leave the office. Where's that Esther? She should have announced dinner half an hour ago."

"Here I am, and I didn't announce dinner 'cause I was waiting for you to dry out. You dried out now, Miz Delaney?"

"You old fool, I wasn't even wet," the old lady said fondly to her shiny-faced housekeeper. "Well, don't just stand there, help me get up."

"No, siree, Miz Delaney. The doctor said you was to eat off a tray, and that's exactly what you're going to do."

"And I pay her to torment me like this! Do you believe it?" Gemini sniffed, making no physical effort to move.

Sam smiled weakly, knowing what the lighthearted banter cost the old lady. Esther knew it, too, as she bustled around fluffing first one pillow and then another, finally placing a footstool at Gemini's feet.

"What do you want me to do with them dumb cats lying in the fireplace?" Esther demanded. "It's their dinnertime."

"You'll be the death of me yet, Esther. Can't you see they're sleeping? They can eat anytime; leave them alone."

"They ain't sleeping; they're drunk, and when they wake up they're going to have a hangover and I'll have to walk them on a leash. No self-respecting black woman walks cats on a leash. I ain't going to do it, Miz Delaney," Esther muttered as she stomped from the room.

"I worry about her," Gemini said softly as she leaned her frail head back into the softness of the daffodil-colored velvet chair. "She doesn't know it yet, but she's leaving for Seattle. I made all the arrangements this afternoon. I don't want her here when I...when I...she needs a vacation," she said lamely.

Sam's throat constricted at the haunted eyes and the bluish tinge around Gemini's mouth. She forced herself to strive for a light tone. "What has Esther prepared for dinner? Do you know, Gemini?"

"Let's both ask her. Here she comes now with the trays. What have you cooked tonight?"

"The only thing you're allowed to have. Sliced lean chicken and a cup of Jell-O. For Miz Blakely, a sweet potato and a small steak with salad."

The old lady's voice was a shade firmer when she baited the housekeeper still again. "No imagination at all. I'm allowed to have an egg, and you know it. Why didn't you bring me a poached egg?"

"*You* said you could have an egg; the doctor didn't say so. No egg," the housekeeper said adamantly.

Sam's fork was poised midway to her mouth when the soft chime of the telephone bell permeated the room. "I'll get it, Gemini," she said, rising from the chair. "I have it, Esther," she repeated to the housekeeper, who had entered the room at a fast trot. "Hello. Yes, this is Gemini Delaney's residence. Who's calling, please?" Sam covered the receiver with the palm of her hand. Her cinnamon eyes asked a question, but all she said to Gemini was, "It's the overseas operator. Your nephew, Christian Delaney, is calling from Turkey."

The old woman's face lit up momentarily and then settled into grim lines. "Sam, tell him I'm sleeping and that I can't be disturbed. I'll get too emotional, and, right now, I can't handle that." Sam nodded.

"Go ahead, operator, I'll take the call." Sam's heart fluttered wildly. At last, after all these months of working on the portrait Gemini had commissioned, she was finally going to hear the man's voice. It would be deep and husky; she could almost feel it. "Aunt Gemmy, it's Chris here. I've been delayed...*squawk*... *sputter*...*crackle*...sometime toward...what's that... who is this...*crackle*..."

"This is Samantha Blakely. I live next door to your aunt.... Hello! Can you hear me...?"

"*Sputter*...*crackle*...*squawk*...what man? Where's my...*crackle*...home..."

"Try to get the operator back!" Sam shouted into the crackling phone.

"*Squawk*... When did you say she would be back?" *Crackle*...and the line was dead. Sam replaced the phone and shrugged her shoulders. "It was a very poor connection, Gemini. I could barely make out what he said. I think he's been delayed, but he is coming home. You heard my end. I'm sorry. Don't worry, he'll make it."

Gemini waved a clawlike hand. "It's all right. Don't fret, Sam. I'm tired now and I think I'll retire for the night. Call Esther for me and have her help me. Her nose gets out of joint if I don't lean on her every so often. Tell her to bring the phone to my room and plug it in. I have several calls I have to make before I call it a night."

Sam threw her arms around the thin woman and choked back her tears. "Not to worry, Gemini. He'll get here in time; I know it."

"I know it, too, child. You finish your dinner and then run along and work on that portrait so you can have it done by the end of the week. Good night, Sam," she said, kissing the young girl's cheek.

"Gemini, thanks for the pumpkin."

"Later you can make Christian a pie—when he gets here, that is."

"Of course, I'll be glad to."

"It's his favorite," Gemini said wearily.

Sam obediently finished her dinner as Gemini had instructed. The food, so carefully prepared by Esther, was bland and tasteless on her tongue. As she ate and chewed methodically, Samantha reflected on the unknown well of courage that she had found in herself ever since the truth about Gemini's failing health had become known. Talking so matter-of-factly about death was one of the most difficult things Sam ever had to do. Yet, it was necessary. Gemini demanded it. Confident and pragmatic, Gemini reassured Samantha that death was also a part of living and that eighty-one years was more than enough time for any woman to accomplish a full, exciting life. Sam told herself that Gemini was right, but that didn't help to erase the pain she felt when she thought about the time that the wonderful old woman would no longer be there.

Thanking Esther for dinner, Samantha went back to her own apartment and changed her clothes in favor of a pair of faded old jeans that were streaked with vari-colored paint, and a comfortable, worn shirt. The portrait of Christian Delaney stood on an easel in the spare bedroom in the direct light of the track lamps she had installed. The handsome, intelligent face of Christian Delaney stared back at her from the canvas. The silvery-gray eyes looked out at her from beneath unruly, dark brows and, as always, Sam thought she detected a trace of humor in his otherwise formal and serious pose. Short-cropped hair that held a hint of a wave dipped over his broad brow, and his head was held arrogantly on the thick column of his neck.

Samantha shook herself. It had happened again. Sometimes, when she turned on the light and stood before the portrait of Gemini's nephew, the canvas seemed to breathe life. It was silly, really, for while her painting was true to life and closely followed the photo Gemini had given her, it certainly wasn't so lifelike that she should have these feelings.

Setting a tall stool before the easel and reaching for her palette and various tubes of paint, Sam prepared the quiet browns and umbers she needed for the background and remembered the long, quiet conversations she had shared with Gemini concerning the subject of Christian Delaney. It was possible that Gemini's descriptions of her nephew were so detailed that Samantha imagined she knew the subject of the portrait personally. Even more foolishly, Sam's dreams were more and more often concerned with the real flesh-

and-blood Christian, and once or twice she had laughed at herself when she suddenly realized she was actually talking to the dabs of color and paint that created his image on the canvas.

"Stupid fantasies of an old maid," she chided herself as she dabbed and mixed her colors. Yet her gaze was drawn again and again to the eyes that stared back at her, and a tingle of anticipation raced down her spine as she thought that soon, very soon, she would be meeting the real Christian Delaney.

Brush poised in midair, Sam frowned. It wasn't possible...it just couldn't be possible that she was falling in love with the man in the portrait. True, Gemini had spoken so often of him that Sam had the impression that she actually knew him. But the rest was pure foolishness. No self-respecting, halfway intelligent girl who was trying to carve out a career in photojournalism for herself right here in this day and age could become so mesmerized with a man in a painting that she felt she was falling in love with him!

Her eyes locked with those on the canvas and the anticipated tingle danced the length of her spine. "Foolish!" Samantha scolded herself as she slammed down her palette and concentrated on the background of the portrait, purposely refusing to permit her eyes to stray to the handsome, compelling features of her subject.

CHAPTER TWO

THE HEAVY PORTFOLIO TUCKED under her arm, Sam waited patiently for a bus at the corner that would drop her off at the *Daylight* door. Inside her purse, in the zipper compartment, was a neatly typed list of corrections for her new contract. Would the man called Mr. Conway be amenable to the changes she was going to request, or would he laugh and tell her to peddle her work somewhere else?

Sam settled back in her hard seat on the bus and willed herself to relax. She felt good and at this precise moment in time she felt she exuded confidence. For some strange reason she always felt that way after a few hours of work on Christian Delaney's portrait. The work last night had gone well, and Gemini would be pleased. Even Christian Delaney, if he ever saw the finished product, would find himself hard pressed to find fault with her work. What was he like? Gemini had said he stood well over six feet and had steel-gray eyes that saw through a person to the very soul. At Gemini's death he was to inherit the family-owned business, and at that time he would settle down and raise a family, or so Gemini hoped. Gemini had said he was strong willed, yet gentle and vulnerable, but she hadn't explained how or why he was vulnerable, but had said someday Samantha would find out for herself. It would be easy to fall in love with Christian Delaney, and if Samantha admitted the truth, even to herself, here on this noisy bus, she was already half in love with his likeness.

"K Street," the bus driver called loudly to be heard above the busy chattering.

Sam slid from her seat and walked to the middle of the bus and waited for the double doors to swish open. She held the portfolio tightly and settled her canvas shoulder bag more comfortably on her shoulder. She made the half block in minutes and walked through the revolving door. "Mr. Conway, here I come, ready or not," she muttered, pressing the Up button. Her heart fluttered wildly when the elevator door opened and she squeezed past the departing occupants. She pressed number 16 and leaned weakly against the wall. Did she have the nerve? Could she do what Gemini told her to do? Of course she could. She had come this far, and besides, how would she ever explain her lack of courage to Gemini?

Sam's eyes did a slow once-over of the elaborate reception area and came to rest on a lacquered china doll-like woman sitting behind a desk with an intercom system at her fingertips. "I'd like to see Mr. Conway, please," Sam said in a voice she didn't recognize.

The receptionist spoke softly, her voice a musical chime. "May I ask your name?"

"Samantha Blakely. I'm a photographer and I work under the name Orion."

"You're Orion!" the tiny woman exclaimed. "May I say that I saw the pictures you took of the boat people and...and they were just...you captured... What can I say? I liked them."

Sam literally gasped. "Did you really like them? I

always feel that I did well if just one person says so. Thank you, thank you so much for the compliment."

The other woman smiled. "Mr. Conway is busy, but I'll interrupt him. He's just putting in his office." She gave Sam a wicked wink and pressed a small white button. She spoke softly and motioned with her hand. "Just give him time to put away his golf club and get behind his desk," she whispered. Sam let her left eye close and walked slowly to a heavy oak door. At the receptionist's nod, she opened the door and then closed it softly behind her. *Here goes nothing,* she said silently as she walked forward to a monstrous desk.

A pink, balding-type man rose from behind the desk and held out his hand. "Charlie Conway," he said jovially, "and you're Orion. Sit down and take a load off your feet. What can I do for you?"

Samantha licked at dry lips and remembered Gemini's words. "Look, Mr. Conway, I'm a good photographer—not the best, but good. Your Mr. Jebard offered me a contract yesterday to work for this magazine. I led him to believe I would sign it, and I had every intention of signing it until I read it more thoroughly. What I'm trying to say is, it's not satisfactory. I'd like to tell you what I would like, and then perhaps we could compro—then perhaps we could come to terms. On second thought, Mr. Conway, I can't compromise or come to terms." Before the man behind the desk could utter another word, Sam was reading off her list of corrections to the contract. "Not a penny less, Mr. Conway. I'll be honest with you. I want this job more than I ever wanted anything, and I know I'll be an asset to your staff, but you have to be fair, too." Sam leaned back, a fine beading of perspiration dotting her forehead. She waited.

"You got it. Listen, kid, what do you do for an encore?"

"Got it? You mean you...you agree to my terms and I don't do an encore?"

"I don't think so. You shot your load the first time around. Look, kid, I knew your old man and I liked him. You've got the same kind of guts he had. There aren't too many people who would march in here and make demands, not even the seasoned pros. You've got guts, and I like that. Your old man and me, we went through some rough times back in the old days. I bunked with him for three solid months in Beirut, when neither one of us could take a bath in all that time. We remained friends, and let me tell you something. Your old man smelled about as raunchy as I did when we finally made our way home. I heard he died a couple of years ago. I'm sorry. He used to talk about you and that Brownie Hawkeye you had. He was proud of you, kid."

Sam was stunned. "Mr. Conway, are you giving me the job just because you knew my father?"

"No! You said Jebard gave you the job yesterday. I just cleaned up his contract for him. What kind of camera are you using?"

"My dad's Hasselblad."

"Kid, that camera has a soul. Don't ever lose it. You using your dad's Leitz lenses?"

"Every last one of them." Sam smiled.

"Looks like we're in business, then. You can start work Monday morning. I'll see what's on the roster, and your first assignment will be ready whenever you are. Welcome aboard, Orion," he said, holding out his hand. "I'm glad you're using your old man's handle. Old cameramen never die, that kind of thing," Conway said sheepishly. "And, kid, call me Charlie. Oh, one other thing—if that's your portfolio, leave it here. Our new president will be in Monday, too, and I'm sure he's going to want to check over our newest addition. I'll give you a good buildup, kid."

"Mr. Con—Charlie, thank you, thank you for everything, but mostly, thanks for telling me about my dad. Maybe someday we can get together and swap stories. I'd really like to hear about some of your experiences."

"I'd like that, too, Orion."

Sam walked on air all the way back to her apartment. She felt good. Thank God for Gemini. She was supposed to call her from the office and let her know how she made out. Darn, she thought wretchedly, how could she have forgotten something so important? A taxi. She would take a taxi and get home as fast as she could and tell Gemini in person.

She was too late....

ON THE DAY OF the funeral, it was fitting that it should rain. Complying with Gemini Delaney's wishes, the services were simple and private. Esther had been given the name of the law firm that handled the old woman's affairs, and the lawyers had taken it from there.

Flowers arrived at the funeral home, and notes of condolence came to Christian Delaney, who still had not returned home. When Samantha questioned Esther as to how Mr. Delaney could be reached, the dark-skinned woman shook her head and shrugged. "All I know, Miz Blakely, is that those lawyers are trying to reach him. But you know Miz Delaney never waited for no man. Her instructions were to have the funeral and get it over with quickly. She used to say that life was for the living, and that the dead don't deserve much more than a passing respect."

Sam smiled bleakly. How like Gemini that was. Never thinking of herself. Gemini was a giver, not a taker. Samantha was aware of the old woman's affection for her nephew and what a comfort his presence would have been during those last days. And yet Gemini hadn't summoned him home. Even though Gemini had been so forgiving concerning her nephew's lack of interest and understanding, Sam wasn't so certain she could.

At the yawning grave site, Samantha gave way to the tears that were building inside her. The rain slashed down unmercifully. The only other mourners present, as per Gemini's instructions for privacy, were Esther, several friends from the neighborhood where Gemini had lived for the past twenty years, and a wizened old gentleman in a shabby, black raincoat and a slouch hat whom Sam rightly suspected was one of Gemini's lawyers.

As the last prayers were murmured and silent good-byes were said, Samantha found it increasingly difficult to choke back her tears. She knew she had to look forward, not backward. She would grieve for Gemini in private, late at night. For now, she had to carry on with her life just as Gemini expected. She mustn't betray the confidence that Gemini had had in her. She would give her best to *Daylight Magazine* and prove her own worth.

Esther and Samantha rode back to the brownstone together, each silent with her own thoughts. When they approached Connecticut Avenue, Esther dried her eyes on her handkerchief and blew her nose. "I'll be taking a late-afternoon plane to Seattle, Miz Blakely. I've written down my address." She dug in her handbag and withdrew a slip of paper. "If there's anything you need and I can help, that's where I'll be."

"Thank you, Esther," Sam said warmly, suddenly realizing how much she was going to miss the housekeeper's warm concern. "You've been a good friend, and I'm going to miss you."

"You won't have time to miss anybody, Miz Blakely. Those two cats Miz Delaney left to you are going to keep you busy enough. Why, you'll be working at your magazine just to keep those two devils in gin."

The two women laughed, each remembering Gemini's devotion to her cats.

"Tell me, Esther, did Gemini name them Gin and Tonic before or after she discovered their penchant for the drink?"

"Miz Blakely, just like everybody else who ever had anything to do with Miz Delaney, they just lived up to what she expected of them!"

ALONE THAT EVENING, Sam automatically switched on the track lighting in the spare bedroom, intending to work on the portrait of Christian Delaney. Fresh tears stung her eyes as she realized that Gemini would never see the finished product. Still, Gemini had commissioned the portrait and, in fact, had paid her in advance. The money she had given Sam had gone for expenses while job hunting. That advance had meant that Samantha had been able to hold out for the best job she could land, instead of being forced by dwindling finances to grab the first thing that came along. Her commitment to Gemini had been to complete the portrait, and complete it she would. Then she would have it sent on to Christian Delaney with a note of explanation.

Lifting her eyes to the easel, her gaze fell on the face of Christian Delaney. She knew it was only her imagination, but there seemed to be a calculating look about the silver-gray eyes. Samantha bit her lip. The one person Gemini had loved more than anyone else in the world had been absent from the private funeral ceremonies.

Tonight was definitely not the right time to work on the portrait, she decided as she switched off the light, and she wondered if she was more disappointed for Gemini than angry. One of the cats snaked around her ankles and purred loudly. "All right, all right. I promised Gemini I would take care of you, and I will. Let's go into the kitchen, and I'll warm up some milk for the three of us."

JUST AS SAM WAS dressing for work on Monday morning, the doorbell shrilled. Startled, she laid down the hairbrush and raced to the door. Who could be ringing her bell so early on a Monday morning? She glanced at the sunburst clock in the living room as she opened the door. It was only seven-ten. "Registered letter for Sam Blakely," a tired-looking older man said quietly.

Sam frowned. Now, who would be sending her a registered letter? Please, God, don't let it be the magazine saying they had second thoughts. She scribbled her name and closed the door. Hmm. Hartford, Masterson, Quinlan, Jacobsen, and Zigenback, Attorneys at Law, followed by a prestigious address on Wisconsin Avenue. With trembling hands, Sam slit open the envelope and quickly scanned the contents. She was to be present in Addison Hartford's office at twelve noon for the reading of Gemini Delaney's will. Sam grinned. Gemini wasn't leaving anything to chance. The two cats, Gin and Tonic, were to come to her for care. Gemini was making it legal. It wasn't so bad; she could take a taxi and still be back in the office by one o'clock. She stuffed the crisp, crackling legal letter into her purse and resumed her dressing.

After setting a small bowl of water, a second of tonic water, *sans* gin, and a dish of cat food on the kitchen floor, Sam was ready to leave for her first day at her new job. She felt good and knew she looked just as good in her tailored navy pantsuit. At the last minute she crushed a matching beret on her head, covering her short-cropped curls. Her camera case over one shoulder and a smart burgundy shoulder bag completed her outfit.

Her heart skipped a beat and then steadied as her eyes fell on the orange pumpkin. *Don't think of that now. Today is the first day of the rest of your life,* her mind mumbled over and over.

She reached the corner just as a bus pulled to a stop. She boarded and settled herself for the short ride downtown. No worries, no problems. She had given her word to Gemini, and she would keep it. The cats were hers and she would see to their proper care. She smiled as she remembered what they were doing when she left. Gin had found a spot in the clothes hamper and had managed to wrap himself in a bright scarlet towel, while Tonic had dragged her boots from a heavy box and settled herself half in and half out of her fur-lined left boot. They were making themselves right at home, but she promised herself that she was going to put both of them on the wagon and turn them into respectable cats if it was the last thing she did.

"K Street!" the bus driver shouted loudly. Sam followed the other debarking passengers and headed straight for the *Daylight* offices.

Her coworkers turned out to be a friendly group of people. Easygoing, willing to help, and an endless supply of stories to tell. By eleven o'clock she had had the grand tour, been assigned a cubbyhole of an office, been introduced to the supply room with wall-to-wall film supplies, and had been informed that her meeting with the publisher and president was set for two o'clock. A memo on her clean desk also informed her she was to report to Charlie Conway at three o'clock for her first assignment.

Sam busied herself for another forty-five minutes by hanging up some of her favorite shots on the small cork bulletin board that came with every cubbyhole. She stood back to admire her handiwork. Photos by Orion. It did have a ring to it. Dad would be proud if he could see her now.

If she half raised herself from her chair and stretched her neck, she could just make out the bank of clocks hanging on the newsroom wall. She did both and then reset her watch. Time to leave for Hartford, Masterson, Quinlan, Jacobsen, and Zigenback.

Sam waited patiently in the dusty, fern-decorated room of the old, prestigious law firm. Eventually, a middle-aged secretary appeared and crooked her finger in Sam's direction, which she took to mean she was to follow. Monstrous double doors creaked shut on dry hinges as Sam crossed fifty feet of worn carpeting. She looked around. Old furniture, bookshelves filled with legal tomes, and a desk the size of a billiard table with a row of diamond-shaped windows took up one corner of the room. To the left of the heavy-looking book-cases were two leather chairs, one in burgundy cracked leather and the other black. A brass lamp and a spittoon ashtray rested on a dusty table. The only words Sam could think of were "old" and "dry," just like the aging man behind the desk. Sam stared down at the wizened gentleman with the sparse white hair and pince-nez and recognized him from the cemetery. She held out her hand, which he ignored. "I'm…"

"Sam Blakely," chirped a reedy voice. "Sit down and let me read you Mrs. Delaney's will. Mr. Delaney can't be here, so we might as well proceed. My eyes aren't what they used to be, and I can't seem to…I don't know where that infernal will is," the old man fretted. "It doesn't make any difference; I know what was in it. Someone will send you a letter confirming what I'm about to tell you. Settle back, Mr. Blakely, and…now, where did I…never mind."

"Mr. Hartford, it's not Mr. Blakely—I'm Ms. Blakely. Mr. Hartford, is your hearing aid turned on?" Sam asked as she noticed a braided wire that ran into his shirt collar.

The old man ignored her words and laced his fingers together. "If I recall rightly, what Gemini's will said was that you, Sam Blakely, are to receive the dividends from fifty-one percent of the family-owned stock for ninety days. After the ninety days an addendum to the will is to be read—if I can find it," the old man said peevishly. "It seems to me that you can't vote, but I'll have one of the younger men check that out and get back to you."

Sam gasped. "Mr. Hartford, are you sure you don't have me mixed up with someone else? I was supposed to get the cats—cats, Mr. Hartford. Mr. Hartford, what about the cats?" Sam shouted.

"Those drunken animals! It's a disgrace and a sin the way Gemini turned them into alcoholics. There's no need for you to shout, Blakely. The battery in my hearing aid is low, but I assure you I can hear just fine. There was something about the cats in the will. A neighbor, I believe, was to be entrusted with their care, plus a cash annuity to pay for their alcoholic comfort. I'll have to check that out."

"I'm that neighbor—I'm Samantha Blakely. Never mind, Mr. Hartford, just send me the letter. I have the cats and they're being well cared for," Sam said wearily as she watched the frail attorney fidget with the button in his ear.

"Oh, pish and tush, this infernal gadget never works when I want it to work," the old man muttered. "It's no never mind. May I say I admire that hat you're wearing, Mr. Blakely? I had one quite similar to it when I was a boy. Everything's gone now—the hat, my hearing, my eyesight. I'm retired, you know, and just came into the office today because Gemini and I were friends for sixty years. It was the least I could do. I'll keep in touch, Mr. Blakely."

Should she protest again and hope to get through to the old man, or should she just leave? Sam shrugged. What was the use? Before she could button her jacket she heard loud snores permeate the room. No use at all. In the waiting room with the dusty ferns and threadbare carpet, Sam looked around. All the doors were closed and there was no sign of anyone. Probably taking a nap. She giggled as she tiptoed out of the office and hailed a cab.

There must be a mistake, and, hopefully, it would be righted in the form of a letter. Fond as Gemini was of her, she certainly wouldn't leave her a controlling interest in her business. After all, hadn't Gemini said that her nephew was the sole heir? And, come to think of it, just what was Gemini's business? She had never said, and Sam had never asked. Ninety days and then an addendum was to be read. What exactly did that mean? It was all a mistake, and one she couldn't worry about now. If she was lucky, she could catch a sandwich in the snack bar at the office and freshen up before she was to meet the new president of *Daylight Magazine*.

SAM KNOCKED SMARTLY on the door of the president's office promptly on the stroke of two o'clock. A terse, cold "Come" made her draw in her breath. He sounded like an ogre, an angry ogre. Squaring her shoulders, she entered the office and walked over to the desk where a man was shouting into the phone, the high back of his chair turned toward her. Impatiently, he waved a hand in the air, motioning for her to sit.

"Just what does that mean? Mr. Hartford, I have great respect for your age and your ability, but how in the name of heaven did you allow Gemini to be duped by some…some gigolo named…what was the name…? Sam Blakely? You were Aunt Gem's closest friend and should have seen to her last needs and wishes. Well, it won't hold water, I can tell you that. There is no such thing as an unbreakable will. I'll break it, and I'll break the neck of Sam-whatever-his-name-is. Find him, Mr. Hartford, and I'll show you a chiseler out to bilk old ladies. Gemini must not have been of sound mind. What do you mean, she drew up the will herself? Don't give me any sermons, Hartford, I want that will contested. I'm the heir, the only heir. No, I don't begrudge Gemini's gifts, but I do intend to find that weasel, Sam Blakely, and wring his neck. Do you hear me, Hartford? Don't you pay out one cent of those dividends. Get it through your head I'm the heir—the *only* heir. No, not for later, for now. How old is this Sam Blakely, anyway? Twenty-three! What time was he in your office? You should have kept him there till I could get there! Hartford, I don't care what kind of hat he had on! I'm advising you now that I'm going to break that will long before the addendum is to be read. You're right I want to see a copy of the will!" Silence. "In that case, Mr. Hartford, I won't just break his neck—I'll kill him before I let him prey on some other poor, unsuspecting old lady. Of course I don't mean it. He'll never be the same, though, I can assure you of that. After work I'll stop by your home and pick up a copy. Do you still reside in Georgetown? Around seven, then."

Sam stifled a gasp. Good heavens, it wasn't possible, was it? He couldn't be...he was! The new president and publisher of *Daylight Magazine* was Christian Delaney, Gemini's nephew. Sam's head reeled as she stared at her new boss. How could this happen to her? And why hadn't Gemini told her? Sam remembered the old woman telling her that Christian would inherit the family business when she passed on, but she hadn't known that publishing was their business. A lump formed first in the pit of her stomach and then worked its way up to her throat. And to think he actually thought she had bilked dear, sweet Gemini! Well, she would just tell him he was mistaken; that was all there was to it. Mr. Hartford was a different story, but this man wasn't wearing a hearing aid. Talk about your comedy of errors. How could a reasonably intelligent man like Christian Delaney jump to conclusions like this? He was going to turn around and she would tell him. Oh, how had she ever gotten into this mess? It was so simple, if this lump would just go away, she might be able to get the words out. Fifty-one percent of the stock was going to her, and that meant the man with his back to her only had forty-nine percent. Would it make a difference if she was male or female? He thought she was a gigolo. *Gemini, do you know what you did?*

The man turned abruptly, the phone clenched in his powerful-looking fist. Slowly, deliberately, he replaced it and spoke, his words chips of ice. "Orion, isn't it?" Not bothering to wait for her reply, he continued: "I must apologize for the conversation you just heard. It's a family problem and I allowed myself to get out of control for a few minutes. I've looked at your portfolio and I liked what I saw."

She was supposed to say something, acknowledge the compliment. "Thank...thank you," she said lamely.

"You're new, according to Charlie Conway, but then so am I—in the capacity of president, that is. Until recently, I've been in charge of foreign publications and keeping our diplomatic doors open overseas. We should get along fine since we're both starting out at the same time. You bear with me and I'll bear with you. What do you say?"

His eyes were just as beautiful as in the photograph. "That...th-that would be fi-fine." Fifty-one percent, fifty-one percent, fifty-one percent! her mind shrieked silently.

"I wanted to spend some time with you and go over your portfolio, but I have some personal business I must take care of starting right now. How would you like to have dinner with me? I have an evening appointment, but I think instead I'll take care of the matter now, before I get any hotter under the collar. Let's say Jour et Nuit. Are you familiar with it? No? M Street at Thirtieth in Georgetown. You'll like it—fireside dining, and the food is served Continental style. Very impressive wine list. I guarantee it. Well," he said abruptly, "will you have dinner with me?"

Sam's mind raced. "Of…of c-course."

"Do you always stutter?" Christian Delaney asked, frowning.

"Well…I…I…this is my…my first day…and…and I never met a president before."

Christian Delaney laughed, a deep, rich baritone. She knew, she just knew he would laugh like that. "I have news for you; I've never been a president before, either, and I'm not all that sure I'll be any good at the job."

"Of course you will. You look just the way a president should look," Sam babbled and then was instantly embarrassed at her words. She flushed.

"Amazing! Absolutely amazing!" Christian said in a voice that resembled awe. "A woman today who can still blush. I like that, Orion. You've got yourself a date with a president." The steel-gray eyes were merry and showed just a shade of devilment. Did presidents do things like "that." If the president was a man, he did. The flush darkened, to Christian Delaney's amusement. "Look, do you think you could meet me at the restaurant? I don't usually make my dates do this, but I'm going to be running late, and…and I want to get to know you better."

Before or after you kill me? her whirling brain questioned. "I don't mind, Mr. Delaney."

"I think I'm going to like you, Orion. A woman who stutters because I'm a president and who can still blush and who says she doesn't mind meeting me at the restaurant. Do you even check the prices on the menu?"

An invisible broom handle stiffened Sam's spine. "As a matter of fact, I do. And," she said airily, "I don't eat much."

"Seven o'clock. And I was complimenting you, whether you know it or not. I appreciate promptness."

Was he mocking her? "I'll be on time."

"Are you one of those women who dawdle and pick at their food, or do you eat to enjoy?"

"I know what fork to use and I've never been known to use my fingers. I usually eat fast because I'm hungry and my dad taught me never to leave anything on my plate. Did I leave anything out?" she asked, a cutting edge to her voice. "And," she said, holding up her hand, "I do not pick up the check."

The silvery-gray eyes narrowed to slits. "We'll discuss that over dinner. That's a smart-looking outfit you're wearing. More than suitable for the restaurant."

"Yes, I know. I've been to a restaurant before, Mr. Delaney. I won't embarrass you."

Christian Delaney inclined his head slightly as Sam left the office. At the door Sam turned and almost missed the speculative look in Christian Delaney's eyes. Those gray eyes that stared back at her every day from the portrait. She said nothing, but merely closed the door quietly behind her.

Once again Sam craned her neck to stare at the clock. Another half-hour till her meeting with Charlie Conway and her first assignment. Where would it be, and what would it be? Might as well go to the supply room and stock up on film and other supplies while she was waiting. But first she would get a cup of the rancid coffee the cameramen called ambrosia and think a little. She really had to decide what she was going to do. Christian Delaney was no fool. Gemini was right—he saw straight through to your soul. She didn't like the thought and felt frightened. What would he do when he found out Orion was Sam Blakely? Would Charlie Conway tell him before she could? Not likely; nor would the other cameramen and newsmen. They were introduced to her as Orion, and first names held. As far as they were concerned, that was her handle and they cared nothing for her legal name; and, if by some chance someone mentioned it, they would promptly forget it; it was the nature of the trade.

Why was she so edgy, so frightened? She hadn't done anything wrong. A mistake had been made, and as long as she didn't accept any money from Gemini's estate, she was in the clear. A sinking feeling gripped her innards. She had every reason to be frightened. Christian Delaney was ruthless and without sentiment. Business always came first. Hadn't he proved this by putting business ahead of being with Gemini in her last hours? Europe was only ten or eleven hours away by air. He hadn't even come to the funeral. Gemini's estate was business of the first order. Why should she expect him to be any less ruthless and understand the mistake that had been made? Surely, Christian Delaney wouldn't want the alcoholic cats. That issue she would fight him on simply because she and Gemini had many discussions and she had given the old lady her word that she would care for the animals. She would honor her promise no matter what.

Gemini—kind, gentle, feisty Gemini, owning *Daylight Magazine*. It was unbelievable. No wonder Gemini had known what to tell her to ask for in the contract. "Don't be such an upstart that you can't accept help." Those were Gemini's words. So what if she used the unisex name? So what if Gemini helped her with the contract? And so what if Gemini put in a good word for her? She was a darned good photographer, and she would prove it or die trying. There was no way she would let Gemini down, not now, not ever.

Sam stretched her neck. Five minutes to three and

she hadn't gotten any coffee, after all. Her musings had taken up a good twenty-five minutes. Now it was time to meet with Charlie Conway and see what she would be doing and where she was going.

Evil, blue-gray smoke as thick as marshmallows greeted Sam as she rapped smartly on Charlie Conway's door and entered. Coughing and sputtering, Sam collapsed against the wall and burst into laughter as she waved her arms to ward off the obnoxious fumes. "Now I know where my dad caught his habit. I didn't think there were two people in the whole world who would find the same cigar and actually smoke it."

"Let me tell you something, kid," Charlie said, working the fat, brown cylinder between his teeth. "These cee-gars were the only thing that kept me and your old man sane during some darned fool uprising in South America. We decided early on that if we were meant to be killed, it wasn't going to be by some guerrilla, but by a fifteen-cent cee-gar. They're up to thirty cents now. Would you believe it? You can open the window if you want," Charlie said generously.

"I wouldn't think of it," Sam retorted as she dabbed at her watering eyes.

Charlie worked the cigar to the side of his mouth and fished around his cluttered desk for a sheaf of official-looking papers. "Okay, Orion, you're going to partner with Ramon Gill. In case you don't know it, he's got the fastest pencil in the east. He's a good man—lascivious, but good. You can handle it. If he gets out of hand, threaten to take a shot of his left profile; he hates that. You're going to California tonight. Here's your plane ticket, along with some expense money. Right now, that fire raging in the canyon is nothing more than a brush affair, but in another twelve hours it's going to

be the biggest bonfire you ever saw. I want you and
Ramon to be the first ones there."

Sam nodded. It never occurred to her to ask the man
seated behind the desk how he knew the brushfire was
going to rage. He was a newsman, and if he said it was
going to go, then it was going to go. Newsmen had a
sixth sense, and that was good enough for her.

"I want you and Ramon right there in the front. Don't
be afraid of a little soot and ash. Just get me good
footage. You got that?" Sam nodded. "And don't let
some jackass try to ward you off because you're a
woman. Around here you're Orion, cameraperson. Is
that clear?" Sam nodded. "Well, what are you waiting
for?"

Sam grimaced. "I was sort of hoping for a 'good
luck' or 'take care' or something."

"You make your own luck, and if you have any
brains, you'll take care of yourself. My wishing you
anything isn't going to make a bit of difference. Hang
in there, kid, and I'll see you back here in three days,
give or take a few either way."

Before she left the office, Sam phoned Ramon Gill
and arranged to meet him at National Airport at eleven
o'clock. They would take the "red-eye" together,
getting in to Los Angeles in the wee hours of the
morning.

She took another taxi she couldn't afford back to the
apartment to pick up the cats for boarding. Time for a
quick shower and time to pack a duffel. Then dinner
with Christian Delaney. Sometime between the appe-
tizer and dessert she would tell him *she* was the Sam
Blakely mentioned in Gemini's will. With a little luck
she could run out of the restaurant before he fired her,
and she could at least get one assignment for *Daylight*

under her belt. She had to make it perfectly clear to him that she had known nothing about the will. Also, she'd make him understand she never knew Gemini owned *Daylight Magazine.* Her heart pounded all through the taxi ride and only returned to normal when she exited at her doorstep.

Her hand trembled as she fit the gold key into the lock. The phone in the living room was shrilling as she closed the door and threw the dead bolt. She raced across the room only to hear the dial tone as she placed the receiver to her ear. Whoever it was would call back if it was important.

First things first. She stripped down, showered and redressed. Makeup went on sparingly, as did a dab of perfume. She packed heavy twill pants and sweatshirts along with a week's change of underwear. Toilet articles in a leather case were next, along with a pair of hiking boots. In this business you traveled light and smelled a lot.

Now the cats. She called them and, as usual, they ignored her. She'd have to do what Gemini did. Craftily, she bent down to the liquor cabinet in the corner and managed to clink the gin bottle and tonic water at the same time. One cat was on her shoulder, and the other twined himself around her leg. "Look, guys, this was a fake. There isn't enough in either bottle for a shot. You're a disgrace. The vet isn't going to cater to your problems, so let's go on the wagon right now. A few days of milk will do you both a lot of good." Both cats looked at her disdainfully and swept out of the room, their lush tails straight out to show their disapproval. "Come on, now, you have to get into your basket," she said, chasing them and scooping both up at the same time. "I don't want to hear a peep out of either one of you. You're sober now and you're going to stay that way." Both cats hissed their anger as she snapped the lid of the carryall and lugged it to the front door. Now, where was the vet Gemini had used for the cats? Quickly, she flipped through her address book till she found the name of the animal hospital. Rockville! A fast look at the sunburst clock told her if she avoided the rush-hour traffic, she might make it. She still had the keys to Gemini's vintage Mercedes. As much as she disliked doing it, she would have to use the car.

The cats hissed and clawed at the wicker as she lugged them to the garage at the rear of the brownstone. She slid open the doors and placed the cats on the floor in the back of the car. A yowl of outrage made the fine hairs on the back of her neck stand on end. "Both of you be quiet. I can't drive with all that screeching," she called over her shoulder as she maneuvered the heavy car down the alley and onto Connecticut Avenue. Sam drove fast, her eyes glued to the rearview mirror for any sign of the city's finest. Walter Reed Medical Center on the right. She was making progress.

Sam popped a stale mint into her mouth as she swung north on Georgia Avenue and made her way to the Capital Beltway. The Interstate green read: NORTHERN VIRGINIA. Sam took the second right, looping back to merge westbound with Interstate Maryland 495. Noticing a gap in the middle lane, Sam pushed down on the directional lever and eased into the slow-moving traffic. She heard the snap of the wicker lid as her eyes sighted the Mormon Temple. To Sam's eye it looked like a glacial cathedral sculpted from a massive chunk of ice. The cats were loose and hopping onto the front seat. Playfully, they hissed and scratched at the plush seats to celebrate their freedom.

Twenty minutes later Sam stood at the reception desk in the vet's office, the heavy basket next to her on the countertop. Loud hisses and snarls swept through the office. Quickly, Sam explained who she was and the situation with the cats.

"Miss Blakely," the receptionist said, a look of panic on her face, "the doctor can't treat Mrs. Delaney's cats. He simply refuses. The last time they were here we all had to go on tranquilizers. They're disruptive. We couldn't determine what their problem was and decided they were just riddled with neuroses. I'm sorry, really sorry."

It was Sam's turn to panic. They had to take the cats. "If I tell you what's wrong with these cats, will you take them?"

The receptionist inched away from the counter. Her eyes were shifty as she stared at the noisy basket. "Well, that depends on whether the condition is treatable. I'm Dr. Barstow's wife, and I can't have my husband upset with those animals like the last time. What is it?" she asked fearfully.

"They're alcoholics."

"Alcoholics?" Mrs. Barstow said stupidly.

"Yes. I've got them on the wagon, but I can see now that I'll have to wait till I get back to dry them out. Just give them some gin and tonic and they're as docile as two kittens. Believe me," Sam pleaded as she made her way to the door, hoping against hope that the woman wouldn't call her back and demand she take the hissing cats with her. "I'll pick them up in a week, sooner if I get back before then. Thank you, thank you so much," she babbled as she ran from the office.

If she didn't hit traffic, she could make her seven o'clock appointment for dinner with Christian Delaney right on schedule. She prayed silently all the way back to the city and didn't draw a safe breath till she hit Wisconsin Avenue. She drove through Rock Creek Park, admiring the rich colors of late autumn, silently congratulating herself on a job well done. The cats were safe, for the moment, and she had Gemini's car back, secure in its space in the double garage. Carefully, she locked the garage and slipped the keys into her purse. Along with her confession, she would turn the keys over to Christian Delaney. Surely, he wouldn't mind that she had used his aunt's car for the trip to Rockville. After all, it was for the cats, not a joyride.

She raced around the corner to her apartment. She dialed and waited for the crackly voice of the taxi dispatcher to tell her how long she would have to wait for a cab. "Three minutes," she was told.

Sam heard the phone ring as she locked the door behind her. Should she go back and answer? She was saved the decision when a blue and white cab slid up to the curb. Whoever it was would have to call back later. A lot later.

The cab ground to a smooth stop in front of the restaurant just as a yellow Jaguar cut in front of it. Christian Delaney emerged from the low-slung sports car just as Sam paid the driver.

Christian Delaney eyed the worn duffel bag and the heavy camera case. Sam explained and was surprised to see her escort frown. "It's no problem; you can check both of them at the cloakroom."

"You're wrong. I'll check the duffel, but this camera never leaves my side."

"It must make a cold bedfellow." Christian grinned as the maître d' showed them to a cozy table near the monstrous fireplace. "What will you have to drink, Orion?"

"Scotch on the rocks." Sam watched as Christian's eyebrows shot up in surprise. What did he think she was going to order, a Shirley Temple? He ordered the same thing for himself and then lit a cigarette. "That's the second time I've surprised you in the space of a few minutes. Why?"

Christian answered bluntly, "I was surprised that Conway assigned you to cover the pictorial side of the fire, and I didn't expect you to order Scotch—it's a man's drink."

"Two sexist remarks in one sentence." Sam grinned. "I don't see what my gender has to do with my ability to photograph a fire, and I happen to like Scotch."

"Well said." Christian grinned, showing a flash of strong white teeth. "What time does your plane leave? Who's the journalist? Normally, I would know all about this assignment, but as I told you, I had family business to take care of this afternoon and didn't go back to the office after lunch."

Sam was glad she had both hands around the squat glass in front of her. She blinked and felt her heart resume its normal beat. "And did you settle your family business?" Was that calm, casual voice hers?

"No, I didn't." Christian's tone was vehement. "If there's one thing I cannot and will not abide, it is professional, slick con artists who prey on defenseless old ladies. Tomorrow, I'm hiring the best private detective firm in the city to track down that slick weasel, and when I find him I'm going to..." Sam gulped and wished she could drown herself in the amber fluid she was holding. Now. She should tell him now! Samantha opened her mouth, forcing the words to her lips. But before she could utter a sound, he interrupted.

"I'm sorry. That's the second time I allowed family

matters to intrude. Pleasantries only from now on. Tell me how you came to be a photojournalist."

Sam relaxed. This was familiar ground and she was comfortable. What seemed like hours later she glanced at her watch, dreading to see what numbers the hands rested on. Soon it would be time to go; and, suddenly, she didn't want to leave this man's presence—not now, not ever. She must tell him now, before she left. She couldn't continue playing this game of hide-and-seek. In essence, she was deceiving him, and that deceit was making everything a lie—her job, the assignment, this dinner, even the way Christian's eyes were smiling into hers. Her confession would change everything. Samantha gulped, feeling a shudder run through her. Taking a deep breath, she began: "Christian, I must tell…"

Christian's voice was cool, almost mocking when he interrupted: "That's the third time I've seen you glance at your watch. Am I boring you?"

Sam stared at the man across from her and flushed a deep crimson. "On…on the contrary. I just…just realized that…that it's getting late and I'm going to…to have to leave…soon. I'm having such a good time I don't…I don't want to leave," she said honestly and could have bitten her tongue the minute the words were out. "But before I do, I have to tell…"

Christian leaned across the table and took both of her hands in his, stifling her determination to tell him about his aunt's will. "Then don't go. Stay here with me. I'll call Charlie Conway and tell him to get another photographer. I like you, Orion, and I don't want you to leave, either."

"Christian, there's nothing I would like better, but I can't do that. I gave my word, and as much as I want to stay, that's how much I want to cover this story.

Please understand. Photography is part of my life. I can't just…just throw it in on a whim." At the look on Christian's face, she added hastily, "Not that this is a whim, it's just that I have to tell…" Not knowing what else to say, she sat miserably in her chair.

"Believe it or not, I understand. There will be other days and other nights," he said meaningfully.

Sam forced a chilling note into her tone when she replied, "Mr. Delaney, I think I should tell you that I do not sleep around, nor would I be any good at one-night stands. I have a tendency to lock into situations. Now, if you would like to revise that last statement of yours to read, 'there will be other days and other evenings,' I can go away on this assignment with a clear head and have something to look forward to on my return. I do like you and I want to see you again, but I also don't want you to get the wrong idea or later say that I misled you. That's why I want you to know…"

"I do know. And you could never mislead me, Orion." Was she mistaken, or was his face registering shocked disbelief at her words? Had she really said those things aloud? Evidently. Up front. Always be up front with everyone, Gemini had said. People always respected honesty and forthrightness. Sure they did, Sam thought cynically. *I think you blew it that time, Gemini.*

"I have to leave now," Sam said, looking at the circlet on her wrist. "But before I do…"

"I'll drive you to the airport. I can't let you take a taxi. What would you think of me?"

Exasperated, Sam tossed her napkin onto the table. Would this man never let her speak? If she wanted to make her plane on time, she'd have to give it up as hopeless. The first thing she would do on her return would be to sit him down and tell it like it was. A minuscule twinge of guilt nipped her conscience. Had she really done her best to tell him, or was this assignment more important than the truth? "It's not necessary to take me to the airport, but I would like it, if you're serious," she was astonished to hear herself say in a smooth voice.

"Orion, you have no idea just how serious I am. This probably sounds a little corny, but I enjoyed that little speech of yours a minute ago. I hope we do have many days and evenings together. Let's pick up your duffel and get out of here."

Sam walked on air out to the yellow sports car and was in seventh heaven all the way to the airport. At least it was seventh heaven as long as she didn't allow herself to think about what a coward she was for not revealing to Christian that she was the Sam Blakely he was seeking—seeking to wring his neck, she reminded herself. It was all a mistake; she was certain of it. As soon as that doddering old lawyer looked into the matter, everything would straighten itself out. Gemini couldn't have left her anything besides the two cats. It was unthinkable. All Gemini had ever said was that the two cats were going to be Sam's responsibility, and Samantha had assumed that taking the cats would somehow repay Gemini for the countless kindnesses the old woman had shown her. Besides, this was no time to be revealing anything to the publisher and president of the magazine that was giving her the first big break at becoming a successful photojournalist. She couldn't take the chance of having Christian become so angry that he took the brushfire assignment away from her.

To Sam's surprise, instead of dropping her off at the terminal, Christian parked his car and escorted her to the ticket counter. Ramon Gill was standing just beyond the ticket line, sporting his *Daylight* press badge so she would recognize him. Ramon's Latin eyes flicked over her appraisingly. "So, you're Orion. Somehow, I wasn't expecting someone as pretty as you."

Sam's trigger had been pulled, and she almost bristled with a stinging retort about how being a female photographer didn't necessarily mean you had to look like a dragon. But she thought better of it. If she was to work successfully with Ramon Gill, that would mean they had to be on good terms. Instead of giving him a sharp retort, she smiled a coy thanks for his compliment.

"Ramon, have you met our president? Mr. Christian Delaney."

Gill's eyebrows raised in surprise. "Yeah, I've heard there was somebody new in the front office. How do you do, Mr. Delaney? I've followed your work on the foreign market, and as a journalist, I appreciate it. You've gotten our reporters into some newsfronts where even *Time* magazine was unwelcome."

"I did my best," Christian answered, shaking Ramon's hand firmly. "Listen, why don't you go and grab a cup of coffee? There's still time before the takeoff. Orion and I have a few things to discuss."

"Yeah, sure," Ramon agreed affably. "Say, Orion, want me to take your duffel with me? It's good to see a woman who can pack sensibly. I was sort of worried that you'd come with fifty-nine suitcases and that we'd have to wait all night for the baggage. I always travel with carry-on bags myself."

Sam handed Ramon her duffel. "I appreciate it." As Ramon reached for her camera and gadget bag, Sam stepped backward. "These stay with me, always."

"Sure." Gill shrugged. "I know all about it. I ought to. I've been working with you camera people long enough. The camera never leaves your side, right?"

"Right."

"Okay. See you at the boarding gate." With a nod to Christian, Ramon hefted his own duffel plus Sam's and headed for the coffee shop.

"You handled that very well." Christian smiled down at her. "I could see that you were just ripping to straighten out Ramon's thinking about female photographers. Restraint and discretion are the better part of valor."

Sam laughed. "Am I that transparent?"

Christian looked down into her upturned face, a long, penetrating look that seemed to steal her breath away. "Come on," he prodded. "You're going to get a proper send-off."

"And what is that?"

"A beer in the V.I.P. lounge and then a very sound kiss just before you board."

All the while they conversed over their beers in the softly lit V.I.P. lounge, Sam's thoughts were focused ahead on the kiss he promised her just before she boarded the plane. The conversation was lighthearted and she joined Christian in some teasing banter, but all the while her eyes drank in the familiar planes of his face, the tiny cleft in his chin, the lines around his eyes that said he had spent a good deal of time in a hot, sunny climate, the slight salting of gray near his temples, and, most of all, the lights that glowed from the depths of his silvery-gray eyes.

She liked the way the corners of his mouth lifted when he smiled. The slight tilt at the end of his nose hinted at his Irish heritage. His heavy, almost unruly, brows added a sternness to his features that was waylaid by the humor in his smile. Fleetingly, she wondered if anyone, even a great artist, could capture this man's vitality and masculinity on canvas. Now, to her discerning eye, she realized how flat and inaccurate the portrait in her spare bedroom really was. It was the image of this man, not the great personality and charm he exuded.

Christian glanced at his watch. "I'd better get you down to the gate now, or I'll just sweep you up and refuse to let you leave me. You're very beautiful, you know. And I like the way your eyes flash when you laugh. You have a very nice laugh, Orion, and I intend to hear it often when you get back from your forest fire." His tone was deep and husky; the expression in his eyes excited her.

They ran, hand in hand, toward the gate where her plane was waiting and had just arrived when the flight was announced over the public address system. Sam's heart beat like a trip-hammer at the thought of his promised kiss. She wanted that kiss, needed it, and shamelessly knew that she was anticipating it.

Her hand shook slightly as she handed her boarding pass to the flight attendant. Suddenly, Christian had wrapped his arms around her and drew her close into his embrace. For a long moment he gazed down into her eyes before he lowered his head and pressed his lips to her mouth.

The touch was light, fleeting, teasing. His strong arms held her, refusing to allow her to escape. Again, he looked down into her eyes, an expression of surprise glowing in the depths of his own. The room seemed to spin; all sound was muted; only the drumbeat of her heart sounded in her ears. And when again his head lowered to hers, his mouth possessed hers, demanding an answering response, giving a promise of things to come.

"Sir. Sir!" the flight attendant insisted. "Sir, you are hampering the other passengers from boarding the plane. Sir!"

Reluctantly, Christian released Sam. Bewilderment and surprise were struck on his features. "Orion..."

"Please, sir, you are blocking traffic!"

"Off you go, Orion. I'll be waiting," he murmured huskily. "Get going before I steal you away," he added gruffly.

In a trance, Samantha hurried down the corridor to the plane. Dazedly, she found her seat beside Ramon and fastened her seat belt. Her lips were still tingling with the touch of Christian's kiss. Her body felt the hot imprint of where his arms had held her. Shaken, she pushed her camera bag beneath the seat and tried to control her rising emotions. She was almost looking forward to the long flight to California. She needed time. Time to think.

Ramon stirred beside her. "That was quite a little scene you and Delaney performed out there. And, by the way, it's nice to know there are still some girls who can blush."

CHAPTER THREE

TIRED, GIDDY WITH SUCCESS, Sam stopped dead in her tracks in the middle of the airport parking lot and stared at her companion, Ramon Gill. A surge of laughter overcame her, and she wiped tears away with the back of a grimy hand. "You should only see what you look like! I swear, Ramon, there's a decided odor of singed hair and charcoal wafting this way."

"Ha!" Ramon snapped. "They'll never place you on the ten best-dressed list. And that isn't exactly Arpege clinging to you. I'd sell my soul for a shower and a fresh change of clothes right now. The least you could have done was to make a later flight reservation so we could have showered. You in a hurry or something?" he asked, unlocking the door of his Corvette.

"Or something." Samantha grinned. "If I never smell smoke again, I'll be just as happy." Jackknifing herself into the Corvette, she settled herself and leaned back against the seat.

"That's it, sleep," Ramon chided as he slipped the key into the ignition. "You women are all alike. Here I am, wounded in battle and just as exhausted as you, and yet I have to drive. Where to, lady? And it better not be Maryland."

Sam smiled. "Wounded, are you? Since when do they give the Purple Heart for singed eyebrows?"

Ramon returned her smile. They had formed a mutual appreciation for one another during the assignment of following the forest fire. Together, they had discovered that they were both unyielding when it came to covering the news story to the best of their ability. Instinctively, they had assisted one another, falling into an easy rapport. Ramon put the words on the paper, and Orion's photographs brought them to life.

"I repeat, Orion, where to?" he asked as he paid the parking fee at the booth near the edge of the lot. "In other words, where do you live?"

Sam was instantly awake, her mind racing. She had forgotten. How could she go back to her apartment? Christian Delaney said he was hiring private detectives to track down the "gigolo" who had befriended his Aunt Gemini. If she went back to the brownstone before she could make her explanations to Christian, she would be spotted and then the fur would fly. She was too tired for confrontations, for explanations, and there was no way she could face Christian at the moment. For now, at least, evasion would be the best tactic. And it might continue to be until she could straighten out this mess. With any luck at all, the ancient lawyer would have discovered his error by now concerning the fifty-one percent of the stock being left in her name.

Samantha drew a deep breath and exhaled slowly. "Actually, Ramon," she said airily, "I was thinking that perhaps you could drop me off at the airport Holiday Inn. It won't be out of your way. I'm just too tired to go back to my apartment and wait for the water to get hot and for the heat to come on. All I want is a shower and sleep. Just drop me off." Before Ramon could answer, Sam had taken her duffel bag from the backseat and had her camera slung over her shoulder.

Ramon glanced at his companion suspiciously. "If Holiday Inns are your thing, it's okay with me. I'm going to stop by the magazine. Do you have any messages to deliver?"

"I'll call Charlie after I take a shower and brush my teeth. Do you think it's possible to have cinders and soot in your teeth?"

"Anything is possible," Ramon muttered as he swung the Corvette down the ramp to pull alongside the entrance to the Holiday Inn.

"Thanks for the ride, Ramon." Sam grinned at the journalist's second suspicious look and waited on the curb for the sports car to swing onto Jefferson Davis Highway. The second the fast-moving car was out of sight, Sam hefted the duffel over her shoulder and headed for the Crystal Underground Shopping Center. An hour later she was laden with two burgeoning shopping bags, compliments of her American Express and Visa cards. She had to have clothes, and since she had decided not to go back to her apartment for the time being, she had no other choice but to buy new clothing from the skin out.

The motel room's door double-locked and the chain in place, Sam turned the shower on full blast and stripped down. She stood under the needle-sharp spray, letting the tiny beads of water wash away the top layer of soot and grime that had worked their way through her clothes. She lathered her silky skin twice and managed to shampoo her hair at the same time. What seemed like forever later to her, she stepped from the cascading water and wrapped herself in the skimpy motel towels.

First things first. How much had she charged with her plastic money? Recklessly, she rummaged through the shopping bags until she had a neat pile of receipts in her hand. Mentally, she tallied them up and gulped. Cash—how much cash did she have? With one eye closed to ward off disappointment, she peered at the thin sheaf of bills in her wallet. A grand total of sixty-three dollars. Darn, why did she feel like such a criminal? She hadn't done anything except be nice to an old lady of whom she had genuinely been fond. Another one-eyed look in her checkbook told her she wouldn't be able to camp out in a motel much longer, not at forty-two dollars a day plus food. She would have to face Christian Delaney, and soon.

Sam returned both the checkbook and credit slips to her purse. She popped a crystal mint into her mouth and dialed the main number at the magazine. The switchboard operator put her on hold. Sam leaned back against the propped-up pillows and was instantly asleep, the squawking phone in her hand.

Sam awoke refreshed, the alarm beeping on her digital watch, at 8:00 a.m. She vaguely remembered waking up once during the night to total darkness and also vaguely remembered hanging up the phone. She opened the drapes and peered out at the tall building on top of the Crystal Underground from her fourth-floor room. It was difficult to tell exactly what kind of day it was. It looked cold, and here she was with nothing more than a heavy sweater purchased at the shopping center. She had to get her own clothes or she would freeze to death.

She showered, taking her time, and then called down for room service and was informed that all meals were served on disposable plates with plastic implements. She had time for a leisurely breakfast and the ride into the city. The first day back after an assignment was always a slow day to catch up. It was either a congratulation or gripe-and-complaint day. Either way, it was still slow.

A drab gray light filtered through the window at her cubbyhole office at *Daylight Magazine* and directed Sam's attention to a small stack of mail, which rested on her desk. Before she could begin to open the vari-sized envelopes, Charlie Conway slouched into the office. "You did a good job, kid. The lighting on those pics is some of the best I've ever seen. Just in case you're interested, the front office asked for a complete set of photos. I expect you'll get some praise from on high. You did a good job, and Ramon had only good things to say about the way you work, and coming from him, that's the best."

Sam smiled happily. "Ramon actually said that?"

Charlie rolled his cigar around in his mouth a couple of times and grinned. "Actually, what he said was you were okay but weird, and you had this thing about motels. Oh, yeah, he said you forgot where you lived."

Sam flushed and then laughed. "I was so tired, Charlie, and what with the jet lag, I just didn't have the stamina to go all the way back into town. I tried calling you, but the girl put me on hold and I fell asleep and didn't wake up till this morning."

"You're forgiven. I'll forgive anything you do if you keep giving me pics like the ones of the fire. You got a lunch date? I'd like to hear about the fire."

"No, I don't have a lunch date, but I have to run a few errands. I can stop by your office later if you want and we could have a cup of coffee and talk about it, unless you have another assignment for me."

"You're on call. It's a date, then. Anytime this afternoon is okay, the rag has been put to bed."

"Didn't Ramon fill you in?" Sam asked inquisitively.

"Ramon told me to read about it in the magazine. He's like a superstitious old gypsy. He'll talk my ear off once the rag hits the street, but not one second before."

Sam watched the old editor as he exited the office, an ominous, billowing cloud of foul gray smoke in his wake. She fanned furiously at the air and was startled to see Christian Delaney standing in the doorway. "Welcome back, Orion." He smiled from ear to ear.

Sam felt her heart begin to thud. It seemed to have some kind of bongo rhythm all its own as she stared at the handsome man in the doorway. "Th-thank you. It's good to be back." She waited, uncertain if she should get up and hold out her hand, or if she should stay seated behind the rough, scarred desk. You didn't shake hands with a man you kissed, not if you kissed him the way she had, anyway. Throwing caution to the winds and ignoring her fast-beating heart, she rose and walked over to the publisher. She grinned and said, "Come in, said the spider to the fly." Christian Delaney needed no second urging.

"The question is: Who's the spider and who's the fly?" He grinned back as he drew her to him.

"Hmm, does it matter?" Sam murmured as she nuzzled her head against his chest.

"Not to me, it doesn't," Christian said huskily as his mouth met hers. The kiss was butterfly soft, yet demanding in its intensity.

Sam moved slightly and stared deeply into Christian's eyes. "I liked that. Kiss me again," she said boldly.

They were both shaking when Christian released her and held her away from him at arm's length. Sam stared back, knowing her feelings were revealed in her shaky gaze. She swallowed hard. She couldn't have uttered a word if her life depended on it. Apparently, Christian felt the same way, for he kissed her lightly on the cheek and opened the door. "Dinner," he said gruffly. "After work, around six." Sam nodded.

"How…how di-did you like the pictures?" Sam blurted. Suddenly, she couldn't bear for him to leave her office. From this moment on, she knew she was going to love this small, confining space with a passion unequaled.

"Pictures? What pictures? Oh, those pictures! Good, very good. I liked them." He turned, his face serious, the silvery-gray eyes hooded. "You're some kind of woman, Orion! Did anyone ever tell you that?"

Sam grinned. It was okay for him to leave now. "Only my dad, and I'm not sure that counts."

"Let's keep it that way," Christian said over his shoulder as he strode briskly down the corridor.

A silly look on her face, Sam slumped in the creaking swivel chair. It was a beautiful cubbyhole, and it smelled just as beautiful as she sniffed at the faint, almost elusive, scent of the publisher's cologne. She had to find out what it was and buy a gallon of it. She would spritz it all around. "I'm in love!" she chortled happily. Her happiness was short-lived when she remembered how she was duping Gemini's nephew. She had to tell him. Tonight, she would tell him, after dinner, when he took her home.

Don't think about that now. Why not? her mind questioned. *There isn't anything else to do.* "Yes, there is," she said aloud. "I didn't open my mail." Quickly, she sifted through the mail and sorted it into piles. Circulars, sale flyers from various department stores, bills, two letters from college friends who insisted on keeping in touch, and a legal-looking envelope from the

Women's Bank. Her bank. She slit open the envelope and withdrew a pale green check attached to a letter. One short paragraph that said Sam Blakely was due the enclosed third-quarter dividend check from the Delaney stocks. Beyond realizing that the amount was in six figures, she couldn't comprehend the actual sum. She had no basis for comprehending money in such large amounts. Sam lowered her eyes at the slip of paper she was holding. She gagged and the check fluttered and fell to the floor. Transfixed, unable to move, her eyes followed the square of paper. She gagged again and covered her mouth with both her hands. It couldn't be! There was a dreadful mistake! There just wasn't that much money in the whole world! And they sent it in the mail, she thought in horror. Oh, God! Oh, God, what was she going to do? Pick it up, of course. You didn't leave $667,395.42 lying on the floor. Gingerly, she picked up the check and stared at it again. Did one fold a check for this amount? Was it one of those that you did not fold, spindle, or mutilate? Quickly, she opened her top desk drawer and dropped the check onto a pile of blank paper. She slammed the drawer closed with shaking hands and held it in place. Slowly, she inched the drawer open a fraction. It was still there. Oh, God, it was still there! She would give it back to Christian tonight when she told him who she was. He would know what to do with it. That's what she would do.

Gemini, how could you do this to me? she wailed silently. *He's never going to understand. I can feel it.* Blind panic covered her like a mantle and then coursed through her veins, leaving her weak-kneed and trembling. There had to be a way out of this; she just had to find it. She would put herself in Christian Delaney's place and try to react the way he would. Now, let's see, first she would explain and then hand him the check. He would say something magnanimous like, "Why thank you, Ms. Blakely. There aren't too many people in the world who would return a check for $667,395.42. Believe me, I understand perfectly why you're returning it. You're returning it because it's a mere drop in the bucket compared to what you would get from our relationship if we married. Even the lowliest copy runner at the magazine knows I'm the heir to the Delaney publishing fortune. When you compare $667,395.42 to a fortune, it doesn't take much imagination to know which one you'll pick." A squeal of pure agony escaped her tight lips. She *couldn't* tell him! She *had* to tell him! She would compromise. She would tell him later, much later. For now, she wanted more time with him, more time to feel his lips and arms around her, so when she was in the dark days to come, she would at least have memories. Gemini had lived on her memories for the last forty years. She would have memories and $667,395.42. And this was just the third quarter. If she were to take that amount and multiply it times four, she would have... Oh, God! She had to give it back. Perhaps what she should do was to send it anonymously to the bank president. She was a woman; she'd understand.

An unseen devil perched itself on Sam's shoulder and whispered, "It's yours; Gemini saw to it. It's all legal. You don't really have to give it back. Why not take a 'wait and see' attitude? If Delaney finds out who you are, see how he handles it before you return the money. You could find yourself out in the cold without a job, an apartment. That dividend check will buy a lot of warmth."

"Not the kind of warmth I'm looking for," Sam snarled at the invisible devil. "I won't do it. I'm giving it back!"

A copy boy stuck his head in the door and yelled, "Catch!" And he tossed her a heavy manila envelope. "Charlie wants you to go over Ramon Gill's story and space the pics."

Sam nodded and flipped open the envelope. Thank heaven for work. Thank heaven for anything that would take her mind off the slip of paper in her desk drawer.

Working industriously for the next several hours, Sam managed to finish up her work a few minutes before six. Time for a quick spruce-up and a dab of fresh makeup and she would be ready to meet Christian for dinner. Her heart fluttered wildly at the thought and then thumped heavily in her chest. What was she going to do with the check? She couldn't carry it with her; you just didn't carry that kind of check around. She couldn't leave it in the office drawer. The safe. She would ask Charlie Conway to put it in his safe. Too late; he was gone. Vaguely, she remembered smelling his cigar as he walked by the office and said something about seeing her in the morning. Now what was she going to do? The first thing she should do was put the green slip in another envelope. *Hide it!* her mind screamed. *Where?* She answered herself. The only place left—Christian Delaney's safe. What better place. She would seal it, scribble her name on the envelope, and forget about it. Ha! How did a person who had $889.88 to her name forget about a small green piece of paper bearing her name and the sum of $667,395.42? One didn't forget; what one did was ignore it. Immediately, she felt better and she felt positively lightheaded once the check was safe inside a manila envelope. Carefully, she sealed the metal hook beneath three layers of Scotch tape. Her hands were trembling so badly she tangled the tape around her fingers and finally ended up pulling the sticky tape apart with her teeth. The matter tended to, she literally fell into the swivel chair and collapsed. She wasn't meant to have money, not if it did this to her. Disgust washed through her as she stared at the square envelope in front of her. Disgust gave way to pity for herself as she continued to stare at the fateful envelope. *Gemini, you shouldn't have done this. Whatever possessed you to do such a thing?* Finding no answers, Sam mentally affixed an invisible ramrod to her spine and stood up. Before she could think twice, she picked up the envelope and marched down the hall to Christian Delaney's office. The door stood open and she knocked lightly before entering.

The scene was an exact replica of the first time played out in the publisher's office. The handsome publisher stood with his back to her, shouting into the phone. Sam blanched at the words and dropped the manila square she was holding. She didn't want to listen, didn't want to hear more ways the man was going to kill her. She should leave, run as fast as her slim legs would carry her, but she couldn't. Not yet. She would punish herself and listen.

The words were ice-cold and the harshest she had ever heard. "It's been seven days! What do you mean you have one lead and you aren't even sure of that? Fine, if money is your problem, then put more men on the case. I told you before I didn't care what it costs. Find Sam Blakely! Did you check with the postman? His mail was being held at the post office and was picked up today. Right, it was picked up today! Do you want to know why it was picked up today? I'll tell you why!" Christian Delaney thundered into the phone. "The dividend checks went out in the mail this week for the third quarter. Right now, this minute, he's probably winging his way to the Mediterranean intent on bilking some other old lady. Check the airlines. Now that that weasel has money to burn, he's apt to go first-class. Gigolos do that. What do you mean, how do I know that? I just know. What about the Division of Motor Vehicles? He doesn't own a car. It figures. Try the rental agencies. I understand you can rent a Mercedes for a very small down payment. My aunt would never ride in anything but a Mercedes or a Checker cab. I'm certain you never thought of that," Christian said sarcastically.

Christian turned and motioned for Sam to sit down. He rolled his eyes in apology and again turned to face the panoramic view of the nation's Capitol. "I can't wait to hear your lead. Let's have it. A man named Sam Blakely. What street? Spell it; Kilbourne Place, off Mount Pleasant Avenue. Do you have a number? Amazing! Second floor, number 1755. I have it. You're right I'm going up there, and right now. When was he seen last? Of course I'm edgy. And I'll stay edgy until he's behind bars or I have my hands around his neck. I'll call you later."

Sam's brain was working double time and her fingers were fidgeting with the shoulder strap of her heavy canvas bag. When Christian turned to her and smiled, her heart melted and she wanted to leap up and throw her arms around him. He must have felt the same way, because he crooked his finger slightly, beckoning her to him. She fell into his arms and sighed deeply. Gently, Christian stroked her soft curls and held her close. "If I kiss you now," he whispered huskily, "we'll never get around to dinner."

Sam moved slightly from his embrace and smiled.

"Charlie Conway is gone and I want to put this in the safe. Will you do it for me?"

Christian reached for the envelope and turned it over, looking at both sides. "You didn't put your name on it." Not waiting for her to answer, he picked up a black grease pencil and scrawled "Orion" across the front. "It doesn't feel as though there's anything in it."

Sam forced another weak smile and remained silent.

Christian twirled the dial on the wall safe and then deposited the envelope. Locking the safe, he smacked his hands together. "Okay, let's get out of this place. I have a stop to make before we go to dinner. I hope you don't mind, but it really can't wait. I'm sure you heard my end of the conversation, so you know what's been going on. By God, the nerve of that weasel!"

"What...what weasel?" Sam gulped.

"The weasel who duped my aunt Gemini and the weasel we're on our way to see. That weasel!"

"Oh," Sam said inanely, "that weasel."

"He's the one. When I'm finished with him, he'll never prey on another poor, unsuspecting old lady again."

"Is that wise?" Sam asked hesitantly. "What I mean is, you can get yourself into a lot of trouble taking this matter into your own hands. Besides, perhaps there's been a mistake..."

"If there's one thing I can't stand, it's deceit," Christian interrupted through clenched teeth. "I despise lies and trickery. I may have been born into money, but it's meant nothing to me. I receive a salary just like everyone else here at Delaney Enterprises. My parents saw to it that I worked my way through life. At the age of twelve I had two paper routes because I wanted a new bicycle. I worked summers.... What I've done, I've done myself. The money that's come to me through the family has barely been touched. I don't live the life of a playboy. As for the shares my poor misguided aunt left to that Sam Blakely, just let it suffice to say that I want it back. All of it. This has been a family-owned business, and as far as I'm concerned, it will always be. Fifty-one percent of the stock is the controlling interest. How can I ensure the growth of this company if the controlling stock is owned by a Sam Blakely? There's a lot at stake, and I intend to settle it—immediately!"

Sam was stunned. Why was he telling her this? Was this his way of making his threats known? Could it be he already suspected that she was Sam Blakely? Oh, if ever there was a time to bare her soul, this was it. Swallowing hard, she forced her tongue to working order and managed a garbled, "Christian, there's something I think...what I mean is, I'd like to talk to you..."

"Darling, remember what you were going to say. We've got to get moving. Tell me over dinner."

She knew she should have insisted. Allowing him to cut her off was too easy. Now was the time, before things went too far, before it was impossible to tell him, and then he would find out sooner or later and hate her for it. But it was not to be. Christian took her by the arm and led her out of the office.

As Christian drove along the unfamiliar streets, he turned to Samantha. "I left my driving glasses back at the office. Watch for Mount Pleasant Avenue. This is Seventeenth Street, isn't it?" Sam craned her neck backward and managed a jerky nod. "It should be along about here. It's been years since I've been in this area. If the trolley tracks were still here, it would be a breeze. There's something about streetcar tracks that make me melancholy."

"Turn left, Christian. There's Mount Pleasant Avenue," Sam said quietly. What had she been thinking of? She had actually been going to tell him. If she had, he never would have called her "darling." She meant something to him. She was certain of it. And he certainly meant something to her; just how much, she was afraid to even measure. "Kilbourne Place on your left. What number are you looking for?"

"End of the block, number 1755, second-floor apartment!"

Christian guided the car to the curb and sat for a moment. "I shouldn't have brought you with me. This doesn't look like the kind of neighborhood that's safe to walk around in after dark. I'm not even sure the car will still be here once we come out of the building."

Sam looked at the grimy brick building and winced. Venetian blinds that held years of dirt were hanging lopsidedly on the cracked windows. One window on the second floor was being propped open with a portable television set. A tattered blue curtain fluttered wildly. A sudden gust of wind came up, and dry leaves hurtled through the open window. What if some thug lived inside and he attacked them both?

"Lock your door, Orion, and hold on to my arm," Christian said, holding open the door for Sam.

Clutching Christian's muscular arm, Sam walked with him up the brick steps into a filthy hallway that reeked of years of stale food and other nauseating odors. Cautiously, they made their way to the top of the rickety steps with the aid of a fifteen-watt bulb that hung precariously from a frayed electrical wire.

Christian rapped loudly on the door and then stepped back, pulling Sam with him. No answer. He rapped again and kicked at the bottom of the door at the same time. "Yeah, whatcha want this time?" a whining voice demanded. Sam felt faint at the sight of the wizened old man who opened the door.

Christian stepped back another step and asked forcefully. "Is your name Sam Blakely?"

"And what if it is. My old mum gave me that name seventy-two years ago, and I'm still using it, so what business is it of yours?"

Christian ignored the question and asked another. "How long have you lived here?"

"As long as the cockroaches—and that's forever. Who are you, anyway?"

"Did you know Gemini Delaney?" Christian demanded in an angry tone.

"Don't know no Gemini anyone. Crazy name if you ask me. I ain't into that star stuff myself. Matter of fact, I just got out of the hospital today. Was in there for a whole month. I had pneumonia," the old man said proudly. "'Course, I was in the charity ward, but they took care of me just like everyone else, and they even called me Mr. Blakely. It's important for a man not to lose his identity. I was born Sam Blakely, and I'm gonna die Sam Blakely. Say, now, what you gonna pay me for answering all these questions? Listen, you ain't from one of them there TV shows, are you—you know, the hidden camera one?"

"No," Christian said disgustedly. "Look, I'm sorry to have bothered you. Here," he said, handing the old man a twenty-dollar bill. "Buy yourself a good steak and some vegetables and see to it that all the good they did for you in the hospital doesn't go to waste."

"That's mighty nice of you, mister. You sure you ain't from one of them TV shows and they're going to come here and take this money from me after they turn off the cameras?"

"I'm sure," Christian said over his shoulder as he guided Sam down the dim stairway. "Don't touch anything, Orion."

Outside in the fresh air Sam gulped and swallowed hard. Poor Christian. She had to tell him; she couldn't allow him to keep searching like this. He looked so defeated.

Inside the car with the doors locked, Christian drove through Rock Creek Park. He was silent for so long Sam began to feel apprehensive. She should say something to break his mood. She should tell him now before this charade went much further.

"Orion, I'm sorry. This was a beastly thing to subject you to. All I can do is apologize. This business with my aunt has me caught up in a whirlwind. No more unpleasantries. I've been looking forward to this evening since you left for California. This is our evening and I don't want anything to spoil it."

The husky, intimate tone of his voice sent tingles up her spine. She felt herself drawn to him, losing herself in him. When he looked at her that way, with a crinkle of a smile in the corners of his eyes, she was reduced to Silly Putty. All reason escaped her; all determination to confess her true identity evaporated. To keep herself from melting beneath his silver gaze, she struggled to find conversation. "Is anyone at the magazine taking up a collection or planning a party of some sort for Ramon Gill? He's getting married next month," she blurted.

"No. I didn't know. I'll speak to Charlie about having a luncheon or something. Gill has been with the magazine for a long time. It's the least we can do. You're a romantic, are you?"

"All women are romantics." Sam grinned in the darkness. "Are you a romantic, Christian?" she teased.

"Of the first order. But if you tell anyone, I'll deny it. How would it look to my staff if they found out I was all mush inside?"

Sam laughed and the tension was relieved. They were both relaxed now, with a long evening ahead of them. She would tell him tomorrow that the Sam Blakely he was seeking was right here—under his nose. Right now, she needed this man who claimed he was a romantic. She needed to feel him beside her, needed his comforting words, and, at the same time, perhaps she could give him something in return. *I can't fall in love with him; I just can't.* A tiny, niggling voice warned that it was too late. She was already in love with Christian Delaney.

Christian had made reservations at a marvelous German restaurant in downtown Washington. Beer was served in lagers, and hearty pork sausages and cabbage were the main fare. All through dinner, Tyrolean musicians played their wind instruments and strolled among the tables. Samantha was mesmerized. It was immediately apparent that Christian was a familiar patron from the way he was greeted by the waiters and maître d'. The service was impeccable and the atmosphere conducive to quiet conversation. Throughout dinner, Christian kept up a cheerful banter, never once mentioning his search for one Sam Blakely. Time and again Samantha would find herself looking into his silvery-gray eyes and feeling as though she would drown in his warm, lingering looks. His gaze touched her face, her hair, her eyes, her mouth, and ignited a flurry of strange yearnings and excitement that she had never known. Reaching across the table, he touched her hand, holding it, fondling it, possessing it, as though he would never let her go.

Sam wished that dinner would never end. She preened in his attention, became breathless under his sultry glances and in the promise that was in his eyes.

Christian was just suggesting a ride along the Potomac when the pager he wore on his belt beeped insistently. His tone was full of disappointment when he excused himself to phone the office.

Sam watched his retreating back as he made his way to the phones. Suddenly, as though coming out of a dream, she began to panic. The evening was almost over! Christian would be wanting to take her home! It was hopeless. She would not lie to him or, at best, evade the truth again! She would face his rage and fury and tell him who she was. She would pray he would understand. She respected him too much to deceive him any longer. And, heaven help her, she loved him.

As she was pondering her problem and mourning over the fact that she would lose both the man she loved and the job she wanted in one stroke, he reappeared at the table. "Penny for your thoughts. Orion, something's come up at the office. I've got to go back there. It's an important break in the Mideast story. It couldn't come at a worse time!"

"Time and news wait for no man, Christian," Sam murmured regretfully, secretly relieved that once again the decision to confess all was taken from her hands.

"Come on, I'll get you home before I go back to the office," he said as he signed the check.

"You don't have to worry about me. I can take a cab home. It's all right, really." She had to tell him, but she needed his undivided attention, and this was not the time, nor the place. Or was this line of thinking another indication of her cowardice? she wondered, disgusted with herself.

"No, it's not all right. I'll take you home and then I'll go to the office," he insisted as he took her arm and led her out of the restaurant.

As they waited for the attendant to bring his car around to the front, Samantha became rigid. "This is really silly, Christian. I can take a cab right from here to my doorstep. Really. I'll be fine."

"If you're certain," Christian compromised. "Tell you what, I'll leave my car here and send for it in the morning. I'll ride in the taxi with you as far as the magazine, and I'll make sure the driver gets you home safely."

Christian climbed into the cab beside her. "I'll make this up to you, I promise—as soon as possible."

Samantha smiled reassuringly. "I don't mind, not really. There's always a next time."

Christian pulled Sam into his arms. "There's no time like the present," he whispered against her ear. And when his mouth came crashing down on hers, she felt the earth move beneath her feet. It was a long, lingering kiss, a kiss that dreams were made of. It was a kiss that held promises and soft words. Words like love, and eternity....

Breathlessly, she pulled out of his embrace and leaned her cheek against his shoulder. "God, I hate to leave you. I could hold you like this forever. I've never felt this..."

"Sh!" She silenced him by pressing her finger to his lips. The panic was rising in her breast again. She couldn't let him declare his feelings for her until she confessed her relationship with his aunt. To do otherwise would be unfair, and he would hate her for it.

CHAPTER FOUR

SAM LOOKED AT HER WRIST for the third time in less than five minutes. She had to do it. She had to tell Christian Delaney that she was the Sam Blakely in question. He had to understand. And if he didn't, she would have to work double-time to make him aware that she had nothing to do with Gemini's bequest, that she had been completely in the dark until the day the letter arrived from the lawyer.

A quick look in her tiny pocket mirror told her her face was on straight; nothing was smudged. She was glad now that she had chosen the raspberry silk dress and Halston perfume. She looked her best, and right now that feeling was paramount. Would Christian understand? Finding no answers to her tormenting questions, Sam took a deep breath and marched down the long, narrow hallway to the publisher's office. Blunt. She would tell him straight out and not mince words. Up front. No lies, no deceit. She would say it like it was and take whatever was coming to her.

Sam moistened dry lips and tapped quietly on the heavy door.

"Come in."

Sam's eyes closed momentarily and then she squared her shoulders. She was Daniel going into the lion's den. No, she was Samantha Blakely going into...

"Orion! What a pleasant surprise, and one with which I would like to start every day." How husky his voice was. How sensual his voice was. Yes, he was handsome. He was coming around the desk, ready to take her into his arms. He would kiss her and then she would tell him. No, she had to tell him first. She moved slightly out of his reach and then turned to stare at him for a brief second.

"There's something I have to talk to you about, Christian. It really can't wait another moment." Why was her voice cracking like this? *Because I care,* she answered herself.

"You sound so serious, Orion," Christian said in mock severity.

"I am serious, very serious. I tried to tell you several times, and you would always interrupt me, and then I finally lost my nerve and took the easy way out. I don't want you to do that again until I tell you what I have to…to…to say to you."

Christian's tone, as well as his expression, was both amused and indulgent. "Orion, you have my undivided attention. You may proceed. Look, I'm going to sit down so I won't tower over you."

Sam jammed her hands into the side pockets of the colorful dress so the publisher couldn't see how they were trembling. She took a deep breath and squared her shoulders. "Christian, I know that you will understand what I'm going to say because you are a man of…of… compassion. I know that you will understand that I tried on several occasions to tell you, but…what I mean is…you may at first think I was trying to…but… I wasn't…I am Sam Blakely," she finished lamely.

Christian Delaney neither moved nor spoke.

Sam rushed on. "I'm that...that dastardly person who owns fifty-one percent of this...this company. I didn't know until I got the letter from the lawyer! Say something! Please, you can't blame me! I didn't know! I don't want the fifty-one percent! I tried to tell you in the restaurant before I left for the West Coast, but you kept interrupting me. I wanted to tell you when I got back, but...I didn't mean to deceive you. It was just that things got out of hand and...and..."

Silvery-gray eyes stared at her and through her. How cold and dead they looked. There was no need for words on the publisher's part. His eyes said it all. As far as he was concerned, she, Sam Blakely, ceased to exist.

"It's not the way it seems, and I did try to explain, but you kept interrupting me," Sam said in a shaky voice. "You must believe me! I don't want this magazine or your aunt's money! I don't know why she did what she did. I'm telling you the truth. Why won't you believe me? Please," she pleaded, "don't look at me that way. I thought—I hoped—that you would be fair and understand." What was the use? He was listening to her, but he didn't hear a thing she said. It was over. She turned to leave, her legs like fresh Jell-O, barely holding her erect.

Christian's words, when they finally came, shocked her. "You'll never see a penny of my aunt's money. I'll fight you in every court in the land. Liars make poor showings in a courtroom. So be prepared."

Sam's shoulders drooped. She wasn't a liar. She wasn't. She had tried to tell him. She had wanted to tell him from the very beginning. And now, because of her willy-nilly procrastination, it was all over between the two of them. How he must hate her. Scalding tears burned her eyes as she closed the door softly behind her.

How final, how terminal the small sound was. You closed a door and part of your life was left behind.

Shoulders slumped, feet dragging, Samantha faced the long, seemingly endless corridor back to her office. Her heart was choked in her throat and the world around her seemed dark and without life. Suddenly, someone was holding her arm, shaking it.

"Orion, Orion, have you heard what's going on?" It was Ramon, and from the look of him, he was excited.

Samantha dragged herself back into the world of the living. Sudden sounds of clacking typewriters bounced into her awareness. Noise and confusion made her blink. What was going on? From the look of things, something important. Efficient secretaries were ripping papers from their machines with the speed of sound. Sam glanced around for Charlie Conway, but he was nowhere in sight. Milling reporters huddled into groups, talking excitedly.

"C'mon, Orion, get with it! Haven't you heard? Guess not. Word just came in over the teletype. Break in the Mideast crisis," Ramon told her. "I think I'm going. Cross your fingers. I missed out when it happened, and Conway told me this would be my turn."

Instantly, comprehension dawned upon Samantha. This would be the story of the decade.

Ramon, seeing the fervor shining in her face, prodded, "Get in there, Orion. See if you can get Conway to let you come along. As long as you keep your mouth shut and click your shutter the way you did in California, you can tag along with me anywhere. If I were you, I'd go in there right now and plead your case."

Sam was stunned. It was the answer to her unasked prayer. She could go away and try to forget Christian

Delaney. Lose herself in her work. When she got back, things might be straightened out. When he had time to think, Christian might decide... Oh, what was the use of tormenting herself like this? This, for now, just might be her answer. "Ramon, do you think Charlie will assign me?" she asked, a note of desperation in her voice.

"No. But it will make you feel better. Lizzie is the one who's making the travel arrangements. I've already put in a good word for you. Everyone around here knows Lizzie runs this company."

Sam looked puzzled. "Lizzie is just a secretary."

Ramon shrugged. "So? She runs this company. Even Delaney does what she says. She's one of those people who's never wrong. And Delaney inherited her when he took over. Some say she was old man Delaney's mistress, and others say she was just a platonic friend. All I know is if Lizzie books a flight for you, you go. You'll learn, Orion."

"Have you seen Charlie?"

"He's getting the roster ready. Go on, Orion. What have you got to lose?"

What did she have to lose? Nothing. Without Christian there was nothing left. This assignment could mean her emotional survival, and it was suddenly the most important thing in the world. She wanted to go, needed to go. "Ramon, are you sure? About my tagging along with you, I mean."

"Orion, you make me look good. I'm no fool. I saw your pics, and with my story that makes us a winning team. And—" he grinned, lasciviously "—you aren't half-bad to look at, either."

"Gee, thanks."

"Your turn." The journalist grinned.

"Well, you aren't half-bad yourself. I like the way you dead-dog a story. Of course, that Latin charm goes a long way with the ladies, and they're the ones who spill to you."

"It's the teeth, Orion. They flash like a beacon in the night. Gets them right here," he said, pounding his chest. "Get going before Conway thinks you aren't interested."

Sam inched her way between the milling journalists and photographers and finally made it to Charlie Conway's office with one bruised elbow and a skinned shin. Cautiously, she opened the door a crack and then walked in hesitantly. "Charlie...oh, Charlie! I want to go!" she said adamantly.

"So does everyone on the magazine. I want to go myself. Heck, I'd drop all of this in a minute, but they tell me I'm too old. How do you like that? I'm too old! Seasoned, maybe, but old—never! Those young pups out there, think they know everything. I'll let you know, Orion, at the same time everyone else knows. If it's any consolation to you, Gill was in here three times pleading your case. You're late," he snapped.

"I just got here. I really want to go, Charlie."

"Check it out with Lizzie," Charlie said, relighting his stubby cigar.

"Does she really run this magazine?" Sam asked curiously.

"I think so. She sure tells me what to do. This roster is a farce. The real story is who she's making the travel arrangements for. It's a game we play around here. When the smoke clears, we match up our lists just to see how close I came to hers. It's a stupid way of doing business, but, she hasn't goofed once in all the years I've known her. Go on, see if she's got your name on the list. Get out of here. Can't you see I have work to do?" the old man said gruffly.

Sam watched Conway pick up a dart and throw it at a penciled likeness of Lizzie that was tacked to the door. "Ha! Right on the nose!" Charlie chortled as the dart found its mark.

Lizzie was built like a dowager queen and that was how she reigned in the front reception area. Sam made her way to the marble foyer and stood staring at the woman behind the desk. Her pencil was flying over a sheaf of papers, making notes and canceling out other notes. She peered over the top of her glasses and picked out a pencil from her top knot of spiky gray curls.

"You got a problem, Orion, or do you just naturally stare at people?" she asked in a gravelly voice.

"Both, I guess. Am I on your list, Lizzie?"

"Did Gill send you in here?"

Sam nodded. "I just found out you run this place. I thought Mr. Delaney was…"

"He is. I am. I'll get back to you. Run along now, I'm busy. Ah, by the way, did the dart hit my nose or my top lip?"

Sam watched in horror as the old lady whipped out a dart and aimed it at a faded newspaper clipping of Charlie Conway. Peals of scratchy laughter erupted from the receptionist as the dart found its mark.

Panic gripped Sam's stomach muscles. Had that been a look of pity in Lizzie's eyes when she posed her question? Or was she becoming paranoid about everything? What had she been asked? Whatever it was, the woman was obviously waiting for an answer. "Yes," Sam muttered weakly as she walked back toward Ramon.

"Well?" Ramon snapped, clutching at her arm.

"She said she would get back to me. I have a gut feeling I'm not going to go, so be prepared. The gods aren't looking on me too favorably right now," Sam said morosely.

They waited for over an hour before Christian Delaney made his appearance in the newsroom.

Lizzie and Charlie stood behind Christian, each holding a slip of paper. First Charlie handed the publisher his, and then Lizzie held hers out. Sam watched, holding her breath, as Christian compared both slips of paper. "It's a tie." His eyes narrowed as he scanned the list a second time. "I want to say, here and now, that I am the one who has final approval of this list, and there are one or two changes I think should be made." Sam's heart thudded, knowing what was coming.

"According to this, Orion is the only woman selected. It's too dangerous, Lizzie. Charlie, what about Mac Williams? Orion hasn't been in the Mideast. Take her off the list."

Sam's spirits fell to her shoes. How could he do this to her in front of a room full of people? Tears stung her eyes as the journalists and photographers dropped their eyes to avoid seeing her humiliation and hurt. This was a deliberate slap in the face, his way of getting back at her. How could he do this to her! How dare he!

Sam stared at Christian Delaney, hardly believing his words. How could he humiliate her this way? And then another feeling coursed through her——that alien feeling she had come to know so well. She was hurt, hurt to the core of her being. Did he really think she wasn't good enough to go with the others? Was he really denying her the chance to go along because she was a woman, or was he getting even with her because he hated her? Tears of self-pity flooded her eyes and she gulped back a threatened sob. Her shoulders squared imperceptibly. She couldn't let him know how she felt. She was a professional, and professionals didn't weep and wail when something wasn't to their liking. She had to put on a good face and make out the best she could. Maybe he thought he was fooling the others, but she knew why she wasn't being permitted to go.

The looks on the men's faces told her all she needed to know. She was on her own. You didn't cross the boss or ever tell him what to do. It was part of their code. Christian Delaney was the publisher and president. He was supposed to know what he was doing; that's why he was a boss. Ramon Gill shrugged and walked away, the others following.

Sam's throat constricted. She had to say something. How could she just walk back to her cubbyhole office without making a fight of it? She couldn't. Her voice, when she spoke, surprised her; it was even and calm, belying the turmoil she felt. "I think I'm good enough to go with the others. It saddens me that, as my employer, you feel I'm lacking in ability…and other things, as well. I know that…"

"Spare me, Orion, whatever philosophy you're about to spiel off." Sam was stunned at the cold, arrogant look of the man as he towered over her. He was so close she could smell the faint minty aroma of his breath. "My decision stands; you remain behind. You may own fifty-one percent of this magazine, but I am still president and publisher."

"It was a mistake. I don't really own the controlling interest," Sam said, a note of panic creeping into her voice.

A muscle twitched in Christian Delaney's cheek; and, if possible, his voice was even more chilling, his eyes more steely, his stance more arrogant when he spoke. "Oh, there's no mistake; you own the controlling interest, all right. Even if you owned ninety-nine and eight-tenths percent of the stock, you still wouldn't be permitted to go with the others. It's not safe; you'd hinder the others. Regardless of what you say or think, a woman is a woman, and all the men would feel responsible for you. Get it through that airhead of yours—E.R.A. hasn't caught up over there. My orders stand. Now, get back to work before I decide to dock your pay."

Sam was mortified beyond words. She stared a moment at the publisher's retreating back and then ran to her office and slammed the door shut. Great choking sobs tore at her throat. Airhead! He had called her an airhead! He had added insult to injury. The slender shoulders shook with the intensity of her sobs. All of this was happening to her because of Gemini's generosity. Why couldn't he realize it was all a mistake? That fifty-one percent was going to make trouble for her in more ways than one. What hurt most of all was he didn't believe her; he sincerely believed that she had duped his aunt into leaving her the controlling interest in *Daylight Magazine*. He was so wrong. Why wouldn't he listen to her? Did he really hate her so much?

"I didn't do anything wrong," Sam whimpered to the empty office. "The only thing I'm guilty of is falling in love with him. I love him, I love him," she sobbed heartbrokenly. She sniffed and dabbed at her eyes and then blew her nose lustily. "I'll show him. I'll show him that I don't care about the assignment. I'll make him understand, somehow, that I don't want or need his aunt's legacy. If it takes me the rest of my life, I'll make him understand." It was a hopeless thought, and Sam knew it in her heart. Christian Delaney hated her. A chill washed over her when she remembered his steely eyes and his icy words.

ONE WEARY DAY after another passed. Sam's eyes hungered for a glimpse of the publisher as she went about the mundane chores that Charlie Conway assigned her. Once she had literally collided with him at the water cooler. She wasn't sure if she imagined it or not, but he had appeared shaken at her nearness, and for a brief second she thought he was going to reach out and take her into his arms. Instead, he had nodded curtly and strode off down the long corridor. Her heart had fluttered wildly all day long.

Sam finished her sandwich and tossed the waxed paper and half a deli pickle into the trash can when Charlie Conway's voice shouted for her attention. "Orion, do me a favor, will you? I can't seem to locate that confounded office boy. Take Mr. Delaney's lunch in to him and set it up."

"Charlie, isn't there someone else…? What I mean is, I can't do…go…in there…Lizzie—can't Lizzie do it?" She felt like a rabbit caught suddenly in a snare. She wanted desperately to see the handsome publisher, wanted desperately to… "I can't do it, Charlie!" Sam bleated.

"Guts, Orion. You can do it. You *will* do it. That's an order. Now, move it!"

Sam picked up the plastic tray with Christian Delaney's lunch on it and carried it precariously down the long corridor that led to his office. The door was partially open and she debated a second before kicking lightly with the toe of her shoe to announce her arrival.

Christian Delaney's back was to Sam as she placed the tray on the neat, uncluttered desk. She was just removing the napkin from the sandwich tray when he swiveled abruptly and knocked her off balance. The ham and rye and the two halves of the kosher pickle slid across the desk. In her attempt to reach for them, she leaned too close and fell into Christian's lap. This couldn't be happening to her. It was. Strong arms held her close, too close.

"This is one way of announcing your arrival. A simple 'Here's your lunch' would have worked just as well." The voice was controlled, with no hint of amusement in it.

Sam felt herself drain of all color. Why did she feel so weak, so...trapped? The viselike hold on her arms hadn't lessened. Her senses reeled with the scent of the man holding her. This was what she wanted, what she needed—to be near him, to have him hold her and whisper sweet words. Evidently, he was expecting her to make some comment or he would have released her. "You moved...I wasn't expecting...Charlie said there...I'm sorry," Sam muttered. In her agitation in trying to defend herself, she found herself cheek to cheek with the man holding her.

Silvery-gray eyes stared into hers, drawing her into their depths. Sam waited, wild anticipation coursing through her like a riptide. She knew he was going to kiss her, and she made no move to extricate herself from his strong hold. His lips were featherlight upon her own and she responded in kind. It was Christian who withdrew first, his eyes blazing into her own. Before she could draw a breath, his lips seared hers, sending fire through her veins. When he released her a second time, she was shaken to her very being. He must care for her; otherwise, how could he kiss her like this? Her heart soared and then plummeted when she heard his next words as he somehow thrust her from him, still keeping his hold on her arm. His voice was cold and clipped. "That was a mistake, and I apologize. Have the office boy get me another sandwich." She was dismissed.

Sam shook her head slightly to clear it. Her eyes narrowed. He had done it to her again. He had humiliated her and, worse yet, he had taken advantage of her by kissing her. Never mind that she had wanted him to kiss her, even willed it. An angry retort rose to her lips. His cold eyes were mocking her as she turned on her heel. "Yes sir, Mr. Delaney, sir." At the door she clicked her heels and snapped a salute.

The publisher's deep, mocking laugh followed her all the way back to her office. It wasn't till an hour later that she remembered to order him another sandwich. Christian Delaney wouldn't starve—he ate people alive, especially photojournalists.

HER DESK CLEARED for the day, Sam spent the remaining minutes watching the hands on the wall clock creep toward the five and twelve. Soon it would be time to go home and spend another lonely evening watching television. She knew she could work on the painting of Christian, but all the life seemed to have gone out of the project. The plain and simple truth of the matter was she couldn't bear to even pick up a brush.

Christian Delaney's voice thundered over the partition. "There must be someone around here. Where's the assignment sheet? Lizzie," he roared, "where's Matowski? Where's Blandenberg? And what happened to Jefferies and Arbeiter? Well?"

Sam rose and stood in the doorway. If the angry publisher thought he was cowing Lizzie, he was mistaken. His arrogant, insufferable attitude only worked on dimwits like herself. The man hadn't been born who could cow Lizzie.

"Matowskie is in Seattle. You sent him yourself three days ago. Blandenberg is in Israel on vacation. You approved it yourself three weeks ago. Jefferies and Arbeiter are covering an assignment in Venezuela. If you're looking for a photographer, there's one standing right behind you." Lizzie's tone was saccharine sweet, yet firm. She ran the company, and no upstart like Christian Delaney was going to intimidate her. Besides, she was sixty-nine years old, and rank did have its privileges.

Sam's heart started to pound and then she started to bristle. Just let him ignore her this time. Now she was angry. Whatever the assignment was, she wanted it. How could he turn her down this time? He couldn't. If she was all there was, he had to use her. It never occurred to her to even wonder what and where the assignment was.

The publisher's eyes went from Lizzie to Charlie Conway to Sam. He didn't bother with more than a cursory glance in her direction before he locked in with Charlie Conway. "Order the Lear jet to be made ready. The board decided that with the feedback coming in so steadily from the Mideast, we're going to take a crack at the energy problem from here. The destination is the Southwest. You're it, Orion."

Lizzie answered for her. "That's what she's here for. Two hours, Orion. Be at the airport."

"Who…who's going with me?" Sam stammered. Not that she cared. She didn't care about anything except that Christian Delaney had said she could go, that he was giving her the assignment, and Lizzie, God bless her, approved. If Christian assigned her to cover Dracula's castle, she couldn't have cared less.

"Me," came the curt reply.

Sam swallowed hard and then she grinned from ear to ear. "You got it, Mr. Delaney." Now let him make whatever he wanted out of that statement. She was going to the Southwest with him. Together, in one plane. They would be working side by side. Truth was truth. She was going to have him all to herself, and by some stroke of luck she just might be able to convince him of a few things. Whatever, she had a fighting chance now, and she was going to make the most of it.

Lizzie favored Sam with a heavy-lidded wink, and Charlie Conway shifted his evil-smelling stogie to the left side of his mouth.

CHAPTER FIVE

SAM HADN'T REALLY KNOWN what to expect when she arrived at the private airstrip on the outskirts of Baltimore, where she was to meet Christian Delaney to embark on their assignment of American energy resources, but the shining Lear jet, with its engines whining in warm-up, certainly wasn't it. And when she lugged her camera equipment and duffel bag out to the winged machine and curiously looked into the cockpit for a glimpse of the pilot, Christian answered her unspoken question.

"I'm a qualified pilot, Orion. This little beauty is all mine. Personal property; not an asset of Delaney Enterprises."

Samantha felt herself flush with anger. She wanted this assignment, but at what price? Was he going to be caustic and riddle her with his sarcasm during the entire trip? Holding back a tart reply, she threw her duffel up the gangplank and into the plane. Forcing a smile to her lips, she turned to meet his stare. "She is a beauty, Mr. Delaney, and I have every confidence in your ability as a pilot."

"Good. Then you won't mind sitting up front with me." His eyes watched her, daring her to demur.

Sam's spirits sank lower. She wanted nothing more at this point than to hide away somewhere near the tail of the plane, far away from this man who created such conflicting emotions in her. This job would necessitate working very closely with him to complete the assignment. Was she prepared to be so near him, close enough to touch, and yet, at the same time, recoiling from his presence? Inhaling deeply, as though breathing in the courage she would need, Sam reminded herself that this very same man who held such a great attraction for her was the one and the same who refused to believe her innocence concerning Gemini's will.

"I'd enjoy sitting up front," she heard herself say lightly, refusing to meet his eyes, fearful that the lie would show itself there in the windows of her soul.

"Good. Got everything? We won't be anywhere near a drugstore where you can buy flashbulbs or anything else."

Samantha bristled in spite of her resolve not to allow him to get to her. "Mr. Delaney, I'm a professional. I assure you I've got everything I need."

Her sharp tone seemed to go unnoticed. "Great. Climb aboard."

THE SILVERY WINGS reflected the gold of the sun as they leveled off at twenty thousand feet. Christian's command of the Lear was impressive, just as Sam knew it would be. Everything Christian did was with an inborn confidence and certain ability. His hands on the instruments and controls were steady and knowledgeable, and his voice was crisp and authoritative when he called in to the control tower far below.

Their first destination was a uranium mining plant in southwestern Arizona. Hours alone with Christian Delaney.

"There's a coffeemaker in the back. Want to try your hand at it?"

Wordlessly, Sam unhitched herself from the seat belt and, stooping slightly, made her way into the body of the plane and to a small counter near the tail section. Everything she needed was readily available, including coffee cream in the small refrigerator beneath the shiny counter.

As she waited for the coffee to brew, Sam sat and chewed at her thumbnail, realizing a sense of tension drain out of her. Just being near Christian set her teeth on edge. There was a sorrow that settled somewhere between her second and third rib because he believed she was a fortune hunter of the worst kind. There was nothing to say and nothing she could do to convince him that she hadn't preyed upon an old woman's sentiments.

The coffeemaker gurgled and indicated its cycle was completed. She prepared two mugs, remembering Christian preferred cream, no sugar. Cautiously, she made her way forward again and handed him the steaming mug. For an instant their fingers touched, and Sam felt a bolt of electricity shoot through her. How long had it been since he had touched her? How long since he had taken her in his arms and claimed her mouth for his own? Ages. Centuries past a lifetime.

Slowly, she sipped her coffee, covertly watching Christian's every movement. She realized his casual expertise in handling the plane. How confident he was. How masterful. It was little wonder that he had come to loathe her. This was an open, straightforward man who was used to taking up the reins of responsibility. Lies and deceit had no place in his life. He would never believe that she had tried to tell him the truth about her identity time and time again. And now, she had begun to wonder just how hard she had tried. Was it possible that she had unconsciously allowed him to interrupt her every time she was about to tell him that she was Sam Blakely? Had she been so greedy for his kisses that it had jeopardized her own honesty?

FOR WHAT WAS BEGINNING to seem like a lifetime, Samantha sat beside Christian Delaney while their plane headed due west, and the plains of America rolled beneath them. The publisher's silence was deafening. He hated her, she was certain of it. There was no use trying to explain her relationship with his aunt Gemini and the fact that she hadn't even realized the old woman's connection with Delaney Enterprises, much less connived to dupe her into writing her into the will.

If Samantha had somehow hoped that this time alone with Christian would be an opportunity to mend the wounds, she knew now how wrong she had been. She knew if Christian would turn to look at her his eyes would be shards of steel and his face would be a mask of granite.

She surveyed his uncompromising concentration out the windshield and toward the horizon. Could this be the same man who had swept her off her feet—the same man who possessed her lips with his own? Who had promised her tender moments with his eyes and offered her shelter and a loving haven with his arms?

Why didn't he say something? Anything! How could he expect to complete an assignment under these circumstances? Silently, she willed him to turn and speak to her. Instead, he fixed his steely gray eyes straight ahead and his mouth into a thin, forbidding line. He held her in contempt, and now that same contempt was filling the cockpit and choking off her air.

Sam massaged her temples, warding off a migraine. She watched Christian's every movement and saw his casual expertise in handling the plane. Samantha found it impossible to tear her eyes away from him. She memorized his profile, the arrogant set of his head above broad shoulders and powerful body. She knew every nuance of his features. Knew them and loved them. She had loved this man long before she ever knew him. Long, patient hours of working on his portrait into the lonely hours of the night when only she and his likeness shared the solitude.

She loved him. Didn't he know that? Couldn't he sense it? Feel it? How could he be so stupid and insensitive? Did he think only of the fact that Gemini Delaney had made a ridiculous gesture by willing her that large interest in the family business?

Guilty tears stung her eyes. She had had opportunities to confess to him that she was the Sam Blakely he was seeking. But she had let them go by. And now, when she had finally told him, it was too late. She had made him feel like a fool for not having known much sooner. Little wonder he thought she was a fortune hunter.

A sudden jolt shook Samantha out of her reverie. Her eyes flew to the left wing, where the engine was issuing a cloud of black smoke. Her stomach lurched warningly. She sought Christian with her eyes; panic welled within her. She saw the tenseness in his shoulders and neck and the hard set of his mouth.

"Christian! What's wrong?"

"How do I know?" he growled from between clenched teeth. "But if we're going to crash, it's not going to be from twenty thousand feet up. Hold on, I'm taking her down."

Samantha felt the pressure in her ears as the craft descended and the ground below came closer and closer.

"Where are we?" she gulped, looking for the gray skyline of a city.

"We've been out over the desert for the past hour. That's California straight ahead, Arizona below.

"Better hold on tight, Orion. Take the flotation cushion from under your seat and put it in your lap. Get your head down, way down!" His tone compelled her into immediate action.

She heard Christian try to make radio contact and send a Mayday signal. It was all happening so fast, as fast as the rush of air against the windshield as the Lear plummeted toward the earth. She heard Christian swear, trying again and again to make contact, muttering something about an electrical burnout in the instrument panel. "Hold on, Orion, we're going down!"

Long moments. Eternity. Pressure in the cockpit dropped. Her ears popped. A lifetime of prayers skated through her mind, and every one of them included Christian.

She felt the aircraft's speed decrease until she thought they must be hovering in midair. Suddenly, she felt as though the floorboards beneath her feet were rattling, shaking, grinding against something. The wheels touched the ground and the plane seemed to skid through the whirling dust as it swooshed and careened wildly. Samantha's heart was in her mouth as she pressed her head down and felt the safety belt dig into her abdomen, holding her back against the seat when the momentum was hurling her forward.

A terrible wrenching sound filled her world as the Lear tilted crazily to one side. She heard Christian swear again under his breath and the thunderous noise in her ears subsided as he cut the engines.

Cautiously, incredulously, Samantha raised her head

from the cushion. They were on the ground, and although they were tilted to one side, all forward motion had ceased. They were safe!

"This is your captain speaking." Christian laughed with wild relief from where he slumped back against his seat. "At this time I'd like to thank you for flying blind, and *Daylight Magazine* thanks you and hopes your stay in the Arizona desert will be enjoyable. I'd like to say, at this time, that the temperature is a pleasant one hundred ten degrees. Be certain to gather all your belongings and check the overhead racks so nothing is left behind."

Sam unsnapped the seat belt and crawled across the cockpit, throwing her arms around Christian. "I knew you could do it! I knew it! I prayed for both of us!" she cried, planting a wet kiss on his cheek, his nose, his eyes, and finally his mouth.

Hard hands closed around her arms, pushing her away. "Am I really to believe you prayed for the both of us, or just yourself, Orion? Think how much simpler it would be to take over Delaney Enterprises if I wasn't around to stop you!"

This couldn't be happening to her. She must be having a nightmare. When she awakened, all would be well. No, it wouldn't. Nothing was ever going to be right again. An invisible ramrod stiffened in her spine and she locked glares with her accuser. "No matter what I say or how I explain, you aren't going to believe me. I don't have to defend myself, Christian—not to you or to anyone else. You've already judged and found me guilty. I'm sorry for both of us that whatever it was we had wasn't strong enough to weather this." Was that cool, positive voice really hers? Now, when the end of her world was looming before her? The ramrod in her spine slipped beneath Christian's silvery, unblinking stare.

"Get your gear together, Orion. We can't stay here. As the captain of this plane, consider that an order. This is not time for hysterics." His voice was controlled, but there was a thinly veiled note of venom beneath it. Clearly, she had no choice but to follow his orders.

Christian hefted himself from his awkward position in the crazily lopsided cockpit and literally had to crawl through the hatch to the rear of the plane. Silently, he emptied the small refrigerator of soft drinks and a small supply of canned goods. He searched the compartment over the seats and found the one containing the first-aid kit and flashlight.

Red-faced, Sam watched him, knowing that she herself would have set out into the desert without a thought to the supplies to be found aboard the aircraft. Even in crisis, Christian kept his head. And now, here alone in the wilderness, it suddenly dawned upon her that she was completely dependent upon him. Somehow, the thought was not comforting.

THE HEAT WAS OPPRESSIVE. By shading her eyes, Sam could see Christian striding ahead in the distance. Her heart thudded and then was still. If she wanted to catch up and not lose sight of him, she was going to have to pick up her pace. And, she told herself, he had the food and drinks, not to mention the compass she had seen him discover in the first-aid kit.

Quickening her steps over the hard-packed sand, Sam seemed to be gaining on Christian's retreating figure. Keeping up that long-legged stride might have tired him. Or else he was deliberately slowing down so she could catch up with him. She only wanted to keep him in sight; she didn't want to walk beside him.

Sam's pace slackened as she wiped the perspiration

from her brow and dabbed at her neck with the tail of her shirt. This heat was worse than anything she had ever experienced. Her mouth was full of cotton balls and gritty sand. The minuscule grains were in her eyebrows and her hair, and her skin itched. She wished for a drink but would die before asking him for one of the sodas he had taken from the plane.

Suddenly, Sam's heart thumped madly as she saw Christian turn to glance at her over his shoulder. He stopped and faced her, concern written on his features. Coming abreast of him, Sam shaded her eyes against the golden glare of the sun.

"Give me your duffel, Orion." Obediently, she handed him the soft-sided bag. Dropping to one knee, she watched him rifle through it, withdrawing a spare shirt. "Here, wrap this around your head to protect you from the sun."

Clumsily, Sam struggled with the shirt, finding it impossible to do as he ordered. "You've already had too much sun," he said solemnly, taking the garment from her and doing it for her.

"I'd like to offer you something to drink, but we have to conserve whatever we have. Here, take this." He stooped to pick up a smooth pebble from near her feet, wiped it off on his shirt, and offered it to her. "Put this in your mouth. It's an old Indian trick to fool the salivary glands and bring moisture to the mouth." Sam did as ordered and, while it didn't produce the hoped-for results, her mouth didn't feel so parched.

"We'll stop now and rest. We'll continue for a few hours when the sun begins to set. Since I'm responsible for you, you'll do as I instruct. Understood?"

Samantha nodded in agreement, grateful for the opportunity to get off her burning feet. The heat was coming off the sand and penetrating her hiking boots, and she wished for a cool pool of water to put them in.

Christian led her over to a bone-dry, scrubby-looking bush of indistinct genus and faced her away from the sun. He placed the duffel under her head and ordered her to stay put. Then, taking himself to the opposite side of the bush, he settled himself down.

Tired though she was, she hesitated lying back and succumbing to sleep. She wasn't certain that Christian wouldn't leave without her, and she admitted to herself that she was afraid he might. What would she do if he took it into his head that she was more trouble than she was worth, and he left her here alone? She couldn't sleep—she didn't dare.

Back home, when she couldn't sleep, she would get out of bed and work in her darkroom or go through the stacks of old pictures she had collected. Or work on Christian's portrait, she reminded herself bleakly. Quietly, she withdrew the prized camera and squinted into the sun. Why not? There was nothing else to do, and she had a generous supply of film in her gadget bag. Why not take pictures of the desert? When she looked at them in years to come, she would remember. It wasn't fair. How could this be happening to her? There he was, mighty male animal, sleeping like a baby, and she had to stay awake because she was afraid he would leave her.

Sam focused the lens and adjusted her f-stop. She moved slowly, striving for the correct light. She turned, her intention being to snap a picture of the sleeping publisher. His features were relaxed in sleep, making him look vulnerable. Only she knew what kind of lurking monster was hidden behind those handsome features. Quickly, she snapped again and again. In those years to come she could quietly torture herself by staring at his likeness. Tears burned her eyes unexpectedly. Her feelings were too raw, too injured, to make logical thought possible.

Feeling her eyes upon him, Christian woke up with a start. He glared at her and kept his silence. Samantha felt compelled to explain. "You looked so vulnerable, so peaceful...I only wanted to capture it on film."

"A likely excuse. What you probably meant to do was bash me over the head and then you'd meet little resistance to holding on to that fifty-one percent," Christian snarled. "Well, I have news for you, Miss Photographer, you won't get rid of me that easily."

"Is that what you think? Of all the stupid, insufferable...you're detestable! I can't even look at you!" she shot back.

"You have that a little backward. It's you who's detestable. Imagine, taking advantage of a little old lady. It's criminal, do you know that? Criminal!"

"Think whatever you like. As long as I know I didn't do anything, I can live with myself and that fifty-one percent!" she cried savagely. "The only thing I was guilty of is...was...not explaining the mix-up in the first place. Change that to the only *stupid* thing I was guilty of. I grant you the whole situation appears decidedly suspicious, but you won't give me a chance to explain."

"Explain! No thank you," Christian said sourly. "I've had enough lies to last me a lifetime. Besides, I know my aunt Gemini was nobody's fool, yet you seemed to have managed to talk her out of the controlling interest in the family business. Heaven only knows what you'd try to talk me out of before this trek through the desert is over."

Sam backed off a step, hardly believing what she had

heard. She flinched as though she had been physically struck. She wouldn't cry; she refused to give him that satisfaction. Besides, when you were dead inside, everything stopped working, even tears.

Christian Delaney wasn't finished upbraiding her. "And when we get back to Washington, consider yourself dismissed. Don't even bother coming into the office. You're through!"

The words and his anger vibrated along Sam's nerve endings and she felt her fingers curl into claws. The invisible ramrod in her spine stiffened. "You can't fire me! I didn't do anything! I'm good at what I do, and you know it!"

He leaped to his feet and stared down at her, his mouth fixed into an implacable line of fury. "I don't know any such thing. It's my magazine, and I don't want you to have any part of it." His voice had dropped two octaves and held a barely controlled rage. He was an imposing figure, glaring down at her: tall, lean, powerful.

"I have an unbreakable contract. Gemini saw to that. You try to fire me and I go to court. I'll charge you with sexual harassment!" What was she saying? Was she crazy? At the malevolent expression on his face, Sam stepped backward.

Christian blanched. His fury was barely controlled. His white-knuckled fist reached down and picked up his canvas bag and slung it over his shoulder. Turning away from her, he stomped off, dark head lowered over hunched shoulders.

Following behind at a safe distance, Sam seethed inwardly. Had she really said all those things? From the expression on his face, she had not only said them, but he had believed her. As if she would ever do any such thing. She didn't want his company or his money. She had lashed out in self-defense, aiming to stun him, hurt him. Any mean and hateful thought that had flown into her head, she had spit out through her mouth. It was one thing to defend herself, to hurt someone, but it had been totally unnecessary to keep sticking in the knife and twisting it for emphasis.

"There's one other thing, Mr. Delaney," she called to his retreating back. "I want to go on record as saying that I detest people who have the power to shatter other people's dreams and then actually go ahead and do it. You are one of those people! First, you let Gemini down by putting your business first instead of being there at the end when she needed you. And now you suspect the worst about me and refuse to listen to any explanation."

Even as she watched him, he stopped dead in his tracks. Every muscle in his body tensed and he was ready to spring like a wild jungle cat. Fear balled up in her throat, choking off all air. She had gone too far. Reminding him that he hadn't been home in time for Gemini's last days and then her funeral had been a low blow, and it didn't appear he was going to take it lying down.

Paralyzed with terror, she saw him turn. He placed one foot in front of the other, stalking her. Unable to move, unable to think, she was mesmerized by his approach. Threatening, lethal, determined, he closed the distance between them. Powerful, potent and ruthless, he sighted his quarry and hypnotized her with the predatory glare in his silver-gray eyes as though she were a jackrabbit paralyzed by oncoming headlights.

Samantha gasped for breath and felt the shock of motion return to her limbs. She turned and ran, throwing one leg in front of the other, escaping, scrambling away as though a hound of hell were on her heels. And he was.

Her feet slipped in the sand; her breath came in ragged gasps. Her duffel and camera bag banged against her legs in an unrelenting rhythm. Just when she thought that her heart would burst, she felt herself being pulled backward and her legs sprawling out at awkward angles.

Together they rolled over the shifting sands. He bore his weight on top of her, stilling her struggles. She was locked against his heaving chest, feeling his labored breaths against the side of her face.

She felt him draw away, felt his gaze upon her. Panic tearing through her, she cautioned a glance at his face. His eyes were burning through her to her very core. Fear subsided; there was no menace in his silver-shadowed glance now. Instead, there was something else there, something she didn't dare put a name to.

With a force that was almost violent in its intent, he covered her body with his own. Pressing down, bearing down, stilling her struggles and kicks, he held her, dragging her arms upward over her head to prevent her from tearing at his face. Her breathing came in pants and ended in an inconsolable groan of hopelessness.

Deliberately, with barely concealed menace, Christian glared down at his prey. He studied her face for a long, unendurably long moment. Their eyes locked—hers with trepidation, and his with victory. He lowered his head, aware that she was incapable of movement, and his mouth came crashing down upon hers.

The desert sand shifted beneath her weight, and Christian shifted his length to hold her captive. His lips possessed hers and awakened her already heightened senses. Samantha's world became full of Christian. The taste of him, the feel of him, the power of him—they all assaulted her awareness. His sensual demands excited and aroused and ignited her passions.

The heat of the sun was dimmed by the desire that blazed between them. His intimate exploration of her mouth sent tingles of pleasure down her spine. His hands released her arms, allowing them to wind around his neck, holding embracing, answering his.

The touch of his hands aroused and inspired a slow curl of heat that emanated from her offered body and consumed them. He tasted her flesh, where her shirt revealed it, all the way down to the soft swell of her heaving breasts.

His excursion of the smooth curves of her body was sure and designed to please, as though they had roamed and discovered many times before this. The fires licked at Samantha's senses, tearing down her defenses, allowing her to forget all else besides being here, this minute, with Christian, loving Christian.

She had never felt so alive, so vibrant, as she did when she was in his arms, and she knew with a certainty that the only death that would ever exist for her was to be separated from this man who could sizzle her passions and awaken her desires.

His fingers were in her hair, on her throat, teasing the pleasure points beneath her ear. Each of his movements was created and drafted to overwhelm her and to ensure his complete and total possession. A tide of desire ebbed over her objections. There were no objections. There was nothing—only Christian, the man she loved and wanted.

Her back arched, her arms held him close, her lips answered his, and when she felt him draw back and roll over, pulling her with him, she gladly followed. Their legs tangled, their breath mingled, and with a wanton abandonment she undid the buttons of her shirt, allowing him complete access to the heated flesh beneath. With authority his fingers wound through the silky strands of her hair, pulling her head back while his lips made a heady progression along her throat to the valley between her breasts.

Desire became a fire, white-hot and searing them together in a wild and lusty experimentation of lips and hands. On top of him as she was, she was aware of his lean, muscular body between her knees. She felt the sun burn into the newly exposed skin of her back, matched only by the even hotter touch of Christian's lips on her breasts.

Samantha looked down into his eyes, feeling as though she was bathed in molten silver and golden sands. A hidden spring of emotion bubbled to the surface as she whispered, "I never knew love could be like this."

Suddenly, she felt him stiffen beneath her. His hands ceased their tender excursion of her flesh, and his mouth, pressed against hers, became hard and unyielding. Pulling away, staring down into his face, she saw his gray eyes harden and become like forged steel.

"Love, Orion? I thought you called it sexual harassment!"

Sam pulled away from him and struggled to her knees. Wounded beyond belief, she fumbled with the buttons of her shirt, covering herself from his scrutiny. How could she have been so stupid? Did she want this man so much that she could forget her own self-respect?

Christian narrowed his eyes to slits. She watched his lips tighten into a grim, white line. "Why were you taking pictures of me?" he demanded.

A sob rose to Sam's throat. If she answered him, he

would know how close to tears she was. She turned her face to the side and clenched her hands into tiny fists.

"I asked you a question. Answer me!" Christian thundered.

Through superhuman effort she submerged a sob. If she could only stop her body from trembling. Her mind raced; she would not, not ever, admit to this man that she had wanted his picture so she could remember him when he was most vulnerable.

Christian lunged suddenly, reaching out a long arm and pulling her against his massive chest. Samantha's face was within a hairsbreadth of his. Fascinated, she watched a muscle twitch in his cheek. He was holding her much too tight—too tight to breathe. Her breath was coming in short, ragged gasps as Christian cupped her head, with its tousled hair, in his big hand, forcing it back at an awkward angle. His voice was soft and full of menace as he stared down into her tear-moistened eyes.

"You would have allowed me to make love to you a moment ago," he said huskily. He thrust her from him; his voice was tight and bitter. "It won't work, Orion. If you don't believe or accept anything else, believe that I will never permit you to take control of Delaney Enterprises."

Anger and humiliation ripped through Samantha. She didn't deserve this treatment, but she had no defense. He would never believe her, no matter what she said or what she did. She wanted to lash out at him, tell him that she would have given herself to him because she loved him. Not money or his publishing empire. Only Christian. The words never found their way to her lips. She could only stand there with her eyes cast down at the dry, arid ground, and only sheer determination helped her choke back the tears.

A long moment of silence crept between them as he waited for her answer. His eyes bore through her expectantly, and when Samantha found the courage to meet them, she was surprised to find a dark yearning in his gaze. But it was fleeting, and when he decided she had no reasonable answer for her actions, he turned away.

Tears were flowing wildly down Sam's cheeks as she stuffed the camera into its case. She was careful to keep her back to Christian so he wouldn't see how vulnerable she really was. She couldn't allow him to find her with her defenses down again. The hurt was too great, too crippling.

Sam's tears and stuffy nose were replaced with hiccups as she trudged behind Christian. The only thing that made the trek bearable was the pleasure she was going to have when she handed over the sealed envelope in the publisher's own safe. She'd tear the check up before his very eyes. Then she would tear up her contract with *Daylight Magazine.* If Christian Delaney didn't want her, then she didn't want him, either! Even as she thought it, a fresh wave of hiccups seized her, punishing her for the lie. She would spend her life wanting Christian Delaney, and she knew it.

CHAPTER SIX

SAMANTHA WAS SURPRISED how chill and cold the nights in the desert could become after the broiling heat of the day. She and Christian were camped for the night beside a rare outcropping of ancient rocks that still managed, somehow, to hold a little of the sun's heat. They both knew it was a temporary state of affairs since the sun had only gone down a little over an hour ago, and soon those same rocks would be clammy and cold—as cold as the stars that were beginning to twinkle in the velvet blackness of the night.

Her scanty knowledge of outdoor living seemed grossly inadequate now, when it was really being put to the test. Thank goodness for Christian. He, at least, had had the foresight to realize they would need a fire for warmth, if not for the light. So, during their interminable walk he had instructed her to gather dried vegetation when it was available. Their northeast journey had taken them closer to the foothills where the terrain had given way from loose sand to a rocky foundation. There was much more protection from winds and an ample supply of dried, scrubby bushes whose underbrush snapped off easily in the hand.

Working together, they gathered rocks to make a fire ring, and with the cigarette lighter from his pocket, they ignited the brush, feeding the fire from time to time to maintain it.

She was silent as she watched Christian work, and she wondered if he felt she was foolish because she didn't think of this small comfort herself. Out of his duffel he withdrew several packages of cheese crackers and an already-opened can of soda. It was tonic water, and the bitter liquid was more refreshing to their thirst than the sweeter soda that Christian had also taken from the plane's small refrigerator.

Sam settled down on the far side of the fire and after a moment Christian brought her the first-aid kit he had retrieved from the compartment over the seats. "Poke through this, will you, Orion? I've already taken the compass out, and that's what we've been following. Maybe there's something else we could use." Sam looked up, surprised by the almost friendly tone of his voice. Maybe, just maybe, if there was nothing else they could salvage of their relationship, they could develop a camaraderie and help each other through this uncertain situation of being stranded in the desert, miles away from anywhere.

Her hopes were dashed when Christian spoke again. "That's woman's stuff; I don't know a bandage from a snake-bite kit."

Angrily, Sam snapped open the metal lid. Of all the chauvinistic...just because she had long hair and wore lipstick didn't signify that all she was good for was "woman's work"!

First of all, there was a second compass. Wordlessly, she tossed it over to Christian, who immediately checked it against the one in his pocket and nodded his head confidently. Next, Sam dug out a first-aid cream for small cuts. Happily, she opened the plastic tube and smeared the soothing lotion on her weather-dried face, satisfied with the immediate results. Since they had suffered no injuries, not even minor scratches, she had no immediate use for the various ointments and iodines and bandages. But at the bottom, folded into a flat rect- angle, enclosed in an envelope of clear plastic, was a shock blanket—a thin, aluminum-gray nylon sheet designed to keep in thermal body heat. It would appear the nights wouldn't be so cold, after all. Happily, she displayed her find to Christian. "You take it," he told her. "I'll make do with the extra clothes in my duffel."

The extra shirts and light jacket that were stowed in her duffel bag were further protection against the cold. She may have to go to sleep hungry and tired, but she wouldn't be cold. As Christian banked the fire, Sam wearily made a pillow of her duffel bag and tried to assume a comfortable position to sleep. The shock blanket was light, but within a few minutes she happily admitted that it lived up to its purpose. Turning on her side, she was soon fast asleep.

Sometime during the early morning hours, when the sun was just creeping over the horizon, Samantha awoke with a start. Something was holding her and preventing her from rolling over onto her back. Chris- tian. Apparently, the cold night air had had its effect on him, and he decided to share the shock blanket with her.

His arm was flung carelessly around her in sleep, the tips of his fingers just resting on the swell of her breasts. His body had molded itself around her in sleep, and they were nested together like two spoons. His breath feathered against her cheek, and she realized that somehow, during the night, in their exhausted sleep, he had slipped his arm beneath her head and she was resting on his shoulder. For a long, glorious moment,

Samantha knew the joy of awakening in the arms of the man she loved. *Did love,* she corrected. She couldn't, wouldn't allow her defenses to slip now. Knowing what being devastatingly hurt by Christian's unrelenting suspicions could do to her, she was not going to put herself in that position again. To contradict the adage, once was certainly enough!

Christian seemed to sense her wakefulness, or had he already been awake and watching her sleep. The thought was disconcerting and Sam flushed as she thought of how his fingertips had rested so close to her breasts.

"Rise and shine, Orion. We've got a long day ahead of us."

Obediently, she hauled herself out from under the shock blanket and away from his embrace. Immediately, the morning air felt chill and hostile. Or was it just because she had moved away from this man whose masterful confidence in even the most precarious of situations could make her feel protected and secure?

They decided to save a few remaining packages of crackers and cheese for later and broke camp to travel while the air was still cool. Mile after mile, Sam trudged along behind Christian. His tall, straight back became a directional for her, a beacon in the vastness of the desert. She found she was capable of losing all track of time. Glancing at her watch time and again, she realized how slowly the minutes passed when one was miserable and exhausted. She rolled the smooth pebble around in her mouth—having decided it did help—and thought about the two remaining cans of warm soda in his duffel.

The sun had reached its apex, and Christian was searching for a spot of shade where they could rest through the worst heat of the day. He was less than successful, finding only a low stand of sun-burned, leafless trees that had probably been around since the time of Christ.

"This will have to do. Take something out of that duffel and cover your head." He had already stripped off his shirt and draped it, Arab fashion, over his own head.

Following instructions, Samantha then dropped to the ground and lay down with her arm over her eyes. The thought of the wonderfully wet soda was becoming an obsession. After a few minutes she sat up, knowing her sudden movement was noticed by Christian. Working fast and furiously, she dug through her duffel and withdrew the shock blanket and the first-aid kit.

Reading her thoughts, Christian jumped to his feet, and together they carefully laid the blanket over the stunted trees, securing it at the corners with gauze bandage. Sam noted how well they worked together in an amiable silence. Once or twice their hands touched, and Samantha felt as though she'd been jolted by an electric charge. Whatever she felt for this man, it definitely was not indifference.

Settled close together in the shade they had created, they shared a few sips of the precious soda. It didn't quench their thirst, but it was wet.

They continued their march through the coolest part of the day, when the reds and golds of the sun slanted across the ground, making long, dark shadows of every bush and rock. When the sun dipped below the horizon, and it became too dark to walk safely, they again set up camp. This time, Christian gathered the rocks to make a fire circle while Sam scrounged for dry wood.

When Sam was digging through the duffel, the unmistakable sound of metal against metal clinked.

That night they felt as though they'd feasted like kings: half a can of soda, a package of crackers, and half a can of deviled ham. The icy stars twinkled down on them, seeming friendlier than the night before.

Once again, Christian banked the fire so it would burn slowly throughout the night. Sam settled herself down, and placing her head on the duffel, she lay back and threw the thin shock blanket over her.

A moment later Christian crawled in beside her and, back to back, they drifted off to sleep.

Sometime during the night Sam awakened to find her head nestled on Christian's broad shoulder and her arm thrown carelessly over his chest. Her right leg was cradled between both of his, and he held her lightly in an embrace. It was dark, too dark to see him. The fire had almost completely gone out, and the desert night air on her face was cool in contrast to the warmth they generated beneath the blanket. But she knew somehow that Christian was not asleep. She sensed his awareness as though it were a tangible thing.

"You sleeping?" she heard him whisper. She remained silent, pretending sleep. If she admitted she was awake, she would have to move, have to take her arm from around him and take her head from his chest. She listened, hearing the thump of his heart, hearing the slow intake of his breath.

It was peaceful, so peaceful, and they cuddled together beneath the blanket as though they'd slept together for every night of their lives.

Tenderly, he turned to face her; she could feel his breath upon her cheek. Softly, softer than the night air, he grazed her cheek with his lips.

More than anything, she wanted to turn, capture his lips with her own, taste his kiss and feel his arms tighten

around her. But the thought of him accusing her of
seducing him, of trapping him, of making love to him
and making him love her just to get her hands on his
money and the Delaney empire was too great. Her humiliation would be beyond bearing.

Still feigning sleep, Samantha sighed deeply and
turned over on her side, facing away from Christian. In
the darkness, she squeezed her eyes shut and a single
tear of regret escaped from behind her long, upswept
lashes.

Christian stirred, turning toward her, snuggling
close, his body pressed against hers, spoon fashion.
His arm wrapped around her and she relished the comforting warmth, the gentle gesture. Long into the night,
to the first break of dawn, Samantha lay quietly, determined to remember this gentle truce into the long, dark
future.

FOUR MORE DAYS passed and the quiet truce between
Samantha and Christian continued. But just beneath
the surface, lying like a tiger stalking its prey, were the
differences between them. Samantha had surrendered
the need to explain about Gemini, and Christian didn't
mention it.

The Hasselblad camera she had inherited from her
father became part of a game they played. During the day
whenever an interesting ground formation or light study
came to Samantha's attention, she stopped, took out the
camera, and snapped away. She took several pictures of
Christian as their journey progressed and he had come
to the point where he even good-naturedly posed for her.
He had sprouted a scrubby beard, and his hair was
unkempt, as were his clothes. But he now sported a wonderful bronze tan that resembled newly minted copper.

Samantha herself had traded her long-sleeved khaki shirt and slacks for a brief costume of halter top and shorts for an hour or so each morning, and Christian's tan was rivaled only by her own.

The first-aid cream she had found in the kit was a wonderful protection against the drying heat of the sun as far as her face was concerned. She was determined not to return to Washington dried out like a prune, with only her hands and face kissed by the sun. She supposed she was being foolish, and Christian called her a sun worshipper, but vanity won out.

Several times when they stopped at noonday, she had entrusted her camera to Christian and he snapped pictures of her while she posed for him. They laughed that when they finally returned to D.C. and looked at the pictures, it would seem as though they had shared a vacation in the sun. Samantha fleetingly wondered if his casual statement meant that the wounds between them were healing.

CHAPTER SEVEN

EARLY MORNING STARS were still visible in the sky when Christian awakened her. Dragging herself from sleep, Samantha was forced to leave the warmth of the thin blanket. While Christian went about covering the fire with loose earth, she quickly ran a brush through her hair and straightened her clothing.

"If I'm correct," Christian said, breaking the silence, "we should be out of this wilderness within the next two days. California should be right over those hills in the distance."

His words should have been encouraging; instead, they filled Sam with a sense of dread. Civilization and home didn't hold the promise she had wished for at the beginning of this adventure when the plane had gone down. Civilization and home now meant being away from Christian. Their camaraderie had developed out of a mutual dependence on one another. Once back home, that relationship would end and Christian would send her out of his life forever.

As they packed their belongings into the two duffels, Christian shook a soft-drink can experimentally, a frown creasing his face. It had taken all their willpower to refrain from emptying the can of its last few sips of liquid. The scowl on his face communicated to Samantha the seriousness of their situation. The distant hills seemed so far away, too far and too long to be without water or some other liquid to ward off total dehydration.

Glancing in her direction and realizing that he had transmitted his worst fears, Christian soothed, "Come on, now, it's not as bad as all that. We're well into the foothills now. There's bound to be a water source, no matter how small."

Samantha smiled weakly, running her tongue over cracked, dry lips. How would they ever find water in this huge, vast wilderness? The outcroppings of rock were so numerous that they could climb right past a tiny spring and never notice it. It seemed Christian wasn't going to allow her time to worry. He helped her load her duffel, slung her precious camera case over his own shoulder, and pointed her off along the trail they had been following for the past two days.

Hours passed; the sun climbed the sky in a wide, pepper-dry arc. With each hour the trek became more unbearably hot. Even the wind that stirred the dust and threw it in their faces was dry and hot. Still Christian encouraged her to go on. She knew without a doubt that without his strength she could have given up hope days ago, out beneath the burning sun, brain scorched, helpless.

When they stopped to rest later in the afternoon and when they had consumed the last of the too-sweet, flat, nevertheless wet, soda remaining in the last can, Christian pulled his navigating map out of his duffel. As he studied it for the umpteenth time, Samantha saw him look upward, searching the sky. She knew he couldn't be looking for a search plane. That possibility had already been discussed and discarded. The itinerary had been indefinite, and waiting for someone at *Daylight Magazine* to become concerned about their whereabouts and begin a search would be foolish. And deadly.

"What are you looking for, Christian?" she asked as his eyes once again scanned the bright blue sky.

"Birds."

"Birds? You…you don't mean vultures…do you?" she finished weakly.

"No, birds. They need water, too, you know, and some of the bigger ones feed on rabbits and wood-chucks, which also need water. Usually, birds roost near a water supply, and in late afternoon they usually head home." Even as he spoke, a clutch of high-flying figures dotted the sky.

"I've been watching them for some time. According to my map, the treeline of these foothills is just a little way off. Get it, Orion? Trees. Birds?"

"Let's go, then," Sam said as she struggled to her feet. "We still have a couple of hours of daylight to search."

"Atta girl," Christian praised as he helped her sling her duffel over her shoulder. "Say a prayer and keep your eye on those birds."

The trek had become more difficult now that their trail took them on an incline. Soon Sam was able to see a line of scrubby trees and the underbrush looked thicker, more plush, somehow. Christian kept his vigil on the sky, leading Sam upward and to the right, to the west.

By some miracle that Samantha was never able to fathom later, she found herself at the top of a rise, leaning heavily upon Christian's arm, and below her, barely visible in the thicket surrounding it, was a beau-tiful clear rivulet of water that reflected the sun's fading red-gold rays.

SAMANTHA SAT ACROSS from Christian, feeling better than she had in days. The tiny rivulet had quenched their thirst and had miraculously replaced itself from a water source that fed it before spilling over onto rocks and disappearing into the earth.

Handing Samantha a handkerchief that had been dipped in the water and wrung out Christian smiled. "Tomorrow morning, we'll follow the direction of the water. It's my guess that farther up in the hills there's a wonderful spring, and perhaps even a little waterfall."

"You mean we might even be able to bathe?" Samantha asked hopefully.

"That's my bet."

When Sam fell asleep that night, before exhaustion overcame her, she dreamed of the spring and prayed for a waterfall.

In the morning, before the sun had barely skipped over the horizon, both Sam and Christian were eagerly on their way to discover the mother stream. There were times when the little river went underground and became difficult to follow. Other times, they could actually measure it growing in size.

Shortly after noon, they found it. Water. In all its glory. The sun danced over it, creating millions of shimmering lights in its dark blue depths. There was even the prayed-for waterfall, although it was only a few feet in height and was hardly more than a trickle.

"What did I tell you?" Christian laughed triumphantly. "The lady ordered a waterfall, and there it is."

"Somehow, I think I should have made my requirements more specific," Sam teased, already pulling off her shoes for the anticipated plunge into the shimmering pool.

Heedless of Christian's presence, she stripped down

to her bra and bikini panties and leaped into the pool. The water was cool, actually cold, and took her breath away. After diving below the blue surface once again, she came up for air, giggling in delight.

"Do you sleep with your socks on, too?" Christian laughed, calling her attention to himself.

It was then that she saw he had already discarded his socks and boots, stripped off his shirt, and was unbuckling his pants.

"What are you doing?"

"Same as you, only with less."

Squealing with embarrassment, Samantha dove once again and came up on the far side of the pool. When she surfaced she saw that Christian was already up to his waist in the water, and the pile of clothing on the bank attested to the fact that he was naked.

"Why so embarrassed?" He laughed. "Listen, Orion, I'll make a deal with you. You wash my back and I'll wash yours."

"Ha! A likely story. You must think I'm pretty dumb to fall for a deal like that!"

Christian laughed. "Why not? Things got to be pretty nice between us out there on the desert. As a matter of fact, there were some nights there when you were pretty darned friendly."

Sam flushed. His manner was only half-teasing; his eyes were telling her something else altogether. "Christian, I expect you to behave like a gentleman. You keep to your side of the pool and I'll keep to mine."

"Talk about likely stories," he said, advancing on her. "More likely you'll take over fifty-one percent."

Staggering beneath the weight of his words, Samantha stepped backward. It had been so long since Christian had accused her of duping Gemini out of his inheritance that she had almost forgotten that the argument existed. The careless sting of his words and the decreasing distance Christian was putting between them sent a spur of panic into her chest. She stood, wading toward the far side of the pool where the water was more shallow. Beneath the sheer material of her bra, which was even more revealing when wet, Samantha's breasts were firm, and the rosy crests were erect from the coolness of the water. She saw Christian's eyes drift to them, his pleasure evidenced by his sultry look.

Still he advanced on her, closing the distance between them. In defense, not in play, she splashed him, heaving quantities of water at his head. He bent, grasping her knees, and pulled her down, the water closing over her head. Whooping for revenge, Samantha splashed and tormented him by threatening to run from the pool and steal his clothing. "Then see what kind of macho image you create running through the desert stark, staring naked!"

Laughing, Christian captured her and threatened to dip her under again. Screaming for mercy, Sam clung fiercely to him, her arms locked around his neck, her face pressed close to his.

Suddenly, it seemed as though time ceased to tick. Nothing, no one, existed in the whole world, only the two of them. Gently, he embraced her, cradling her head in one hand and supporting her back with the other. Backward, back, he dipped her and into her line of vision swept the sky and the scudding clouds. Slowly, deliberately, he bent his head, beads of water shining on his dark hair. Closer and closer his mouth came to hers.

Samantha gave her lips without reservation. She

knew she would always give herself to this man,
knowing with her whole heart and soul that he truly
loved her. If only he would admit it—to her, to himself.
She knew with that one, gentle kiss that she could never
belong to another.

Christian lifted his head, questions in his silvery-
gray eyes, his brows furled together over the bridge of
his nose. He disengaged her arms from around his neck
and stepped away from her.

"The water's getting cold," he growled, making
her wonder if he was half as angry with her as he was
with himself.

LATE THAT AFTERNOON, Samantha began to gather their
freshly washed clothing from the surrounding bushes
on which she had placed them to dry. She glanced over
at Christian, who was busy gathering firewood with
which to roast a small rabbit that he had successfully
trapped earlier. When Sam had first seen the pathetic,
limp little carcass before Christian skinned and dressed
it, she swore she wouldn't touch a bite of it. Now, with
her stomach complaining with hunger, she knew she
would set her squeamishness aside.

As they had gone about their chores to make a comfortable camp for the night, there had been little com-
munication between them. Christian seemed to be
pondering his own thoughts and she was still remembering his remark about taking over of fifty-one percent of
the pool. Money. Why did everything have to come down
to money? *Gemini,* Sam said to herself, *you don't know
what a curse that legacy has been. Why, for heaven's
sake, did you do it? You must have had a reason, but for
the life of me I can't think what it could have been.*

When the first stars were shining in the velvet-black

sky, and the little fire was sputtering into glowing embers, Samantha rested against the rocks and patted her midsection. Much as she hated to admit it, the roasted rabbit was the best meal she could remember ever eating.

"I was afraid you'd be too squeamish to eat." The sudden sound of his voice in the still night startled her.

"Only my sensibilities are squeamish. My stomach had other ideas." She tried to keep her voice light while measuring his mood. There were times that to say Christian's moods were mercurial was an understatement.

"Orion, I've been thinking. Do you really mean what you say—that you never wanted and still don't want your inheritance of Delaney Enterprises?"

Sam's eyes widened. "Of course. I know I've never had a right to that inheritance. I still don't know why Gemini did that. It certainly had nothing to do with her feelings for you. She adored you; you know that."

"Well, I've got my own ideas about Aunt Gemini. However, if you listened closely to the terms of the will, there's an addendum to be read in the near future. Also, it forbids you to either sell your shares or to sign them away."

Now Sam's interest was definitely piqued. "I remember something to that effect."

"Now, before you go off the deep end, Orion, hear me out. If my calculations, and also my navigational skills, are correct, right over that ridge is California. If you're sincere about the inheritance, you'll marry me there. Community property laws would relieve you of twenty-five and one-half percent of Delaney Enterprises, still leaving you a rich woman, but putting the family business back into my control."

Stunned, Samantha leaped to her feet. "What are

you trying to do? Test me? I've already told you I don't want it—*any* of it! Take it! Take it all!"

Christian's hands grabbed her arms painfully. "I can't take it, Orion. And you can't give it to me. You can't even sell it to me. This is the only way."

Samantha looked up into his face. There was a shadow in his eyes, a shadow she was certain wasn't created by the moonlight. There was an urgency in his voice she had never heard there before, and as the full reality of his proposal dawned on her, she thought her heart would break. Marry him? She would have cheerfully followed him to the end of the earth just to hear him say he loved her. Now, the thing she had wanted most ever since the first moment she had set her eyes on Christian Delaney had been made a mockery. A sham. Lowering her head so he couldn't read the pain in her eyes, she nodded, unable to hold back the biting words that she threw up in defense of her emotions. "As you say, I'd still be a rich woman. I'll go to sleep tonight dreaming of how I'll spend all that money—if we ever get out of this predicament alive, that is." Even to her own ears, her voice was dead sounding and unconvincing.

"Oh, we'll get out of this alive, all right," Christian said positively. "Come over here. I want to show you something." Unceremoniously, he led her to the top of the rise where he had been gathering firewood. Off in the distance, in the direction he was pointing, he told her to watch. After what seemed an endless moment, a sharp light appeared in the distance and swept across the horizon.

Not comprehending what she was seeing, Sam looked baffled.

"It's the highway, Orion. It's the road back to civilization!"

That night, while Christian slept, Samantha lay awake, huge silent tears dropping onto her cheeks.

CHAPTER EIGHT

LOS ANGELES AIRPORT was a hub of confusion, and Samantha followed closely behind her new husband as they struggled through the crowd of businessmen and tourists. The confusion surrounding her was insignificant compared to the bewilderment she was feeling. So much had happened in the past three days that she believed she would never again gain a firm grip on reality.

Christian led her to a seat near Gate 53, where they would board their plane taking them back to Washington, D.C., and then murmured something about picking up a few magazines.

As he walked away, Samantha sat amidst the flurry of arrivals and departures as she reflected over the events that had led to her becoming Mrs. Christian Delaney. After trekking out of the hills and hitching a ride on the highway, they had found themselves in the little California town of Primo. While she had sat by, Christian had called the offices of *Daylight Magazine* and made several other quick phone calls. A quick shopping trip through Primo's minuscule business district and then a visit to the City Hall where they applied for their marriage license. Then Christian had taken her to the town's medical clinic, where she had stayed for rest and treatment from their desert ordeal.

That was the last she had seen of Christian until he had checked her out of the clinic and then taken her to the magistrate's office, where they were married. Next was a chartered plane flight to Los Angeles and the airport.

A rapid machine-gun fire of events that were fuddled and baffling had brought her to the here and now. Mrs. Christian Delaney. A marriage of convenience. A marriage to prove that she wasn't the gold digger he accused her of being. A marriage that was a sham.

Aboard the jetliner that would take them back East, Samantha watched Christian and she saw that it wasn't until they were airborne that he relaxed. She hadn't realized just how uptight he had been. And he looked so tired. Drawn and fatigued. Suddenly, she wanted to cradle his head to her breast and whisper comforting words. She wanted to tell him she loved him and please not to contemplate divorce once they were back in Washington.

If sleep were the order of the day, she might as well do as Christian was doing. She slept fitfully, her dreams invaded by Christian Delaney chasing her across the desert. His sun-bronzed face was contorted in rage as he shouted angry words at her. Tripping and falling, she raced through the sand, screaming and yelling, begging him to believe her. *Let me explain!* she shouted over and over. *At least hear me out!* He was gaining on her, faster, faster. Her heart thundered as she fell in the sand, unable to get to her feet to escape him. *You don't understand. I had nothing to do with Gemini's will! I didn't even know about it. Listen to me! Why won't you believe me? Please, please love me!*

Samantha shuddered and woke up to see Christian leaning over her, a strange look on his weary face. "You were having a nightmare," he explained.

She felt disoriented, shaken, remembering the vivid dream. Had she cried out? "I'm sorry if I woke you up," she said quietly, trying to fathom the expression in his eyes.

"You didn't wake me up. Are you all right now?"

Was that concern she heard in his voice? Instead of answering him, she closed her eyes again, feigning sleep. From beneath her heavily fringed lashes, she watched as he settled himself in the seat. She had never actually seen a man's shoulders slump before, indicative of defeat. She must be wrong, she told herself. It was merely fatigue. Men like Christian Delaney were never defeated.

Now that she was married, her life was bound to be different somehow. Even though her marriage would never be consummated. Even though it would quickly end with divorce. When they arrived back in Washington, she would go her way and he would go his. Lawyers would handle everything. There would be no chance meetings, no pounding hearts, no tears for what might have been.

IN THE *DAYLIGHT MAGAZINE* offices the marriage between Christian Delaney and resident photographer Orion was completely misinterpreted and met with overwhelming good wishes and congratulatory handshakes. Neither Christian nor Samantha explained that the real reason behind the marriage was to relieve Samantha of the twenty-five and one-half percent of Delaney stock in order to return a controlling interest to the publisher.

Sam deduced that Christian must have made the announcement of their nuptials by phone from California because Lizzie and Charlie seemed to have planned the whole shebang. There were canapés and champagne and well wishes all around. When a toast was made to the new bride and groom, Christian pleased his staff by planting a kiss on Samantha's lips.

It was with relief that Sam noticed Charlie pull Christian away from the festivities on urgent office business. Seizing the opportunity to escape the festivities, Sam gathered up her camera case and slung it over her shoulder. It was time to go home. She frowned. Where exactly was home? Home was the basement apartment next door to Gemini's where she paid the rent. And then she must make arrangements to have the cats returned to her. They were, after all, still her responsibility until the respective attorneys settled the question of their custody.

Sam laid the camera case on the nearest chair. How could she have forgotten? Christian Delaney said she was fired. That meant she had to clean out her desk and take her belongings with her. She might as well do it now and be done with it. This way she wouldn't have to make another trip back to the office and chance a stray meeting with her publisher husband. It would be clean and quick. Forget all those brave, indignant things she had said and thought about on the long plane ride home. If he didn't want her working for his company, she wouldn't. The day would never come when she would force herself on an employer or a man. The fifty-one percent could rot for all she cared. For now, all she wanted was to pick up the pieces of her life and get on with it the best way she knew how.

Her task took all of ten minutes. She would have to hurry or the taxi would leave without her. Two manila envelopes full of pictures, a spare makeup case, and her camera under her arms, she left the tiny cubbyhole that had been her short-lived office. She didn't look back; she couldn't.

Inside her own small apartment she very carefully locked the door, shot the dead bolt, and then slid the chain into place. Even a SWAT team couldn't break down this door with its grille over the paned glass. She was safe. But who was she safe from? Christian Delaney?

Sam walked around the small apartment, touching this and that. Her personal things that she had left behind held meaning only for her. Something was bothering her, and then it hit full force. She really was stupid. Coming back to this apartment was the most stupid thing she could have done. Hadn't he told her that he was taking over Gemini's apartment? Right now, this very minute, he could be upstairs. Her heart began its wild fluttering. Why had she done such a stupid thing? *Because,* a niggling voice said quietly, subconsciously, *you knew he would be there and you wanted to be as close to him as possible.*

Dejectedly, Sam sat down on the sofa and let the tears flow. It was true. She did want to be near Christian, in the hopes that he would come to her and say the past was past and he did truly love her. Would she ever hear him say those words to her?

Panicking with the turn her thoughts were taking, Sam looked around for something to do. The cats. A quick call placed to the vet's and the cats would find their way home in a taxi. Then a shower—a long, cold shower. And an aspirin. Two of them!

An hour later the cats, Gin and Tonic, were stretched out under the cocktail table. "I really feel sorry for you guys, the way you've been shifted from pillar to post. I have some chicken livers in the freezer along with a few gizzards. And I'm going to cook them for you right now. Now that I'm a married lady, I suddenly feel very domestic." Gin nipped at Tonic, who, in turn, snarled his revenge by way of a clout with his paw on Gin's head. Gin's back arched and he spat his anger, which Tonic ignored. "Go to it, guys. Get it out of your system, because you aren't getting high on me. This is a dry house as far as you're concerned."

Sam added a few onions and a little salt and pepper to the livers and gizzards and decided they would be wasted on the cats; besides, she was hungry herself. She quickly plucked a package of cat food from beneath the sink and filled two small bowls. She poured milk into a medium-size dish and added a drop of rum flavoring as an inducement and then whistled for the cats. As always, they ignored her. "So starve," she muttered, spooning the chicken livers and gizzards onto a dinner plate.

The hours crawled by, and to Sam's disgust there was no visit or even a phone call from Christian Delaney. The least he could have done was make some sort of overture so she could reject him. This should have been her honeymoon. She was spending her honeymoon with two reformed alcoholic cats. "This is the pits," she snapped at the cats as she crawled into bed.

THE FIRST THING SHE DID the following morning was call the Women's Bank to ask an officer to recommend a woman attorney. She scribbled down the number and called for an appointment. She circled a date a week into the future and then stared at the calendar.

She should start thinking about her future and what she was going to do. Should she take a trip to the unemployment office? Was she fired or had she quit? And what about the name change? Already she was getting a headache and it was only midmorning. She had to do something constructive like shower and dress. Then she'd make a trip to the market for some food and stop at the post office to pick up her mail. She would buy a few newspapers and see what the job market was offering for unemployed photographers. That should take care of her time till early afternoon. Then she could do some laundry, prepare a little dinner, watch some television, and go to bed. "Some honeymoon," she grimaced. Was she really legally married?

Sam completed her errands and was back in front of the television screen in time to catch the four-thirty movie. A Chinese TV dinner was heating in the oven. The cats were napping contentedly. She kicked off her shoes and propped her slim ankles on the edge of the cocktail table as she sorted through the mail. A sale flyer from Woody's, an American Express bill, the utility bill, scads of letters addressed to Occupant or Resident, and a legal-looking letter from Gemini's lawyer. The most important first. She decided she could live with owing American Express $123.46. She would have to pass up Woody's sale and write out a check for the utility company or have her power cut off. The stiff, crackling, legal paper informed her that she was to be in the attorney's office on Monday, the seventeenth, for the reading of the addendum to Gemini's will. The meeting was to take place at ten-thirty in the morning. Did she have to go? Probably not, she answered herself. After all, she was engaging her own attorney to handle matters. Still, perhaps she should go so that when she met with her private lawyer she would have more knowledge about the current state of affairs. She would go and demand copies of everything in triplicate.

Gemini had always said to get everything in triplicate. They can fool you once, even twice, but three times? That was another story. She wouldn't sign anything unless it was in triplicate.

Sam stared at the sleeping cats and then her eye fell on the silent phone. Why couldn't it ring? Why couldn't Christian call her to see if she was all right? New husbands shouldn't be so…blasé about…about their wives.

The timer on the stove buzzed. The TV dinner was done. She peeled back the foil from the tray and stared at the messy-looking concoction. Yuk! She couldn't eat this…this mess. She had to eat something. The refrigerator yielded little in the way of food: a mushy apple, some cheese that was stiff and hard around the edges, and some grape jam. She should have bought real food when she stopped by the neighborhood deli. A stale breadstick in the breadbox did nothing to enhance her appetite. She was back to square one and the TV dinner. Morosely, she picked at the steamy, stringy chow mein and chewed on the barely visible rubbery shrimp.

It took her less than five minutes to straighten out the kitchen and replenish the cats' dishes with canned milk. Listlessly, she walked back to the living room and the noisy television. Whatever Woody Allen was doing, it must be funny. She decided if the Allen movie couldn't distract her, nothing could. Irritably, she switched off the set.

Time was lying heavily on her hands. Samantha needed to interest herself in something, yet she admitted that she found she would pause, stand stock-still, and listen for some movement upstairs—footsteps, the clatter of a pot, something that would tell her Christian was upstairs in Gemini's apartment. She fully realized the need to feel close to him.

As she wandered through her apartment, she entered the spare bedroom where she had spent so many hours working on Christian's portrait. She would probably never finish it now. How could she? Every line of his face had become dear to her. She would have tried to breathe life into that painting, wishing it could become the man she had come to know so well.

Her lazy gaze fell on the camera and gadget bag, the same ones she had carried through the desert. Suddenly spurred to action, she hefted the bag and carried it to the portion of the spare bedroom off the bathroom where she had set up a darkroom. Her blood tingled and her interest sparked. The film, the pictures that she and Christian had snapped of one another throughout their time in the Southwest.

Working quickly, but deftly and untiringly, she developed the twelve rolls of film that held the memories and images of those seemingly long-ago days when Christian had been within reach of her fingertips.

The long strips of positives and negatives hung from a makeshift clothesline to dry. Finally, admitting her exhaustion, she crept to her bed, to sleep, to dream, to relive her adventure with the man she loved. She had worked blindly, her hands going through the motions. She hadn't dared to pause and dwell on the pictures developing before her eyes. She had to sleep, and that wouldn't be possible if she studied the photographs. The memory was too fresh, too new. Soon, hopefully, she would be strong enough to look at them, cherish them. But for now, she would escape her pain and sleep.

WHEN THE PHONE RANG shortly after noon the next day, it sounded like an alarm. Sam stared at the phone a moment before she realized it wasn't ringing. The alarming sound had been the doorbell. Was it Christian? If it was, what was she going to say to him? What was there to say? Nothing, she grimaced as she released the chain and slid the dead bolt. Before she opened the door, she asked, "Who is it?"

"Barbara Matthews from the *Post*. I'd like to talk to you, Mrs. Delaney."

Mrs. Delaney! She was Mrs. Delaney. "Why?" Sam demanded through the door.

"I think my readers might be interested in your new marriage to one of the most eligible bachelors in the country. I want to do it for the Sunday section. I'll only take up an hour of your time."

How could she refuse? She knew how hard journalists worked and how difficult it was sometimes to fill space. Why not? What did she have to lose? Sam opened the door to admit a vivacious, sparkling redhead who was at first glance a sizzling size three. Sam hated her on sight. "Come in," she said graciously. She motioned for the petite reporter to sit on the sofa and then sat down across from her in a shabby leather chair.

Barbara settled herself comfortably and flipped her notebook to a clean page. "I'll ask the questions, and if you have something you want to interject, feel free to interrupt me. First of all," she said in a lilting, musical voice, "tell me, how does it feel to be Mrs. Christian Delaney?"

This was a mistake. She must have been out of her mind to agree to this interview. "Well...I...it's..."

"There's no way to describe it, right?" Barbara said, making squiggly marks on her pad. "My readers will understand that. All that money! You'll be able to go anywhere, do anything. How have you handled that?"

What's to handle? Sam thought huffily. "I personally think...actually...you see..."

"It's mind-boggling. I understand, and my readers will certainly relate to that. Wishful thinking, if you know what I mean. How do you think you'll like having servants to wait on you and cater to your every need? You *were* a working girl like the rest of us."

"I've always been...been rather in-independent and..."

"You'll handle it like you were born to it, right? Good, good answer; my readers will identify. Now, tell me," Barbara said, leaning over and whispering confidentially, "is he as romantic as the tabloids make him out to be? Does he really have steely eyes that can cut you to ribbons, or do they go all soft and melting, making your head swoon?"

"That's...that's a...a fair..."

"I knew I was right, I just knew it!" Barbara chortled, making a quick row of scratches on her pad. "He'd make a perfect Adonis!" she all but squealed. "Gifts. Has your new husband showered you with gifts yet?"

"Well, actually...you see, it's been such a short... what I mean is..."

"You don't have to say another word. I understand perfectly. He'll do the showering when you leave for your honeymoon. By the way, where is that to take place?" the reporter inquired.

Would the reporter believe her if she told her she was honeymooning alone? Not likely. Sam flushed a bright crimson. "I don't think Chris... Listen, you don't understand. I really shouldn't be talking to you. You've got it all wrong..."

"But of course, I understand. It's a secret, right? I don't blame you for one minute. It's just that my poor readers are so starved for romance that they eat this sort of thing right up and beg for more. I'm sure a round-the-world cruise is not out of the question, right?"

"Right," Sam squealed. She had to get this girl out of here before she suffered a nervous breakdown.

Barbara Matthews coughed to clear her throat. Holding her hand over her mouth, she complained, "Too much talking. Gets me right here." She coughed again.

"Can I offer you something? A drink? Coffee?"

"I would like a drink if you don't mind. Bourbon, straight up," she said firmly.

That was good. No ice in the drink. The cats would continue to sleep. Once they heard the clink of ice or the opening of a bottle, it would be all over. Deftly, Sam poured the bourbon into a squat glass, one eye on the snoozing cats. She extended the drink to her guest and let her breath out in a deep sigh. The cats hadn't noticed.

The petite Miss Matthews downed her drink neatly and immediately asked another question. "Now, Mrs. Delaney, for the record and for my more liberated readers, tell me what you're going to do about your job. Do you plan to continue with your work, or are you going to become, how shall I say it—" she pursed her mouth, seeking the right word and finally came up with it "—domesticated?"

I wonder what she would think if I told her I'm applying for unemployment compensation tomorrow? Sam mused. "I haven't decided exactly…I think what I'll do is…"

"Play the housewife bit for a while. Perfectly understandable. I'd do the same thing myself. Children… what about children? Do you see any in your immediate future?"

Sam's neck was beginning to perspire. "At least a dozen," she said bluntly.

Barbara Matthews scribbled furiously. "Mrs. Delaney, when can I meet Mr. Delaney? I would like a few good quotes from him. I guess he isn't home from the office yet. I really have to get back to my paper and get started on this. Listen, what do you say we fudge a little?"

Sam blinked, not quite understanding what the reporter meant.

Barbara Matthews continued. "What I mean is, if I were to ask Mr. Delaney if he was madly in love with you, he would naturally say yes, right? And if I asked him if he was going to show you the world and shower you with presents, he'd tell me yes to that, too. So, why don't I just say that and this way I won't have to hang around and wait for him and spoil your evening? By the way, why are you still here? Oh, never mind. I know, you're getting a few things together. Sometimes," she said, throwing her hands in the air, "I get so flighty, I don't know what I'm doing. But don't you worry about a thing. I'm really going to knock myself out on this interview. Did you by any chance see the piece I did on the two pandas at the zoo?"

"No, I guess I missed it," Sam said defensively.

"Not to worry. I'll send you a copy. Say, would you mind if I used your powder room?"

"No...no...it's right through there." Sam pointed. Anything, anything at all to be rid of this woman.

Barbara Matthews went into the bathroom through the spare bedroom and Sam tapped her fingertips impatiently on the arm of the chair. Her eye fell on the empty glass that had held the bourbon the reporter had downed in one gulp. Quickly, she picked up the glass and brought it out to the kitchen before the girl could suggest another drink to whet her whistle. Sam wanted Miss Matthews out of her apartment—as soon as possible!

When Sam returned to the living room, she had expected to find the reporter waiting for her. Instead, after a few minutes, Miss Matthews exited from the spare bedroom. Somehow, imperceptibly, her attitude was altered.

"Thank you so much for your time, Mrs. Delaney." She winked slyly. "I do so envy you. You really did snare yourself some hunk. Every woman in the country is going to hate you with a passion for taking Christian Delaney out of circulation." If anything, Barbara Matthews's speech was even more rapid than before. For some reason, Sam felt that the reporter wanted to leave the apartment even more desperately than she wanted to be rid of her.

"Don't you worry about being envied, Mrs. Delaney," the reporter chattered while she slipped into her coat. "You just take it in your stride. Once the women of America get to know you as I have, they'll all take you to their hearts. 'Poor little working girl marries super-rich tycoon.' I'm going to do a fabulous piece of work on this one. Thanks again and much happiness." The girl literally lunged for the door. In the space of an instant, she was gone.

Samantha leaned against the door. What in the world was going on here? A dizzy reporter from the *Post* shows up and harasses her into an interview and then takes off out of the apartment as though the hounds of hell were on her heels.

CHAPTER NINE

THREE DAYS PASSED WITHOUT Christian Delaney getting in touch with her. Sam sat down on the couch, her mind racing. Today was Sunday; tomorrow was the reading of the addendum to the will. Today was also the day the article Barbara Matthews was working on would appear in the special section of the Sunday paper.

Sam glanced at her watch. She had all day to get through before her meeting tomorrow at the attorney's office. Tomorrow she would see Christian. Still, she had to get through the rest of the day. The zoo! She would go to the zoo and see the pandas herself. She would stop at the deli and ask them to pack her up a picnic lunch, and she would spend the day wandering around the zoo. No decisions to be made today. Tomorrow it would be all over.

Donning warm clothing, Sam left the apartment, stopping at the deli for her lunch and a copy of the Sunday paper. Her eye fell on the left hand corner of the newspaper and a square box with a Santa climbing down a chimney. It was a reminder that there were only eight more shopping days till Christmas. Sam was appalled. Eight days! Where had the time gone?

Her purchases intact, Sam left the corner store and walked up Woodley Road on her way to the zoo.

She tramped through the zoo, getting colder by the

minute. Lately, it seemed that all she did was make mistakes. She really didn't feel like roaming around looking at animals in cages. She admitted that the steamy, smelly birdhouse would do nothing for her except possibly curb her appetite. It was only three-thirty, but it would be dark soon. And if she wasn't mistaken, it felt like snow. A sudden wind whipped up, blowing her coat collar high around her neck. Sam clutched at it and buttoned the toggle securely and huddled down into the warmth the heavy coat provided. She wished she had a hat, something to keep her ears warm.

Sam started the uphill climb to the exit, holding on to the iron rail. She raised her head slightly as she felt something wet hit her nose. It was snowing. How she loved the first snowfall of the year! She might as well go home now. She hitched the heavy Sunday paper and her paper bag, holding the lunch she hadn't gotten around to eating, more firmly under her arm. Small children laughing and giggling raced ahead of her as the giant clock at the entrance sounded the time. She smiled as she listened to the tune. The wind was stronger now and the snow seemed to be falling a bit more heavily. She was surprised to see a soft carpet of the white stuff covering the ground already. And she had been oblivious to it all afternoon. It certainly didn't say much for her state of mind.

Inside her snug apartment Sam dropped the soggy Sunday newspaper onto the cocktail table and removed her coat. She'd make herself some soup and have crackers with it for dinner, take a warm bath, and then read the paper. After that she would sort out her thoughts and make plans for what she was going to do with the rest of her life after her visit to Gemini's lawyer tomorrow. There were no two ways about it; she had to get on with her life, without or with Christian Delaney.

Her light dinner finished, her bath completed, Sam powdered herself lavishly with Esther's last birthday present to her—Zen bath powder. She wrinkled her nose appreciatively; she loved the sweet, intoxicating scent. She slipped into a scarlet velour robe and tied the sash.

Wind whistled outside the grilled windows and Sam shivered. The small bedroom was drafty. Her eyes traveled to the free-standing fireplace in the corner of the bedroom, the main reason she had rented the apartment from Gemini. A quick-burning Duraflame log and she was set. Was it her imagination, or did she feel warmer already? Power of suggestion, she mused.

Settling herself comfortably beneath the floral comforter, Sam snuggled back against a mound of pillows. She felt rather like a bird in a nest. Deftly, she tossed aside the first three sections of the heavy, wet newspaper and searched for Barbara Matthews's article. She found it on page two of the Living section.

What she saw shocked her as though she'd stuck her finger in an electrical socket. Pictures! Her pictures! The pictures she and Christian had taken of one another with her father's Hasselblad during their trek in the desert!

Throwing back the comforter, stumbling on it as it caught around her legs, she leaped for the spare bedroom. Those were *her* pictures! The ones she had developed and had left hanging from the clothesline in the darkroom. How…how had Barbara Matthews gotten her hands on them?

Switching on the light in the spare bedroom, her eyes first fell on the easel holding Christian's portrait and saw it was still covered with the paint-stained old sheet she had thrown over it. Almost fearfully, hoping against hope, she looked toward the end of the room where she had created the darkroom. The long strips of negatives still hung there, but the positives were gone. And she knew who had taken them!

"No, no, no!" she heard herself cry aloud as she rushed over to them. Quickly examining them, she saw with her own eyes the figures in the negatives were one and the same with the pictures in the Sunday paper.

Her mind snapped back to Barbara Matthews's visit. The reporter must have taken them when Samantha had allowed her to use the bathroom. That was why she had seemed in such a hurry to get out of the apartment.

Samantha felt her knees buckle under her. It was a dirty, low-down trick. But there was no help for it now. The damage had been done. Christian would either see the article or, at the very least, hear about it. Whatever, the end result would be the same. He would think she had maliciously offered the snapshots to the reporter, and he would hate her with a passion!

In a flurry of panic, Samantha rushed back to where she had dropped the paper. She was compelled to read it, to examine the photos. Somewhere in the article they would have to give credit for the photos. Somehow, she felt she couldn't believe what was happening to her until she saw her name in print. It was just a bad dream, she repeated over and over in her mind.

Diving for the paper, her eyes tried to take it all in at once. Disciplining her attention, she slowed and looked more carefully. Christian would think she had selected them to make him appear foolish. There was one of him looking over his shoulder at the camera, a silly wink and a silly smile on his face. Another taken by an outcropping of rocks...sitting beside the camp-fire...and one in which they had used the delayed timing and both were in the shot together, sitting close, the campfire casting shadows and light on their features and making them look incredibly romantic. There were eleven photos, each more compromising than the one before.

Sam's eyes raked the column of print. It appeared the reporter was big on pictures and small on words. Sam's eyes widened as she read the text and she gasped. She had said no such things!

Good heavens! Where had the reporter gotten such an idea? This was beyond belief! People were actually going to read this and believe it! Correction: it was an early edition of the paper; people had already read it. Christian must have seen it. Oh, no! She whimpered into the pillow. She would sue; that's what she would do, the first thing in the morning. It must be libelous; it had to be. She hadn't said anything like this. Where did that stupid reporter get such ideas? She would never be able to face Christian Delaney again. This couldn't be happening to her; it just couldn't. A bright flush stained her fresh-scrubbed face. Even her ears felt hot. She felt ashamed, mortified, and darned indignant. Tears welled in her eyes at her predicament. Now, what was she going to do?

The blue-white flame from the fireplace blurred her vision as she stared into the flickering flames. She had to do something about a rebuttal. A letter—she would write a letter to the paper and one to Christian Delaney denying...denying what? She had to get her thoughts together and think this through, and she had to do it before the meeting tomorrow morning.

Sam tossed back the covers and walked over to the shuttered window. She opened the louvers and stared at the whiteness beyond the pane of glass. It looked like a winter wonderland in the mellow glow of the street-light. The wind was strong and she could hear it shriek-ing in the trees near the curb as the branches dripped and swayed with their mantle of whiteness. It had been a long time since she had seen snow like this in Wash-ington. It would be a white Christmas, after all. The thought depressed her.

The slim girl shivered in the draft from the window. She closed the louvers and looked longingly at the warm bed she had just left. A cup of tea would do her good right now, she decided, and she really should also change the litter box. It would give her something to do while she thought about the interview in the Sunday paper.

Sam had just tossed the tea bag into the trash con-tainer when the doorbell sounded. She frowned and looked at the kitchen clock. It was eight-fifty. Who could be visiting her on such a night? She walked hesitantly to the front door and peeked through the tiny peephole. Christian Delaney! Sam swallowed hard. What did he want? The doorbell chimed a second time. He had read the paper! Oh, no! She swallowed again and released the chain. Her shaking hands slid the dead bolt and then the regular lock. She moistened her dry lips and swung open the door, her face impassive. "Yes?" she asked quietly.

"May I come in? It's rather blustery out here, as you can see." Sam said nothing but stood aside for him to enter. She watched as he shook the snow from his tweed jacket and brushed at his hair. She was surprised that he wore no overcoat, then remembered that he only had to come from as far away as next door, which meant walking down two flights of stairs. She closed the door but made no move toward the living room. She waited, her heart pounding in her chest. Suddenly, she was aware, acutely aware, of her shiny scrubbed face with its layer of cold cream and even more acutely aware of her naked body beneath the scarlet robe.

Christian Delaney stared at her and then walked into the living room. She had to follow him if she wanted to find out what he wanted. She waited till he sat down on the sofa and then she perched herself on the arm of the wing chair across from him. Still, she said nothing, waiting to see why he was here.

"I came to congratulate you on the article in the *Post*. I had no idea that you were so...so articulate or that you cared so much." Sam felt a chill wash over her at the sarcastic tone. Would he believe her if she explained? And why did she have to explain? Let him believe whatever he wanted. She shrugged and remained mute. Christian frowned.

"Did you read the article?" he asked nonchalantly. Sam nodded. "I was more than a little surprised to see the photographs. Somehow, I hadn't expected you would sell them to the *Post*. *Time* would have been my guess." His voice was quiet, dangerously quiet, and his face betrayed no hint of what he was truly feeling. If anything, he seemed faintly amused.

"I...I didn't sell them..."

"No? Foolish girl. *Time* would have paid you a small fortune for them. Oh, that's right, I almost forgot." He snapped his fingers. "You don't need money, do you? Not with what Aunt Gemini left you. So, why did you do it? Spite?"

"No, you don't understand. I developed those photos the other night, and when that reporter asked to use the bathroom... Oh, what's the use? You'll never believe she stole them."

"Try me," he said, a strange, soft note coming into his voice. His silvery gaze penetrated her, beseeching her to make him believe her.

"It's just as I told you. I let her use the bathroom. She went in through the spare bedroom. I never thought..." Samantha drew herself to full height and squared her shoulders. "Barbara Matthews *stole* those photos from this apartment! That is the truth. I would never, could never, be so low-down as to publish them. They were ours, Christian." A sob rose in her throat. "They belonged to us, and I'm angrier than a hornet to think that they've been made public!"

Christian moved close to her, making her dizzy with his mere presence. "At one time in the desert you threatened to publish the photos."

"I'd never do it. It was only a threat. I wanted to rile you."

"That you did, most successfully." A slow smile crept onto his face, softening his features and bringing humor to his mysterious silver-gray eyes. "The one I liked best was the one of you with your shirt wrapped around your head. And that silly one of you washing our clothes in the spring like an old Indian woman." He laughed, relaxing, believing her.

"It would be nice if you offered me a drink—a celebration, so to speak."

If she fixed him a drink, she would have to move, and she knew her shaking legs and trembling hands would give away her emotions. "Help yourself," she said, motioning to the small cabinet holding the liquor. Christian stared at her a moment, then rose to make his own drink. He carried a bottle of liquor and a glass to the cocktail table and set them down. He frowned a second time as he removed the cap from the vodka and poured a drink. "Ice would be nice," he said quietly.

Sam blinked. Both cats were on the cocktail table in a second, clawing and spitting in their quest for the liquor. "Stop them!" Sam screeched. "Don't let them have any liquor! I'm drying them out!" Feverishly, she reached for Gin, who leaped out of her way and landed on Christian's lap, clawing at his jacket. "Now, look what you've done!" Sam cried as she tried to wipe up the spilled liquor with the hem of her robe, revealing a shapely, satiny leg and thigh.

"What the...?" Christian sputtered as he saw the vodka bottle topple as Gin fought Tonic for the aromatic spirits.

"Do you know what you just did? Why couldn't you pour the drink over the cabinet? Oh, no, you had to bring it over here, and now see what happened? I've had those cats on the wagon for a long time, and you just undid all my good work. Well, they're your responsibility now, and you can just take them with you when you leave here. They're all yours," Sam said angrily.

"The least you could do is help me clean it up." Frantically, she ran to the kitchen for a dishcloth and tried to wipe up the spilled liquor. Once her eyes met Christian's as she mopped at the table. The scarlet robe had parted and an expanse of creamy bosom was visible to his sleepy, silvery gaze. Hastily, she dropped the cloth and drew the robe tighter around her. A dull flush worked its way up her throat and into her cheeks.

"I'm sorry," Christian said huskily. "I had no idea the cats were still boozing it up. You should have warned me. I can see now that we have to do something about them."

"Not we! *You* have to do something about them! I'm giving them back to you—now!" Deftly, she scooped up the drunken cats and placed them in their basket. "Here's your cats and there's the door."

Christian grinned. "Would you really turn me and those poor, defenseless cats out on a night like this? According to that article I read today, you are a hopeless romantic. I refuse to leave!" he said adamantly.

"Well, you aren't staying here," Sam shot back.

"Of course I am. We're married, and those cats are both our responsibilities. I think," he said, grinning widely, "the best thing to do right now is let them sleep it off, and we should turn in ourselves."

Sam blanched. "As far as *I'm* concerned, we're not married! The whole idea was to legally transfer the Delaney stock to you. A marriage of convenience."

"You told the whole world, via the *Post,* that we were married and wanted dozens of children. I'm here to make that wish come true. In the eyes of the *Washington Post,* we're married, and that's good enough for me," he said in an amused voice. "Are you ready?"

Sam pretended ignorance. "Ready for what?" As if she didn't know. One moment she was spitting and hissing at him with her eyes, and the next she was pinned in his strong arms. He held her firmly, diminishing her struggles and overpowering her gasped objections. His lips were on the soft skin beneath her ear; his face was buried in the soft curls that clung to her neck. Insistent, persuasive, his mouth explored her skin, finding and pursuing the pleasure points that sent shudders through her body and made her weak. In spite of herself, Samantha clung to him, relishing this one heady moment, expecting it to be ripped away from her, leaving her bereft and alone and missing him.

Tenderly, he held her head in his hands, lifting her face for his kiss, touching her lips with his in a way that was both familiar and exciting. His hands traveled the length of her body, molding it and pressing it closer to his. She strained toward him, allowing him to hold her this way, loving it, loving him. Softly, so softly that at first she thought she imagined it, his voice rumbled deep in his chest and he whispered her name, "Samantha." A whisper so soft, so poignant, it fed the fires of her desire and echoed in her heart. Again, he whispered her name, telling her the things that lovers say, whispering them for her, words she had given up all hope of ever hearing from Christian.

He gathered her up in his arms, carrying her to the bedroom, taking her from the light into the dark, taking her with him into a world filled with the sound of his voice and the feel of his arms. A safe world, a place where his arms sheltered her and his lips worshipped her. Together they tumbled down the endless corridors created by their love. Together they found the hidden springs of their desires and the gardens of trust and belonging.

Christian was tender; he was forceful. He was all things for all times, and she responded to him, loving him, knowing that he loved her. He made her his own; he turned back the pages of her girlhood and introduced her to the fulfilled future of a woman. And always, he loved her.

For a thousand times his lips touched hers. For an eternity his hands possessed her. He touched her body and evoked an answering cry in her soul. Her heart belonged to Christian, for now, forever. And later, a short eternity later, when the fire had died down to low embers and lit the room with a faint orange glow, it was Christian who looked down at her with wonder in his eyes, softening their silvery hardness to molten pewter. And when he spoke, it was to whisper her name.

CHAPTER TEN

SAM WOKE UP SLOWLY, a feeling of contentment in every pore of her body. A slow, happy smile worked its way around the corners of her mouth. It wasn't a dream. It had been real, every single minute of the long night. She stretched luxuriously, deliberately postponing the moment when she would open her eyes and then touch her husband, lying beside her. She wanted to savor each second until she could no longer struggle against the need to feel his warm, hard body against hers. She couldn't stand it another moment. Squeezing her eyes tighter, she reached out and groped beneath the covers. A sinking feeling settled in her stomach. He was gone! "Christian!" she cried softly, thinking he was in the bathroom. There was no answer.

A sob gathered in her throat as she rolled over on the bed and pummeled the pillows with clenched hands. He was gone. How could he do this to her? How could he go off and leave her without saying something? Anything, even a goodbye, would be better than waking up with this cold, dead feeling. "I hate him! I hate him!" she cried, over and over, as tears soaked the pillow beneath her face, feeling used and foolish.

Crying and making herself sick wasn't going to help. She had to get up and shower. A note. Perhaps he didn't want to wake her up and had left a note. He was considerate. Surely, he had left a note. There was nothing.

Her tears long dried, she sat on the sofa, and it wasn't until both cats staggered to the cocktail table and began licking at the sticky surface that anger rose in her, threatening to choke the life from her body. He had left the cats! Just who did he think he was, barging into her apartment and giving the cats liquor and plying her with soft words and taking her to bed to exercise his matrimonial rights? And she had let him! What a fool she was! Now, she had to go to the lawyer's office and face him.

Sam managed somehow to get through her morning ritual of showering and dressing by habit. Everything she did was automatic, with no thought beyond the moment and what she was doing.

Opening the drapes, she was stunned to see the monstrous accumulation of snow that greeted her gaze. It was a known fact that the District of Columbia fell apart when snow had the audacity to accumulate more than an inch. This looked to her unpracticed eyes like a good eight inches. There would be no buses, and cabs would be at a premium. If she wanted to reach the lawyer's office, she would have to walk. And she would have to start out as soon as possible if she wanted to make the appointment any way near on time.

Sam rummaged in her closet for a heavy sheepskin jacket and also dug out a fur-lined hat from a box in the corner. Bright orange mittens, a gift from Norma Jean back in college days, completed her outfit. She looked down at her serviceable boots and prayed that the manufacturer's label proclaiming them to be waterproof was accurate.

If she hadn't been so miserable, she would have

enjoyed her trek to the lawyer's office. People were scattered everywhere, cheerfully digging out cars and helping one another as playful children pelted one and all with snowballs that dissolved on impact. She trudged on, dodging the flying snowballs, careful to watch her footing. If there was one thing she didn't need, it was a broken bone of any kind.

Exactly one hour and forty minutes later she stomped her way into the lobby of the law offices. The blast of warm air made her blink and wish she was back outside in the clear brisk air. Shaking the snow from her jacket, she walked to the elevator and waited.

The ferns were still intact, as was the smell of lemon polish on the furniture. It was still as dry and dusty as before. Sam wrinkled her nose, fighting off a sneeze. She looked around and was surprised to see a handsome young man advance in her direction. He held out his hand and smiled. "David Carpenter. You must be Samantha Blakely. Follow me. I'll be conducting this meeting. Your aunt's attorney, my uncle, is home in bed with the flu. I'm a junior partner of the firm. I hope you don't have any objections to my handling the affairs."

"Of course not," Sam muttered as she followed David Carpenter's long-legged stride down the corridor. Anything was an improvement over Gemini's age-old friend.

While the young attorney gathered his papers together, Sam looked around the office and liked what she saw. The brown and beige plaid drapes were partially closed to ward off the intense glare from the white world outside. The low-slung beige leather chairs were comfortable and matched the thick pile of the cocoa carpeting. It was a room whose atmosphere was restful and masculine. The rich pecan of the paneled walls reminded Sam of Gemini's library, as did the copper bowls full of daisies and ferns. Her inspection of the room completed, Sam turned her gaze to the lawyer and waited for him to speak.

David Carpenter cleared his throat and then leaned back in his swivel chair. "Back there in the hallway I referred to you as Samantha Blakely. I apologize. I should have called you by your newly married name, Mrs. Delaney. It's just that I've been working on this case for so long, and Sam Blakely has become engraved on my brain. In the beginning I made the same mistake my uncle made in thinking you were a man. Your husband, as you know, was most upset. However, rest assured that he and I both spent several hours this morning going over matters, and he understands his Aunt Gemini's intentions."

"Mr. Carpenter, where is…my…hus— Where is Christian?" Sam asked hesitantly.

"He left here thirty minutes ago. He said he had pressing business at the office. He left a message for you, though. Now, let me see, where did I put it? Oh, yes, here it is. 'I'll be home for dinner, and make my steak rare.'"

Sam's heart soared and took wing. Christian would be home for dinner! She was going to cook for him, and he liked his steak rare. Her smile, when she turned it on the young attorney, was as dazzling as the brightness outside the plaid-covered windows. "Thank you for telling me."

"No problem. Now, let me see. Yes, here it is. This is a letter addressed to you, written by Gemini Delaney shortly before her death. You were only to receive it if you were married to Mr. Delaney. Otherwise, it was to be destroyed." Rifling through his papers, he withdrew an envelope that was addressed to Mrs. Samantha Delaney.

Sam extended her shaking fingers to accept the stiff bond paper. Seeing Gemini's scratchy handwriting renewed a pang of grief. Fighting back tears, she forced herself to open the envelope and read Gemini's last message to her:

Dearest Samantha,

Forgive an old woman's meddling, but the very fact you are reading this letter means my nasty little scheme has ended with you being married to my nephew, Christian. Let it suffice to say that the end has justified the means.

I have made no secret of my deepest regard for you or of my loving fondness for Christian. My problem was in seeing the two of you find each other. I knew you were the girl for him from the moment I set eyes on you. The difficulty existed in having Christian discover this for himself.

It was a simple matter of having him notice you, and I could think of no better way of assuring this than having him think you were the beneficiary of the controlling interest in Delaney Enterprises. I'll bet *that* made him sit up and take notice!

Now the time has come to have the original stock revert to its rightful owner, Christian. Other provisions have been made for you, Samantha, and, needless to say, you are now a very wealthy woman.

Thank you, dear girl, for caring for an old woman. Let your first daughter carry my name.

Remember me,
Gemini

When Samantha looked up through her tears, it was to see the lawyer smiling fondly down at her. "It seems the old matchmaker has had her way."

"Yes, Mr. Carpenter. Gemini Delaney was a wise and wily lady."

"I can see you're not in the mood to have me read the entire addendum to you," he said kindly, offering her a tissue to dry her eyes. "We can go over it at your convenience. By the way, the dividends for the stock that you've already received are yours to keep. I hope you invest them wisely."

"Well, actually, Mr. Carpenter, I didn't cash the check. I gave it to Mr. Delaney in a manila envelope to hold in his office safe. Perhaps you should call him and tell him I'm returning it. I never had any intention of keeping the money. I know Gemini meant well, but I really can't accept it. I tried to explain all of this to your uncle, but he kept getting me confused with a man, and he has a definite hearing problem. I gave up trying to explain, thinking it would all work out. I don't want a cent from the estate. I want you to tell Christian that for me, and I want you to do it today."

"Are you saying what I think you're saying?" the young lawyer asked incredulously. "Don't you think you should be the one to tell Mr. Delaney? After all, he is your husband."

"I want it to come from you, and I want you to explain the mix-up."

"Mrs. Delaney, this is very unorthodox. First, your husband comes in here and tells me he wants things one way, and then you come in and tell me you want it another way. Do you think you could get together and arrive at some sort of mutual agreement so I'm not forced to do double work? We're rather short-staffed here right now."

"What did Christian tell you to do?" Sam asked fearfully. Maybe she wasn't going to get the chance to broil that rare steak, after all.

"To make a long story short, he wants you to have half—fifty percent—of the Delaney estate. Half of everything. Now, you tell me you want nothing, not even the dividends."

"That is it, exactly. And I want you to make Mr. Delaney aware of my intentions before he comes home to dinner tonight."

"I'll certainly do my best, Mrs. Delaney, but your husband has a mind of his own, and he was most adamant this morning when he told me his wishes."

"Thank you for your time," Sam said, rising and holding out her hand.

"Goodbye, Mrs. Delaney, and I also want to thank you for braving that white stuff out there. How did you get here?"

"I walked." Sam smiled.

"I'll get on this right away, and perhaps by the time your husband gets home tonight, we'll have it all settled to your satisfaction."

"Is there anything else, Mr. Carpenter?" Sam asked hesitantly.

"David. Call me David. As a matter of fact, there is. I hope you'll include my name on the guest list for the wedding."

"Wedding?" Sam asked, puzzled.

"Yes. Mr. Delaney and I discussed it at great length this morning." The lawyer paused to smile, a hint of a flush reddening his ears. "To quote your husband, Mrs.

Delaney, he wants to do everything up right, twice, to make sure you don't get away."

Sam gasped, "Christian said that!" Her heart was beating trip-hammer fast. All the love she had locked away in a tiny part of her breast swelled and grew and burst forth, shining in her eyes.

"I seem to be missing something here," David Carpenter murmured quietly, a frown on his face. "I hope I haven't let any cats out of the bag."

"Cats! Cats!" Sam laughed. "All because of the cats!"

"I beg your pardon, Mrs. Delaney, I'm afraid I don't understand…"

"I'm having trouble with it myself, David," Sam called over her shoulder as she sailed out of the lawyer's office, her feet barely touching the floor.

Her first stop was a supermarket where she picked out the biggest steak she could find. Ingredients for a salad and some baking potatoes. Something for dessert, and an apron. If there was one thing a new bride needed besides perfume, it was an apron, and not necessarily in that order.

It was midafternoon before Sam made it back to her apartment, slipping and sliding, carrying two full bags of groceries.

She hung her coat in the tiny closet and immediately set about cleaning the apartment. She cleaned out the grate and added two logs to the fireplace. With machine-gun speed she whipped off the bed sheets and replaced them with fresh ones. A quick once-over in the bathroom and a new bath mat and her house was in order. While the tub filled with luxurious, scented steam, she retreated to the kitchen and began her preparations for dinner. The porterhouse steak was thick and a beautiful beefy red. Deftly, she added a little tenderizer and sprinkled on a few spices. She set the broiler pan on top of the stove and moved on to the baking potatoes, which were long and perfectly shaped. The vegetables were perfection as she rinsed them under cold water. Her only cop out had been the frozen deep-dish apple pie made by the renowned Mrs. Smith. The pie could bake along with the potatoes, and at the last minute she would slip the steaks under the broiler.

She was married, really married. Her hands trembled as she slid the frozen pie onto a cookie sheet. This would be the first meal she cooked for her husband. "Gemini, you fox, this was what you angled for from the beginning. Wherever you are, I hope you know that your plan worked. And I really wouldn't have given him the cats. I just said that because I was angry. I said I would take care of them, and I will."

Sam fished around in the market bag and withdrew the apron she had purchased in the dime store. At best, it was useless. As big as a handkerchief and sheer as gossamer. A delicate ruffle around the edges led into the tie that was of bonbon proportions. She just knew Christian would love it.

The clock in her sunshine kitchen of yellow and orange read six forty-five. The table was set to perfection; the candle was waiting to be lighted. At precisely, six fifty-eight her doorbell chimed. Quickly, she patted at the ridiculous apron—no not ridiculous; sexy—and raced to the door. She flung open the door and fell into Christian's arms. This was where she wanted to be, where she belonged. For now, forever.

"Hey, it's cold out here and it's snowing! Can I come in?" Christian said huskily. Without loosening his hold on her, he managed to slip out of his heavy jacket. "I like your apron." He grinned.

"I knew you would; that's why I bought it!"

"Come here," he said, drawing her closer.

Sam buried her head against his broad chest, burrowing against him. "I have to put the steak under the broiler. Everything else is ready," she sighed.

"Steak?" Christian said in a nonplussed tone.

"David Carpenter said you wanted a steak and that you liked it rare. That's what I'm making for dinner. Did you change your mind? Did David make a mistake?" Sam asked anxiously, not wanting anything to spoil this first dinner for the two of them.

"No! I did say that, but the last thing I want to do right now is eat. Right now, all I want is to make love to you. All through the night until I know every inch of you. And you can start pleasing me by taking off that apron."

Sam giggled. "But what about the steak? I paid seven dollars and forty-three cents for that piece of meat," she whispered against his ear.

"Orion, there are some things more important than eating—and this is one of them." Deftly, he picked her up and headed for the kitchen. Sam wiggled and reached down to turn off the broiler.

"See that pie I baked for you? I was going to lie and say I spent all afternoon slaving over a hot oven. It was one of those frozen creations that are supposed to mesmerize a man."

"What am I going to do with you? Didn't anyone ever tell you that women are supposed to be a mystery to men? You've given away all of your secrets, and this is only the second day we've been together as husband and wife. What am I going to do with you?"

"For starters," Sam said softly, "you can whisper my name the way you did last night, and then we'll think of something after that."

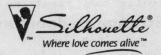

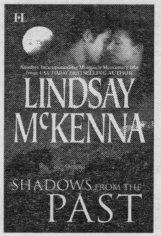

REQUEST YOUR
FREE BOOKS!

2 FREE NOVELS
FROM THE ROMANCE/SUSPENSE
COLLECTION PLUS 2 FREE GIFTS!

YES! Please send me 2 FREE novels from the Romance/Suspense Collection and my 2 FREE gifts (gifts are worth about $10). After receiving them, if I don't wish to receive any more books, I can return the shipping statement marked "cancel." If I don't cancel, I will receive 4 brand-new novels every month and be billed just $5.74 per book in the U.S. or $6.24 per book in Canada. That's a savings of at least 28% off the cover price. It's quite a bargain! Shipping and handling is just 50¢ per book.* I understand that accepting the 2 free books and gifts places me under no obligation to buy anything. I can always return a shipment and cancel at any time. Even if I never buy another book from the Reader Service, the two free books and gifts are mine to keep forever.

185 MDN EYNQ 385 MDN EYN2

Name	(PLEASE PRINT)

Address	Apt. #

City	State/Prov.	Zip/Postal Code

Signature (if under 18, a parent or guardian must sign)

Mail to **The Reader Service:**
IN U.S.A.: P.O. Box 1867, Buffalo, NY 14240-1867
IN CANADA: P.O. Box 609, Fort Erie, Ontario L2A 5X3

Not valid to current subscribers of the Romance Collection,
the Suspense Collection or the Romance/Suspense Collection.

Want to try two free books from another line?
Call 1-800-873-8635 or visit www.morefreebooks.com.

* Terms and prices subject to change without notice. Prices do not include applicable taxes. Sales tax applicable in N.Y. Canadian residents will be charged applicable provincial taxes and GST. Offer not valid in Quebec. This offer is limited to one order per household. All orders subject to approval. Credit or debit balances in a customer's account(s) may be offset by any other outstanding balance owed by or to the customer. Please allow 4 to 6 weeks for delivery. Offer available while quantities last.

Your Privacy: Harlequin is committed to protecting your privacy. Our Privacy Policy is available online at www.eHarlequin.com or upon request from the Reader Service. From time to time we make our lists of customers available to reputable third parties who may have a product or service of interest to you. If you would prefer we not share your name and address, please check here. ☐

BOB09

FERN MICHAELS

77338 PROMISES   ___ $7.99 U.S. ___ $7.99 CAN.

(limited quantities available)

TOTAL AMOUNT $ _____
POSTAGE & HANDLING $ _____
($1.00 FOR 1 BOOK, 50¢ for each additional)
APPLICABLE TAXES* $ _____
TOTAL PAYABLE $ _____

(check or money order—please do not send cash)

To order, complete this form and send it, along with a check or money order for the total above, payable to HQN Books, to: **In the U.S.:** 3010 Walden Avenue, P.O. Box 9077, Buffalo, NY 14269-9077; **In Canada:** P.O. Box 636, Fort Erie, Ontario, L2A 5X3.

Name: _____
Address: _____ City: _____
State/Prov.: _____ Zip/Postal Code: _____
Account Number (if applicable): _____

075 CSAS

*New York residents remit applicable sales taxes.
*Canadian residents remit applicable GST and provincial taxes.

HQN™

We *are* romance™

www.HQNBooks.com

PHFM1209BL